SLIPSTREAMERS

STOLEN SECRETS

ENGEN
BOOKS

Published in Canada by Engen Books, St. John's, NL.

CIP information is available on Library and Archives Canada Cataloguing in Publication website.

ISBN-13: 978-1-77478-077-0

Distributed by:
Engen Books
www.engenbooks.com
submissions@engenbooks.com

First mass market paperback printing: January 2022
Cover Design: Ariel Marsh
Slipstreamers Committee:
Amanda Labonté
Ali House
AJ Ryan
Ellen Curtis
Erin Vance
Lauralana Dunne
Matthew LeDrew

NAVIGATING STORIES

LISA M. DALY & JD RYOT

PROLOGUE

A story:

The door was first found by Lamore. She was foraging in the forest and found a strange plant. She had never seen such a thing. It was tall, with stiff hairs, and most were topped with a tightly curled leaf. On some, the leaves were just starting to uncurl, showing the first signs of a feathery plant. It was new, and she picked a couple, wondering if they were good to eat. She found a concentration of them, and as she walked toward them, the air suddenly changed. It was a little colder, and a little heavier. It caught in her lungs, and she choked in surprise. Looking around, she noticed many of the plants and trees were different; many looked to be starting their first growth after the cold season, even though it was the hottest time of the year. Looking at her feet, she saw not only the coiled plant, but other unfamiliar plants just starting to push through the litter of the forest floor. Turning back, she saw only this unfamiliar forest. Stepping back the way she came, Lamore felt the warmth of the sun on her skin, and breathed deeply of the light air she knew. Turning again, she found her way back to the strange land.

Collecting some of the strange plants, putting them in her basket, Lamore stopped when she heard a noise. Voices, but in a tongue she did not know. Lamore stood and turned toward the sound. Two women came into the small clearing and looked at her. The women were dressed in clothes different from her own. Warmer clothes, better suited to the early growth season. The three stared at each other. Lamore extended her hands, palms up in a gesture of greeting, customary to her people. The women watched, and repeated the gesture and turned their hands slightly, opening them a little more. Lamore took this to be a greeting and did the same. Then, one of the women approached, looked in Lamore's basket, and removed one of the plants. She dropped it to the forest floor and crushed it under her foot. Then she showed Lamore another plant, picked a leaf, and put it in her mouth, chewing. The woman plucked a few more leaves and put them in Lamore's basket. Lamore understood. The plant she had was bad, maybe poisonous, and the other plant was good to eat. Lamore fished in her own basket and removed a handful of sweet berries. She offered them to the women, taking one for herself to show them they were safe to eat. The women each tried a berry, then took another couple, enjoying the sweetness. One of the women reached into a pouch on her hip and took out a small clay pot. Reaching her fingers in, she removed a soft brown substance. The woman took the brown and stretched it until it snapped. She passed a piece to Lamore, broke another for the other woman, and put her own piece in her mouth. Lamore took it and placed it in her own mouth, enjoying the rich sweet flavour. The three women took some time to go through the woods, the two showing Lamore the various edible plants. When they came to a wide river, one of the women stopped and built a fire, boiling water, while the other showed Lamore how to pick the green, curled plants that grew along the bank. They boiled them and ate them together.

Lamore spent the day with the two women, learning about the abundance of the forest. They would try to speak to each other, but Lamore could not make the same sounds as them, nor could they match her words. They gestured and demonstrated, communicating through movement. When she returned to the door, she had a basket full of treasures to bring back. Lamore wished she could communicate with the women about the door, but they refused to go through. Lamore left but returned the next day with a basket full of berries, plants, vegetables and dried meats from her own land. When she could not find the women, she left the basket in the clearing.

A few days later, Lamore returned to the new world. She did not see the women again, but when she checked the basket, her gifts had been replaced with gifts from the strange world. Then the harvest started, and Lamore could not get to the door for many days. When she returned, she had an abundance of gifts. The air was hot and dry, different from the chill of the harvest season. This time, the women were there with gifts of their own. They exchanged food, cooking utensils, cloth, and jewellery. The women gave Lamore a bracelet made from a hollow sort of quill, and Lamore gave them each a pin for their hair. They parted as friends.

Lamore returned each season. Sometimes the women

were there, sometimes others greeted her instead. Always they traded, sometimes taking the time to show how to prepare different things. As time went on, Lamore grew older, and took her granddaughter through the door. Lamore taught her what she knew of the world, took her to the river, majestic in a different way from their own ocean. The granddaughter learned, and, over time, met people from the other world, and traded. The grand-daughter took her own child to learn of the new world.

Generations passed and the worlds changed. Technology changes in this world and that. Our world discovered halfstone and theirs discovered a black belching energy. Our capital grows large, and in theirs, homes and buildings appear along the river. The people we trade with change, but stay the same. The language changes, but it remains impossible to speak. In their cold months, their people start to brave our world, looking for warmth and shelter. Their air becomes heavy and our visits become shorter. Finally, our people can no longer pass through the door, and those who come to us seem to have so little that we can no longer trade. But still, we give them shelter, and ask nothing in return.

CHAPTER ONE

Scritch, scritch, scritch, ting!

"Do I hear another artifact?" asked Jameson.

"Seems that way!" crowed Cassidy as she used a brush to delicately reveal the piece of porcelain.

"You always get the best units. How can I be only a meter away and not be finding anything?"

"I guess I am just lucky like that," she smiled as she picked up her clipboard and measuring tape. "It looks like another piece of that Delftware puzzle jug. I wonder if I've found enough to reassemble some of it." Cassidy started measuring the location of the artifact within her excavation unit.

"Oh, does this mean you'll actually be around for the lab work? You're not going to take off just in time for the 'boring' stuff, as you like to call it," Jameson teased. Unlike Cassidy, he enjoyed the laboratory analysis and the puzzle of the story told by the artifacts. Although cleaning the artifacts could get pretty tedious, he'd admit.

Cassidy wrote down her measurements and slumped slightly. She usually managed to find another project to avoid getting stuck in the lab and the library. Hours of cleaning artifacts, measuring and weighing them, and then typing them in the catalogues. Sure, reassembling the jug would be fun, like a 3D jigsaw puzzle with pieces missing, but there was so much to do before that. Picking up her camera and scale, she carefully took a picture of the fragment of porcelain, checked the image to make sure the blue transfer print was visible, and noted the photograph number. Why couldn't she just stick to the fun parts of being an archaeologist, like excavation and discovering sites? As long as her unit had artifacts, of course. A unit like Jameson's would be just as boring as the lab.

Dropping the artifact and label in a plastic bag, she sighed, "Yeah, it looks like I'll be stuck in the lab. You won't stick me with too much of the cataloguing, will you? Or the cleaning? Or the archival research?"

Jameson laughed, "What kind of an archaeologist are you? I know the lab isn't fun, but it can't just be finding things and that's it. We do have a duty to the job. Plus, this site is fascinating! I mean, at first glance, it looks like a major trade spot, especially with the variety of ceramics we've been finding."

"You mean I've been finding…"

Jameson ignored her and kept going, excited about analyzing the finds. "I think, if we work together and get the preliminary analysis done, which yes, does mean looking for obscure documents in the archives." He gave her a serious look, "You will help, right? I would like to get the first draft of an article out in time for the national conference. The whole team can get it out and hopefully help secure enough funding. This could be a multi-year project."

Cassidy rolled her eyes, "I'll do the work, Jameson. I know it's your project, but I'm just not as worried about the articles. And the students are much better at cleaning and labelling than I am."

"Well, you do tend to vanish, and never tell anyone about your projects. What is the point in archaeology if you're just going to hide all the information away? Don't you have a responsibility to the people you are research-ing? You won't even tell anyone what era or culture group you're working in."

"That's my secret. Like I said, I don't need the articles and the conferences–"

"Or the funding," he cut in.

"Or the funding. I just like the excitement of the finds. And if I don't need to clean and analyze," she paused as she uncovered part of the base of the puzzle jug, "why not just enjoy the finds?"

"You are living the dream, Cassidy. No worries about funding, and never having to present your work. I'm a little jealous."

"I know. It's pretty great," she said with a smile.

***

"Alright team, it's the second to last day of the season. That means we need to finish the excavations," Jameson looked pointedly at Cassidy, "so we can do all of the clean-up tomorrow. If your unit is finished, then help someone else. That might mean screening for others, or helping them with recording. The first two who finish their units need to help Cassidy with hers. That will mean measuring, recording, and using the fine screen for her dirt. She has a lot of artifacts, and some of them are pretty small, but we have been working all summer and I have confidence in your abilities. Okay team, let's finish the season!"

The team of archaeologists gave a small cheer, and dispersed to their units. Most were almost done and just had to finish their final few centimetres of sterile soil to make sure their unit contained no more artifacts. Cassidy would have to rush a little. The number of artifacts she found in her unit took time to record. By mid-afternoon, it seemed like she had ended up with four assistants, and together it looked like they would finish the unit before the end of the day. The rest of the crew had finished before lunch, and were doing the last of the recordings, taking soil samples, and drawing profile walls, plus photographing the site.

Tomorrow they would have to shovel all of the dirt back into the excavation units. They could all agree that tomorrow would be a tiring day, but Jameson had promised to buy a round of appetizers when they got back to the closest town. They had been living in tents for the past six weeks, three hours from civilization, so they were all looking forward to the pub. Some of them would probably have a few drinks, but it was a good crew, and they knew how to have fun without going to excess. There were a few non-drinkers, and they seemed to enjoy the social side of things (and the fried food). Jameson reflected that it had been a good summer, and a good field season.

Jameson was lost in thought while making field notes, when the satellite phone rang. Everyone on the site stopped and looked toward his field gear. He knew sat phones could take calls, but in all of his years in the field, he had never heard one ring.

"Hello?" he asked once he figured out how to answer the phone. The crew looked on, curious. "Um, yes, she is, just a moment please." He took the phone away from his mouth and carefully cupped a hand over the mouthpiece, "Ah, Cassidy, there's someone on the phone for you."

Cassidy dropped the last artifact from her unit in a bag and passed it to one of the students. "You folks can finish off this unit, right?" she asked. They nodded assent, still watching her and Jameson with the sat phone.

Cassidy almost skipped toward Jameson, her red hair bouncing and her grin spreading as she got closer. As she reached out her hand, he hesitated and said, "I guess this is your mysterious benefactor. And I guess this means you'll be leaving us with the lab work."

Cassidy smiled even more as she took the phone and said, "I can only hope," as she walked away to talk privately.

It was Dr. Herbert Gamgee, and indeed he did have a new task for her. Her heart soared as she knew there was no way she'd get stuck in the lab, or, heaven forbid, the archive.

A few minutes later, Cassidy returned to the site, smiling.

"So, I'm guessing from that grin you'll be leaving us?"

***

The next day started with the crew doing a few last minute sketches of unit profiles that had been missed the day before. Then it was all hands shovelling and moving dirt to refill every one of the excavation units they had worked so hard on. Jameson had Cassidy on backfill duty, while he inventoried all of the equipment and made notes about what was broken and needed repair, and what was completely beyond repair and would have to be replaced for the next season. He debated getting Cassidy to do this part, knowing how much she hated the paperwork side of things, but decided against it. Let her go off on her grand adventures; he wouldn't punish her for it. Seeing as he'd be using the equipment next year (as long as his funding came through) it was best for him to manage the inventory. Even if he *really* wanted to pawn it off on someone else.

Cassidy shovelled and dragged dirt across the excavation site. They had a wheelbarrow, but she let some of the crew use it while she piled dirt onto a tarp and pulled it across to the excavation units. There was always something sad, but still satisfying, to finish a field season. Shovelling back dirt was hard, but gave a wonderful finality to the summer. And it was that much better now that she knew she wouldn't end up having to clean the hundreds of artifacts they had recovered this season. She was thrilled to have been the one to find a few of those hundred: every fragment of ceramic, every pipe stem, every button was exciting. Besides her puzzle jug, she hadn't really found anything hugely interesting. One of the students had found a near perfect coin while Jameson had found a clay pipe bowl with an interesting stamp that would need further research to identify, which they were both sure would someday end up in a museum. Maybe there would be enough of her puzzle jug to also be on display, but she probably would hear about it after. Dr.

Gamgee was waiting.

They finished the site partway through the afternoon, and the team piled into the trucks and started back to the nearest town. It was a three-hour drive, and most of the crew napped on the way back, despite the eclectic tastes of music (Jameson favoured electronica, Cassidy epic classical, and another truck shook with heavy metal covers of pop songs). Spirits were high, and that evening a group of tired, dirty, but happy archaeologists piled into the pub. It had been a tough day, as last days of the season often are, and they knew the food would be hot and the drinks cold.

Jameson made sure everyone was seated before ordering one of every appetizer on the menu. After a month of canned food, oatmeal, and surplus military rations, hot, deep fried cheese and zucchini sounded like heaven. Everyone ordered drinks, and a surprising number of people ordered salads, craving fresh vegetables after weeks of wondering what exactly the "vegetable" was in the MRE vegetable pasta.

The drinks arrived, beer and sodas, and Jameson clinked his glass to get everyone's attention.

"First, I want to thank all of you for your hard work this summer. We pretty much kept to the schedule, and made some great finds. And backfill was done in record time," he paused as a server brought out the first of the food. "And I'm sure the prospect of greasy, unhealthy, deep fried food didn't encourage us to work any faster today," he chuckled.

The crew laughed, but didn't hesitate to dig into the finger foods. Jameson continued, "I do have some great news. Since we made it back to internet range, I learned that our funding has been extended. So anyone who wants two weeks of lab work, talk to me tonight or tomorrow. It will mostly be cleaning and cataloguing—"

"Which is the worst part of archaeology!"

"Please, no one listen to Dr. Cane."

Cassidy smiled as everyone laughed.

"But as I was saying, there is lab work available to those who want it. It's great experience, and those of you still in university, it will help you get work terms during the semester. Or help you kiss up to potential supervisors if you tell them you know how to clean, label, and catalogue."

"Wait now," Cassidy interrupted again. "I thought you were going to make me do this work. You never said anything about maybe more funding for the crew!"

"Doesn't really matter, now does it, what with you going away. Maybe, whenever you get back from whatever it is you do, we'll still have some cataloguing left for you," Jameson teased.

"Funny funny," she replied.

"Now, if that is all, Cassidy, I want everyone to raise their glass and toast a fantastic crew and a season well done. Cheers!"

"Cheers!" came the reply from the other archaeologists. Glasses clinked, and everyone drank to the summer.

Cassidy's phone chirped. She glanced at it, drank her cola, grabbed a fried mozzarella stick, stood up and said, "On that note, it's time for me to leave. Maybe see you next summer!"

"Only if you promise to clean some artifacts!" Jameson called after her. "Hey wait! You didn't pay for your drink!"

"Take it out of your new funding!" she called back.

Cassidy left the pub and got into an SUV idling outside the door. *It should be a jeep,* she thought, *like the archaeologists of the 60s, exploring the world looking for artifacts and hominid fossils in their jeep. But they never got to travel by portal.*

CHAPTER TWO

Cassidy loved campus. She hated studying, researching in the library, and long lectures, but she loved campus. Except for exam time, there was always such an element of excitement, especially near the start of the year. In the archaeology building, she wandered the corridors to her office.

Her office was small and cluttered. She had been at the university for a while now, and she could always see the layers of her time there. There were shelves covered in dusty folders of papers, maps spread across a table, books piled around the floor, and items Cassidy had previously collected. Those didn't look as forgotten as some of the piles of paper. For now at least.

Dr. Gamgee was seated in Cassidy's chair. When she opened the door, he stood and greeted her.

"Ah, Cassidy, it took you a while," Gamgee commented.

"Well, I was a day away from any town, so only a helicopter would have gotten me here sooner," she sniped back.

"Perhaps another time." He paused before continuing. "I need you to go to Fredericton, on the east coast of Canada. There's a portal where they used to have an airport," he handed her a sheet of paper, "here's a bit of background. I have you booked on a flight in a few hours. I hope you're okay with sleeping on the plane."

"After sharing a tent for a month, it will be okay." Cassidy glanced at the paper; it was a blog post about the airport, including the location.

"You'll be looking for a mineral. It has special magnetic properties and is important to my work. I need you to get a large sample of it," he indicated with his hands about the size of a carton of milk, "and when you get back, courier it to me, call it a scientific sample, or you might have trouble with airport security."

"Sounds good. Any idea where I'm going this time," she asked, not really wanting an answer. The surprise was part of the fun.

The physicist glared at her through his thick glasses, and turned to walk out of the office. She sat at her desk, looking at the printout about the airport.

***

The flight to Halifax was uneventful, but the one from Halifax to Fredericton was an experience. Cassidy did not know if she had ever been on a smaller commercial plane. Sure, she had been on short flights, just her and the pilot, but there was something strange about flying in the little Beechcraft. In private flights, she could talk to the pilot over the headset, and see what was happening. She had even been briefly offered the wheel before. This was different. Two rows of single seats, only seven seats deep, made up the cabin. There was no room to stow carry-on luggage, it had to be placed on a rack opposite the door. And there was no cabin crew. Before takeoff, the co-pilot came out and gave safety instructions, then went to the cockpit. The door to the cockpit was open and the passengers could watch the pilot and co-pilot work the instruments, but unless you got out of your seat and approached the two, they wouldn't know if you needed assistance. The engines were so loud that you would have to go to the cockpit because no one would be able to hear you.

Cassidy had watched one couple try to talk to each other across the aisle. It involved a lot of "what" and "I can't hear you". She put in her headphones, but could still hear the engines, and tried to get comfortable for the short flight. She watched the lights of Halifax disappear as they climbed through the clouds. With nothing to see, she closed her eyes and dozed.

She woke as the plane hit some turbulence. The blast of adrenaline as she was thrown around her seat made her fingertips tingle. Her phone fell from her lap and pulled free of the headphones as it slid under the seat before her. Cassidy clutched the armrests, her stomach lurching and her heart rate soaring as the plane dropped suddenly. There was no announcement from the cockpit, probably due to the older style of the aircraft. She realized just how comforting that a pilot's announcement could be during turbulence. She looked around the plane and saw the other passengers in varying states of panic. She looked outside. That was a little comforting, but she had to force herself to loosen her grip on the armrests and enjoy the ride. The plane levelled out, and the co-pilot turned around and gave the cabin a thumbs-up. Cassidy leaned forward and asked the passenger ahead of her for her phone, then went back to looking out the window, enjoying the feel of her pulse in her ears.

***

The Fredericton Airport was small. Small enough that they walked from the plane, across the tarmac, and into the airport. She carried her rucksack with her through the terminal. She looked for lunch, but the small kiosk in the airport was not appealing, so she found a cab instead.

"Welcome to Fredericton!" The taxi driver was rather friendly. "What brings you here?"

"Business, but first I'm looking for something to eat and I hope you can suggest somewhere," Cassidy smiled back.

CHAPTER THREE

The end of summer was still warm, but with a touch of the cool of autumn on the wind. Cassidy had a great meal of Caribbean food, surprised to find such a spot so far north. It reminded her of her last trip to Jamaica, and she enjoyed the lingering spices on her palate. She had stopped at a small convenience store and picked up some fruit and vegetables; something fresh to go with her dehydrated and MRE supplies. And chocolate. Always chocolate.

The taxi ride to the old airport was a little strange. The driver did not want to drop her off where there was nothing nearby, until Cassidy pointed out a house and said "That's the one! That's what my friend's house looks like."

The area was residential, not like the 1985 topographic map in the blog post. She was agog at how much the area had built up since the image. From the pictures, there had been a runway in this area, and a couple of outbuildings for the airplanes. The whole area around the airport had been farmland along the Saint John River. That was all gone and now it was a fairly dense residential neighbourhood; very different from the pictures from the 1940s and 1960s. Cassidy looked around, trying to see something that remained of the old airfield. She pulled out her phone and looked at a map of the area. In the middle of all of the backyards there was an area still full of trees. It seemed like an odd thing, this untouched grove, and figured it would be the best place to start.

She found a corner store set close to the grove, stopped in for more snacks, and walked to the back of the building, pushing through shrubs and trees. The undergrowth was thick, and there was a lot of litter and debris she had to climb through. The branches clawed at her back and pulled her red hair, but she forced her way through and the trees spaced out a little, making it much easier to move. Cassidy caught her breath, picked a broken twig out of her hair, tied it back up, and went further into the trees.

There was evidence of people having lived in the area; the remnants of a lean-to off to one side, a small fire pit and a broken frying pan. There was litter around the camp, and Cassidy walked in the other direction. It reasoned that the portal would be away from where people lived.

She walked slowly, between trees, trying to systematically pick through the area. It wouldn't be the first time she had walked past a portal. After about twenty minutes of searching, she felt the familiar disorienting sensation, and walked through to a new world, into a forest. Cassidy looked behind her, not sure if she had really found the portal, but she could no longer see the lean-to and litter, and the trees did look a little different. She stopped and listened, and could hear birdsong, not cars. Definitely a new world.

Cassidy pulled a compass out of the front of her bag. If this mineral had magnetic properties, perhaps the compass could help. The compass point wavered slightly, seemingly pulled in two directions. Unsure where to go, she pulled out a couple of pin flags, thanked Jameson for the donation from the field gear, and marked the portal. She turned back to the compass, and was distracted by a rumble and whoosh ahead of and above her. Cassidy looked up and saw an airplane in line with one of the compass points. Decided, she started in that direction.

"Planes," she said to herself, "looking a heck of a lot like old planes from home."

Wandering through the trees, Cassidy noted that it was an older forest than the one she'd left. The trees were well-spaced and easy to navigate and she enjoyed the stroll. The weather was warm, but not hot, like spring. The air was clean, something she was used to from being in the field. After being at airports and then in a city, even as small as Fredericton, she took a few deep breaths to clean out her lungs. There was always something nice about fresh, clean air. Strange though, as she was obviously close to an airport, that she couldn't smell any sort of fuel on the air. Knowing full well she had a mission, she still took her time to relax and stretch her legs after her travel.

After about an hour of walking, Cassidy came out into a clearing, and before she could decide where to go next, a woman in long skirts and a light, flowing shirt, started to walk toward her with an exaggerated smile.

"Why hello," she said in a chipper voice, "it looks like

we have another one. My my, we didn't expect anyone for another two seasons, but here you are! I know you can't understand a word I say, but you're not a regular are you, so I'll keep talking and hopefully you'll know I'm friendly and won't run back into the forest. I'd hate for you to get lost." She chattered on, but in a happy, welcoming sort of tone.

"Um, I do understand," Cassidy interrupted.

The woman stopped short, her smile faltering for just a moment. "Oh, well. Wow. No one has ever understood us before. Well, isn't that just the insect's appendages. How?"

Cassidy smiled a warm smile, "It's complicated, but let's say a combination of magic and science."

"Magic? I don't understand that one. Science I do know! Well, this will be a slice of occasion bread. Come come, my name is Margaretta, and yours?"

"Cassidy. You don't seem surprised to see me walk out of the woods."

"Oh, tree flower, we get people who walk out of the woods pretty regularly. But you are a little early. The door people usually don't show up for another two seasons, which I believe is when your cold season starts. Then we'll have a group of visitors arrive for a while until it warms up again. We will often see the same faces over time, and sometimes they'll bring new people."

Cassidy was surprised. "You know about the portal? So much so that you expect people?"

"Oh, of course, of course. When the season comes, we go out to the door to greet them with food. They are always cold and hungry when they come through. But you don't seem either. It is very strange." Margaretta looked at her, questioning.

"It's a different season on the other side right now. It is still warm. Not as warm as here, but warm. And I planned to come through, so I brought food with me."

"You have food?! I would really like to try your food. Oh, I hope that's not too forward of me."

Cassidy laughed, "Of course not. I'd be happy to share my food. I think the people who usually come through are homeless, and must come through when it gets too cold to live outside. I noticed a lean-to when I came through the portal."

Margaretta looked confused. "What do you mean homeless? You mean without a home? Why would there be people without homes? Particularly with how hard it is to live on the other side of the door. We have people who live in shelters in the forests, but they can always come back to the town."

"There are long and complex reasons for why people have no homes in my world. Perhaps we can discuss it at another time? I wouldn't want your first conversation about the other side of the portal to be such a negative one," Cassidy said thoughtfully.

"Hmmm… yes, I suppose you are right. I have so many questions. And I must introduce you to the story-tellers. They will have so many questions, too. Perhaps not all at once, though. Would you like to eat first?"

Cassidy smiled. "Yes, that would be nice."

Margaretta laughed, "Then we will start with food, and maybe end as friends."

***

The meal was delicious. Cassidy couldn't recognize most of the fruit or vegetables, but instead of asking, she just enjoyed. It was one of the pleasures of her travel to experience food from everywhere. Usually it was a pleasure, at least.

Margaretta had led Cassidy to the town, which seemed to consist of family houses and a few larger buildings. Not surprising, being surrounded by trees, the buildings were mostly wooden, and a large body of water could be seen a little way past the buildings. A town on the seaside, Cassidy thought. As a contrast, every now and then an airplane would pass overhead. Surprisingly though, the planes were relatively quiet, especially compared to what she was used to.

"Oh, that's the base," Margaretta explained. "They set up last year. You see, the whole world is at war right now; not that you'd guess it from our quiet little town!"

Cassidy was intrigued. A base would probably have the magnetic mineral.

"I've seen the airplanes; we have something similar on my side of the portal, but ours are much louder. If a plane flew overhead where I'm from, it would be so loud that the walls would shake!" Cassidy explained.

"Yes," Margaretta continued, "we know about your, planes you said? I like that, shortening aeroplane to just plane! We got the idea from your side of the door. We always knew about the door, and now and then would visit."

"Have you been through?" asked Cassidy.

"Me, no. We have to be very careful going through.

Every few years someone will go through the door, but they can never stay long. Especially the past three or four generations. Your air is too heavy and too hard to breathe. It makes the lungs burn like a cookfire."

Cassidy contemplated this. The city of Fredericton had been around since the 1600s, but the railway probably didn't go through until the late 1800s or early 1900s, and the area itself wasn't really built up until more recently. In fact, according to the information Gamgee had given her, the area was pretty empty until the 1960s but now it was a residential area, and the whole area was much more polluted than when it was just farmland, or before that, when it was used by the Maliseet people indigenous to the area.

Margaretta interrupted Cassidy's train of thought. "We got the idea for the aeroplanes from your side of the door. My great-grandfather went through and saw the aeroplanes near the portal. He saw one take off and thought it was such a wonder. He went back a few times to talk to the people who flew them and to look at the machines. He figured out how to build them and took his aeroplanes to the capital where they began making them and making them better."

"But if they are based on our planes, how are they so quiet? Especially propeller planes. Those are incredibly noisy. I was just on one a few hours ago and my ears are still ringing!"

"There are other kinds of planes? Grandfather would be so interested!"

"I thought you said it was your great-grandfather?" asked Cassidy.

"Oh it was, but my grandfather helped when he was a young boy. He is proud of the aeroplanes, even if he is not happy with the base. On one side of the leaf, he blames the aeroplanes for the base being here, but on the other side of the leaf, he knows they are a huge accomplishment by his father."

Cassidy was getting a little lost. Margaretta had a lot of information to share, but she was having trouble keeping everything straight.

Margaretta must have noticed that Cassidy was a little overwhelmed.

"Let me get you set up in the visitor house. It's not really ready as you are so early, but you'll be snuggled like a crustacean. You can stay there until you are ready to go back through. Tomorrow, I can introduce you to the storytellers. Then we can tell you more. I know they'd love to meet you."

"That sounds lovely," replied Cassidy. She was going to have to take some time to regroup.

They left the eating area together and walked to a medium-sized house. The door was unlocked, and Margaretta led Cassidy inside.

"During the season, we can have as many as a dozen people here. We expanded the house a couple of times in the past few years, and might have to expand again soon. People are always welcome. We'll make space, but this year they'll be cozy, like seeds in a pod!" Margaretta smiled. "Pick any bed you'd like."

Cassidy walked to a bed near a window on the back wall and laid down her bag.

"Thank you, Margaretta. I didn't know what to expect,

but your hospitality is much more than I ever expected."

"It's what we do!" Margaretta beamed.

Cassidy smiled back, "I will take some time to think about things and make some notes."

"I will collect you in the morning for breakfast," Margaretta said as she closed the door to the house.

Cassidy sat on the bed and took out her notes. She had a notebook with the blog post print-out Gamgee had given her. Earlier, she had noted how what was once an airstrip was now a residential neighbourhood, and over the years, like so many Canadian cities, Fredericton had grown quite a bit. If the people here had been crossing over to Fredericton, she could see how they would have noticed a change in air quality. Hundreds of years ago, if it was just the Indigenous population, the air would have been clean, and still relatively clean with the first Europeans. As the city grew, there certainly would have been more pollution, from coal-burning steamships and trains to more people burning fires to heat the homes. Since the Second World War it would have been much worse. According to the information she had, the area of the portal was farmland, so probably not too polluted, but the railway also passed close by. The area she saw in Fredericton had a major road and a bypass road in the area, which would mean lots of cars, and lots of particles in the air. She thought the air was fairly clean, especially compared to big cities, but given the freshness to the air in this world, she could see how it would cause problems for anyone not used to it.

That brought her to the people coming through. Many portals had stories of people crossing through, but in this world, it was not only known but expected. In fact, they had used the portal to learn about new technologies. Cassidy wondered if they had been over to see the cars yet, and if they had started to learn about that, or if that hadn't been possible since the roads went through. They also expected people to come through. If they were waiting another couple of seasons, could that coincide with winter? When she was looking for the portal, she saw the lean-to of someone who was homeless. Perhaps some of the homeless population of Fredericton would pass through during the winter months. There were news stories every year from many cities about the problems of finding shelter for those without homes during the colder months, so could some know about the portal and use it instead of freezing to death? If the hospitality Cassidy experienced was any indicator, even being an unexpected guest, then it was surprising that they would only get a dozen or so people every winter. Perhaps it was a secret event within the homeless population so only some people would use the portal. And if they were homeless, why would they leave? Would they be encouraged to leave?

Cassidy was surprised at her own foolishness. Of course they would return through the portal; there would be the language barrier. Margaretta was so surprised that she spoke the same language, so whatever the language is, it must be absolutely insurmountable, even after generations of people passing through the area. The strange turns of phrase must be something that the translator had difficulty with; they sounded familiar, if not archaic, but strange at the same time. Perhaps it was taking the closest approximation and trying to turn it into something more recognizable.

That brought Cassidy to the mineral with magnetic properties that Dr. Gamgee wanted her to find. In the forest, the compass seemed to waver between two points. One point seemed to be toward the base, so it is possible that the mineral she was looking for was there. She would have to find out more about this war, and also see if she could visit the base and look for the mineral. She would also have to find out why Margaretta's grandfather was not happy with the base, and hopefully asking about it would not be a problem.

Now with a plan, Cassidy put away her notebook and laid back on the bed. It might be only mid-afternoon at home, but on this side of the portal it was dusk, and she had travelled quite a bit over the past few days. For once, it was a leisurely introduction to a new world, and she planned to take full advantage by getting a good sleep.

CHAPTER FOUR

Cassidy woke to the light coming in through the window above her bed. She felt refreshed after her travels of the previous day. She got up, rummaged through her bag for her toothbrush, and cleaned up at the tap and water basin next to the bed. Just as she was drying her face on a soft towel next to the basin, the door to the house creaked as it opened.

"Hello?" asked a timid voice. "Are you in here? Margaretta sent me. Daylight's up, so it's time to eat!" There was a little bit of excitement in that last statement.

"Yes, I'm here," replied Cassidy.

The door opened and a child, perhaps 8 or 9 by Cassidy's guess, was in the frame.

"Hello, I'm Cassidy," she said as she approached.

"Hiya! I'm Rim. Margaretta's meeting with the storytellers and telling them all about you. I've never talked to a forest person before. How come you can talk like us but none of the others ever can? I always have to act out stuff so they can understand."

"A while ago, I visited a place where they used science," Cassidy remembered Margaretta not quite understanding the idea of magic, but knowing science, "to make it so I could understand language no matter where I am. I have been many places, and no matter how people speak, I can speak with them."

"That's amazing! Can I get one of them so I can speak with the forest people?" Rim asked.

"No, I'm sorry, but I got it very far away and you would have to go back to where I live, and then somewhere else, to get it."

Rim considered this and replied, "No, that won't work, will it? Phia says it's hard to breathe through the door in the forest and that people can't stay there very long." Rim paused, then cheered up. "Did you know it was my great-great-grandfather who last spent lots of time on the other side of the door? He learned about aeroplanes. But now the aeroplanes are here and it makes my great-grandfather sad. He tried to go through the door, but said he could only stay a couple of minutes before he started coughing too much and his lungs hurt. He said the air is thick, like legume soup. Is the air thick?"

"Where I am from, it is not very thick, but it certainly isn't as clean and clear as what you have here. I have never breathed air this clean." She paused and asked, "You said your great-great-grandfather brought back the planes. Does that mean Margaretta is your mother?"

The child laughed. "No, silly. Jeanetta is my mom. Her and Margaretta are sisters."

"Oh, so she's your aunt?"

"What's an aunt?"

Cassidy stopped. They must not follow families in such a way, just looking at linear relations and not sib-

lings. "Where I come from, an aunt is your mother or father's sister."

"Oh. No. She's just Margaretta," Rim said firmly. "Can
we go eat now?"

Cassidy laughed, "Of course. I'm sorry I've been keeping you from your food."

Rim smiled and walked out of the house, expecting
Cassidy to follow.

The meal was delightful. Once again, it was full of
fruit and vegetables that Cassidy couldn't name, although
Rim gave some names for the meals, and warned Cassidy
away from some of the foods. Cassidy tried everything,
and was delighted with the freshness. Anytime she had
been in the archaeological field for any length of time, she
craved fresh foods. That would often happen when most
of what you ate came out of packages or needed to be re-
hydrated first. She couldn't think of a better feast than all
of these fresh foods. She figured Rim was typical of most
children she knew where they were still timid about new
things, and had a laundry list of foods they did not like.

Rim also took the time, between bites, to introduce her
to some of the others at the large breakfast table. While
yesterday Cassidy and Margaretta had eaten alone, the
community seemed to eat together. Cassidy had taken
note of the long tables the day before, but Margaretta had
been giving her so much information so quickly that she
hadn't really thought about it. Now there were 30 or 40
people eating and talking. At the same time, while people
ate together, they didn't seem to all start at once, as she
noticed people coming and going. Even with the delay
of having to collect Cassidy, she and Rim were not the

last ones to arrive. Some people seemed to just sit and eat slowly, or even sit with a mug of hot drink; whatever Rim called it translated to cider, although that was not quite right. It was almost like a fruity coffee. Whatever it was, Cassidy was enjoying it, as were some of the others who just sat and talked over their cups. The whole experience was very welcoming and comfortable, not much different than her mornings out in the field where everyone ate together and discussed the plans for the day.

Once they were done, Rim showed Cassidy where the dishes went to be cleaned.

"In a few more seasons, I'm going to have to help with the dishes. I don't really want to, but we all have to when we get big enough," explained Rim. "But, it won't be many seasons after that until I can help with cooking. I've already done that a little bit during celebrations when they need extra help. I can help with cookies as long as I don't eat too many of them while helping."

Cassidy smiled. "So what do we do now?" she asked.

"Now," Rim stated proudly, "I get to take you to the storytellers."

***

Rim led Cassidy to an open building. It had walls, but large windows with wooden shutters that were all open to the bright day. There was a partial roof, but it was open in the centre, over a large fire pit. There were benches around the inner edge of the building, but still a lot of open space all around the fire pit. It looked perfect for community meetings or celebrations. Now, off to one side of the circular building, five individuals were congregated, some on benches and some on the hard-packed earth. Rim, having seen Cassidy safely to her destination, turned and ran away.

As Cassidy approached the group, she could overhear a little of their heated conversation. They may have been speaking in low tones, but the round room was obviously designed for noise to carry.

"What about this woman makes you want to share our secrets?" an elderly woman asked.

"It's the first visitor that we've seen that we could talk to, and she's very friendly," Margaretta replied.

"But we don't know anything about this woman," a young man said.

"So we talk to her," replied Margaretta.

"You're being too trusting, Margaretta," stated an older man. "I understand that it's exciting that you can talk and learn, believe me, I understand, but don't let a fascination with the other world cloud your judgment. She doesn't seem to be here for sanctuary. You said she's looking for something."

"So maybe we can help her," implored Margaretta.

"She's coming; maybe we should talk about this after we talk to her," said another man, just a few years older than Margaretta.

Cassidy approached the group.

"Um, hello. Are you ready for me?" she asked hesitantly. It was a little worrisome to know how they felt about her, but she was used to suspicion. It was rare for her to get to a new world and to be trusted so readily. Perhaps things weren't going to be as easy as she thought.

Margaretta approached.

"I hope you slept well," she said.

"Yes, thank you. The house is very comfortable," Cassidy replied.

"Good good. Let me introduce you to the storytellers. I already told you about my grandfather, Carlson," she gestured to a man with dark hair and features that were definitely similar to both Margaretta and Rim. Carlson nodded to Cassidy. He seemed like a serious man, with a sadness to his hunched shoulders. Margaretta indicated a white-haired woman to her left, "This is Gertrand. She is the oldest of the storytellers, with the longest memory."

Gertrand protested, "No, my darling flower blossom. You have shown many times that you now have the longest memory."

Margaretta blushed and mumbled a humble thank you before looking up at Cassidy. "Gertrand has taught me many stories, but I believe I have many more to learn." Gertrand smiled at Margaretta as she continued with the introductions. "Sasamuel has lived at the capital but moved here when he was Rim's age, and Olisker is the youngest member. He has shown to be a great storyteller, although he does have trouble keeping all of the ideas together."

Olisker looked down, a little ashamed, "Sometimes I mess up the stories and start telling one but finishing with another."

Sasamuel smiled at Olisker, "It just takes practice. Eventually you will be able to tell one story from start to finish."

Margaretta turned to Cassidy, "Together, we keep the stories of the island and share them with everyone so that we all know where we came from and who we are. We also find new stories that can be passed on. We write down the histories as well, but not everyone wants to read the books, so telling the stories helps everyone remember."

"I understand. We have many names for storytellers where I am from. Sometimes they are historians or folklorists, other times they are elders."

"Elders? Doesn't that mean old?" asked Gertrand, shock in her voice.

Cassidy smiled. The woman looked to be rather old herself. "It does mean old, but sometimes young people can have enough knowledge to be elders. Some societies respect the knowledge that only comes with age, while others respect a combination of age and knowledge that can be passed on."

Gertrand relaxed a little. "Good. I wouldn't want anyone calling me old."

Margaretta laughed, "Gertrand is only teasing. But we do not save knowledge just for the old. There are so many stories that much of a storyteller's younger days is learning them and practising telling them, and then in later years they tell the stories and teach them to the new storytellers."

Carlson had been examining Cassidy during the exchange, and spoke, "My granddaughter says you can speak to us because of a science experiment?"

"That is correct. I have travelled through many portals, or doors, in my world that have taken me many places. In one of those places, I was given a way to understand everyone else, and they to understand me."

"So we will be able to ask about your world? Will you be able to tell us more about the machines of your world?"

Carlson asked.

Cassidy remembered Margaretta telling her Carlson was proud of the planes.

"I can tell you whatever I can. I'm afraid I don't know much about how many of the machines work. I know some basics, but my work doesn't use a lot of machines, but more history. I look at things left behind by people in the past and try to learn about their lives," Cassidy explained.

Carlson's features lightened a little with just the hint of a smile. "So you are a storyteller," he stated.

Cassidy didn't think of herself that way. Between her work with Dr. Gamgee and the fact that she never quite stuck around any archaeological project to do any of the research and analysis, storyteller did not really seem to fit how she did things. But she was not going to argue, especially not if it endeared her to the group.

Sasamuel looked at Cassidy.

"What brings you here?" he asked.

Cassidy liked that he got to the point.

"I am looking for something. A very smart man, a man of science, but not a storyteller, sent me to find something in this world that can be of use to him. He has sent me to other worlds where I have located items that have then been used to heal the sick and to help people in my own world," Cassidy explained. "I don't always ask a lot of questions about why he wants an item," she confessed.

Olisker smiled, "So you like to be part of the stories! I do too. Sometimes I think they asked me to be a storyteller to keep me from exploring and adventuring."

Gertrand gave him a small cuff on the back of the head,

"Foolish boy. Storytellers need to understand stories, and all of your trouble," Olisker blushed a little, "means you know what it is to be part of a story and how to tell it. We know you told enough when trying to explain away your torn clothing."

"What is it you are looking for?" Sasamuel asked, bringing the conversation back around.

"I am looking for a mineral with strange magnetic properties. That was all I was told," Cassidy replied. "When I arrived, I used my compass," she took out the small device, "and on my world it is supposed to point to magnetic north, the top of the world, but here the needle wavers between two points." She reached out her hand, palm flat, to the centre of the group, giving them all a chance to look at the compass and see the needle moving back and forth. "The needle seems a little more focused that way," she pointed back toward the forest, "so I assume that is the equivalent to magnetic north. The needle also points to the base, so I think whatever it is I am looking for, I will find it there."

Carlson scowled at the compass. "Sometimes I wish my father had never told the capital about the aeroplanes. If he had never gone to the capital to try to make them, then they would never have known about the door, and we wouldn't have the base here now. All these people, destroying our quiet little community."

Gertrand gave Cassidy an apologetic smile. "I'm sure Margaretta explained about the base."

Margaretta looked down as Cassidy said, "No, not really."

"I'll explain," said Margaretta before Gertrand could

say anything further. "A dozen seasons ago, war broke out. We are just a small island, off the coast of a large country. There are four countries that control all of the land and all of the people. When two started a war, the other two countries were dragged in through treaties and the like. Now the entire world is at war. Our country was one of the first two. For a few seasons, it had no impact on us. We do not get many shipments from the capital, and we tend to rely on ourselves. There have been many times over the lifetimes where we have all but lost contact with the capital; usually when they are changing governments." Margaretta paused and looked at Gertrand, who motioned for her to continue. "Four seasons ago, military people came to our shores. They had great-grandfather's plans and were using them to make aeroplanes for war. The problem was, your 'planes' fly using a fuel that makes the air heavy, and great-grandfather, though he could figure out much, could not figure out a fuel source that would replace yours. He brought the plans to the capital, where they used halfstones as a fuel source. They also learned about the door. They have not figured out how to stay in your world, but they also want to make sure the other countries cannot go through either."

"That and apparently we are a 'strategic point of land' for the aeroplanes." Carlson's tone indicated he didn't believe that for a moment. "They're just using it as an excuse to keep an eye on us, and that damnable door."

"Carlson!" Gertrand reprimanded, "Do not talk like that. We help those who come through the door; it is a gift and has brought us many wonderful visitors. Sometimes, visitors have been a problem, but that door has been a joy to our people from the first stories."

"I know, I do. But that base has disrupted the hunting grounds, and they drained the wetland, which took away one of our most productive areas for collecting berries, and they even moved some of the graveyard! Imagine, digging up the dead just so you can build a runway," Carlson scoffed.

"It's better than them landing the planes on our dead, isn't it?" asked Sasamuel.

Carlson grunted in response, then went on. "And they've taken so many young people away from their usual work to work over there. Next thing they'll leave and forget the stories of where they are from."

"Hush now," Gertrand cut in, "you know full well our people have been leaving this island almost since we first came to it. And some leave and never return. They forget their stories and find new ones in their new life. But many others do come back, like your own father. The young ones at the base, many will leave, and some are even talking about going to war themselves, but many will also come back. It might be at the end of the war, it might be years later, but they will come back, and we will welcome them and share the stories they might have forgotten."

Gertrand had an authority to her. If Cassidy were to guess about how this community was run, she would guess that Gertrand was the one in charge, even if Carlson liked to think he had most of the authority.

"Cassidy," Gertrand addressed her, "you are welcome here. We do not know what it is you are searching for, but if it is to do good in your world, then we are happy to help you find it."

"Thank you," responded Cassidy. "Your support is appreciated."

Margaretta smiled at Cassidy and started to rock up on her toes, excitedly. Cassidy figured she must have passed whatever test there was in meeting the storytellers.

Margaretta continued excitedly. "I said before this is not when people usually come through the door. We usually don't have big events when we have visitors, mostly because we figure they wouldn't understand the stories, but we decided to invite you to a marriage this evening. Tomorrow we can worry about the base, but I hope you will join us." Margaretta was obviously very hopeful.

"Of course. I am honoured that you would have me," Cassidy replied. She was beginning to think that this trip might not be as much of an adventure as usual. She certainly wasn't used to having so much support, and, dare she say it, friendship, on her travels.

CHAPTER FIVE

The rest of the day was a bit of a whirlwind. This would be the first off-world wedding Cassidy had ever attended, and between Margaretta and Rim, she would be ready. Margaretta had brought Cassidy back to the visitor's house, and within minutes, Rim had arrived with a bunch of clothing. Margaretta had been confident that Cassidy would be invited to the evening's festivities, and had tasked Rim with asking the women of the village for clothing that Cassidy could wear. The women of the town seemed to favour long skirts, often of many colours in an almost patchwork style. These skirts on the other hand, were often a single colour, but had bright beading or dried flowers sewn in elaborate patterns. Cassidy tried on a few until she found a skirt that fit. All of the skirts flowed, and Cassidy could not help but give a little twirl in each of them, much to Rim's delight. The shirts were simple, conservative, wrap styles, meant to compliment the skirts, but not take attention away from the decorations. Cassidy had been worried about shoes, but Rim ensured her that no one wore shoes in the gathering hall. The dirt floor was soft enough.

After Rim made sure they had lunch (no one knows meal times better than a growing child) Margaretta returned with another woman she introduced as Phia. Phia wrapped Cassidy's red hair up and back from her face in large curls, and pinned more dried flowers into her tresses. It had been a long time since Cassidy had been so dressed up, and she was starting to catch the excitement of it.

While doing her hair, Phia and Cassidy exchanged some simple small talk, mostly Phia talking about the happy couple who were to be paired this evening, and how it was going to be Margaretta's first ceremony, so that's why she wasn't doing Cassidy's hair, and how Phia hoped she would be partnered soon, but she had only just started courting someone before the base arrived and now he works on the base and their courtship will have to wait.

Listening to Phia, part of Cassidy remembered why she rarely went to the hairdresser, but at the same time, knew she was learning a lot about the community. This was, after all, a culture of storytellers, and wasn't gossip just another way to tell some of the newest stories?

By evening, Cassidy was ready for the ceremony. Margaretta had been around again to give her some basic tips as to what to expect, though Phia had covered many of them during their time together. Cassidy would stand with both Phia, Rim, and the child's mother, and between the two of them, they would lead her through whatever she needed.

"The most important thing," Margaretta had said, "is to celebrate the couple and to enjoy yourself!"

To Cassidy, it sounded much like any wedding she

had ever attended at home.

***

After being primped and prepared for the ceremony, Cassidy was left alone while Rim and Phia went to get ready themselves. She sat outside on a bench near the village green, and just watched people wandering around, getting ready for the event. After a few minutes, Carlson came and sat next to Cassidy. He sat silently, and joined her in watching the activity.

After a little while, he started to speak.

"My father wasn't the first to visit your world. We've known about the door for almost as long as we've lived here. There are stories of our people passing through, and your people coming here. You are the first one with a shared language though. How does that work?"

"When I was on another world," Cassidy started.

Carlson cut her off. "That's not what I mean. Not the story, but what do you hear?"

"I hear you speaking in my language."

"And I hear you in mine." he said.

"I will admit though, sometimes some of the sayings are a little garbled. I think the translation is trying to make it as close to something I would recognize, but they're often not quite right."

"I can understand. Even people on the base or at the capital say we have some strange language. But it has been incorporated into our stories, so we keep using older language. Many lose it when they go to the capital, it makes them stand out, but they find it again if they come back home."

The conversation ebbed and Cassidy wondered if there was something else Carlson wanted to talk about. After a few minutes of sitting in silence, he spoke again.

"Sometimes I wish my father had never visited your world. Never discovered aeroplanes. Once he saw them, he couldn't get them out of his mind."

Cassidy looked at the man for a moment, then replied, "I have heard pilots say the same thing. Flying becomes a part of them." She thought to herself, *Like travelling to distant worlds has become part of me.* This world was making her pensive, and she wasn't certain she liked that.

"Yes," he said, "I don't understand, but I think I understand. I am a storyteller, it is part of my identity as a person. My father did not really care about stories, but when he first saw an aeroplane it was all he could talk about. He kept pushing himself to stay longer and longer, to learn more. He never got to fly one, but he did get to see them fly and saw them up close. I don't know what they must have thought, this man who would come out of the forest and talk to them in a funny language."

"We do have many languages in our world, so they may have just thought he came from another country, or was one of the land's first people, who also speak a different language from those who owned the airstrip. Although that was likely changing when your father was visiting the area."

"More than one language. Well, that is interesting. And explains some things," Carlson mused. "I could never go through the door and see the aeroplanes. By the time I was old enough, the air was too thick, too heavy. I could only be there a couple of minutes, not long enough to find the aeroplanes."

"They might have been gone. They were only there for a handful of years before they built a bigger airport much further away."

"So even if I could have made it out of the forest, I might not have seen them?"

"Possibly not, depending on when you went. That area has changed a lot in the past century, from farm land, to a railway passing nearby, to an airstrip, and now it is all houses, packed together, and a highway."

"I don't know the word highway."

Cassidy explained, "A road for cars, trucks, and other vehicles to drive a little faster to get to destinations a little further off."

"So for quicker transport?"

"In theory. But that's harder to explain."

"I see." Carlson looked at her. "My father went through the door at the wrong time. He brought your aeroplanes to our land. No. He brought the idea of aeroplanes to our land. He couldn't make them work himself, so he went to the capital where others made it work. And he still never got to fly in one. He died before they finished building the first one."

Carlson stopped, and Cassidy sat quietly, waiting for him to continue.

"If he had never gone through the door and had never seen the aeroplanes, the base wouldn't be here now. We would never have told anyone about the forest people because we never had. Even the people who moved to the capital. If they did tell people, no one listened or cared about island stories. But my father told them about aeroplanes. People from the capital came and went through the door. They even tried to create things to help them stay on the other side longer, but thankfully nothing worked. When the war started, they set up the base. They say it's because we are on the great water and the closest land to one of our enemies, but we all know it's because of the door. They want to make sure, even if they can't pass through, that no one else can. I don't know what will happen when the season starts and people start coming out of the forest. There have been more and more every year.

"Will we be able to understand them now?" he asked.

"No," she replied. "As far as I know, I am the only person in my world who can now understand everyone everywhere."

"That is probably for the best. The base would want to get information from them. Maybe make them bring back information. They may ask you to do that. Please don't. They shouldn't be here. They have taken some of our land that held important resources, they monitor what we do, and they are stealing away our young people with ideas of a modern world. When this war ends, if they ever leave, they will take many young people with them. The young people will leave the village and go to the capital and they may never come back. They will forget the stories and forget who they are.

"Thank you for letting an old man speak. This place is important to me, and I want to impress on you how important. I want to make sure that it stays safe and that you won't do anything to jeopardize our traditions."

Cassidy looked at Carlson and said, her tone as grave

as his was sad, "I won't. You have a beautiful place here, and I wouldn't want to harm it."

Carlson took her hand in his.

"Thank you."

With that, he let go of her hand, got up, and walked away, leaving her to think about what he'd said. This village was so focused on stories and tradition; would modern intervention really be so bad? Cassidy thought of all of the new technologies she had seen in her lifetime, and how exciting future technologies could be. She had seen glimpses of it on other adventures, and hoped for some of the same things at home. Why wouldn't people want these new things? She could never live a quiet life like this one. She knew, deep inside of her, she would be one of those who would leave for the capital, whatever that might bring. Stories were all well and good, and as an archaeologist she had done enough anthropology courses to know how important they were to culture and that they were how some cultures maintained their histories, but she couldn't imagine being so buried in tradition that you couldn't really explore the world. When she had discovered that a lot of archaeology was research, history books, and sitting in laboratories, she was heartbroken. At least Gamgee had given her a way out of the boring stuff.

***

The ceremony started about an hour before dusk. The hearth in the centre of the room had been covered over, and the happy couple stood on the platform, elevated for everyone to see. The townspeople formed a large circle a few steps back from the couple. Close enough to see and hear, but not so close that they were crowded.

Margaretta approached the couple. She looked regal in a dress that hung from her shoulders straight to the ground. Beads formed patterns across her chest and down the dress, creating the illusion of shape on the simple robe. The patterns looked to be symbols, but their significance was not obvious to Cassidy. Margaretta spoke quietly to the couple for a minute. In the meantime, Gertrand approached and laid a small statue in between the couple. The statue itself was of an intertwined couple, well, more of the suggestion of two people in an embrace. It was crudely done, and at the same time, worn smooth with sheen that showed it was not only old, but often touched. The statue was white, like polished quartz, but with an underlying dark colour where it was worn, suggesting a darker stone at the core.

Gertrand stepped back. Margaretta looked toward her, a slight look of panic, but Gertrand nodded, offering support, but still staying within Margaretta's line of sight. Margaretta took a deep breath and turned back to the couple.

"Sim and Darta," Margaretta spoke to the couple, but raised her voice so it carried around the room. "You have come here to pledge yourselves to one another and to be partnered. It is a happy time when two people decide that they will devote themselves to one another, and you make the pledge to be loyal and faithful to each other, to keep each other safe, and to support each other in your daily community life."

The happy couple beamed at one another.

Margaretta continued, "I ask you, in front of the community, do you pledge to be partners?"

Darta and Sim enthusiastically agreed, smiling broadly.

"Do you have your charms, given to you as children?" Margaretta asked.

The couple each produced a small sliver of black stone tied to necklaces from the folds of their shirts and passed them to Margaretta. Margaretta untied the stones from their strings.

"These were given to you on the day of your naming; they show the devotion each of your parents had for you and your love for your parents."

She picked up the idol, turning it around so that the embracing couple were no longer in view, showing a fissure where the milky white stone was rubbed or broken away, revealing the dark mineral at the centre of the statue. Margaretta took the two fragments she had just been given, and brought them to the opening. She held one piece in either hand, but as she brought them closer to the statue, she brought her hands together.

No, Cassidy thought, *they are being* pulled *together*.

Looking closer, Margaretta was trying to keep the pieces apart, but as they neared the idol, she had more and more trouble keeping her hands apart. When she got within inches of the opening, the two pieces joined together and fused. Cassidy had never seen anything like it. There were definite magnetic properties to whatever was in that statue.

Margaretta brought the now single piece of material back to the couple.

"Please cup your hands together," she directed, and

the couple did, one nestling their hands in the other's.

"Your naming charms are now one, bringing you together as one. Keep it, and each other, close to your hearts." Margaretta turned back to the crowd, "Please, let us together celebrate the partnering of Sim and Darta!"

The townspeople cheered, hugged one another, and started moving toward the couple to embrace them. Even Cassidy ended up hugged by more than just Rim and Phia. While everyone was greeting the new couple, the platform was removed and a fire lit, filling the dusk with light and warmth.

Cassidy was pleased to have been invited to the ceremony. Being invited to view another culture's major ceremonies was no small privilege, and Cassidy was more than aware of how much trust they were putting in her. At the same time, she was here on a quest, and it was to retrieve a mineral with magnetic properties. It was not on the base, but rather here, and used for marriage ceremonies. If she could hazard a guess, given that Darta and Sim had pieces from when they were infants, their piece was likely split and given to their children, should they have any. It was obviously a very important part of their culture, but Cassidy might have to figure out how to take it back for Gamgee.

The evening went on. Copious amounts of food came out, laid on small tables around the room, and a group started playing music. Everyone ate and danced and laughed and celebrated. Cassidy joined in as best she could, but kept finding herself distracted by the idol.

CHAPTER SIX

The following morning, Cassidy found Margaretta at the breakfast table. After some small talk, and talk about the ceremony, Cassidy decided to just dive in and ask about the statue.

"So, at the ceremony last night," Cassidy started, "the statue, where did it come from?"

"That is the life idol. It was old when my great-grandfather was young. It isn't part of the first stories, but is part of the earliest stories," replied Margaretta.

"Oh," Cassidy thought about how important such a piece would be to a culture, but continued, "But where did it come from?"

"We don't know," Margaretta's tone changed, becoming the more lyrical tones of someone telling a familiar story. "Ishaul, many generations before, entered the forest on a clear and warm day. He carried a bow and a knife, and wanted to bring home a feast for the high sun celebration. This was Ishaul's first hunt on his own, and with pride, he bid his partner goodbye and ventured forth. Ishaul walked many miles, following the sun, the wind, and the river. On the bank of the river, Ishaul rested. At the waterfall, Ishaul refilled his water skins. Through the rocks he climbed, and saw a beast. It was large and would make a wonderful feast. Ishaul readied his bow and let an arrow fly. The arrow struck true, at the heart of the beast, but rather than fell the beast, it bounced off, landing in the grass. The beast did not notice Ishaul's arrow, and continued to rest. Ishaul tried again. The arrow flew true, and hit the heart of the beast, only to bounce off and join its brother in the grass. Ishaul had a single arrow left. He nocked the arrow, but just as he released it, a crack of thunder overhead startled him, and the arrow went wide. The clouds closed in, and moments later, opened and rained down on Ishaul and the beast. The beast awoke, and Ishaul ran, afraid of a creature that could not be felled by arrows.

"Ishaul hid from the beast and the rain by pressing himself in the shelter of a wall of rock. In the darkness, he found a bright and shining stone. In the darkness, it glowed. With no arrows and nothing for the feast, Ishaul took back the large stone. He used a chisel, and carved the milky surface of the stone. He carved a couple, in honour of his love for his partner. The statue was a gift to her, and she cherished it. When they were blessed with a child, and the child grew, the child knocked the carving from its place above the hearth and broke through the white stone, leaving the loving couple undamaged. The child tried to repair the damage by pushing the dark flakes of stone from the inside back into the statue. Ishaul caught the child.

"'I am sorry father,' the child cried, 'but I am fixing my mistake. See, the rocks fix themselves.'

"Ishaul observed, and as the child brought a sliver of black rock to the opening at the back, it healed itself, becoming one with the statue once again. As the child went to pick up the last piece, Ishaul stepped in.

"'No,' he said, 'this last piece is for you. This statue shows the love between myself and your mother, but you are part of that love, and you should carry this stone to know that you come from our love.'

"The child took the stone, tied it with string, and wore it. When the child was grown, he asked for a second sliver for the woman he loved. Ishaul gave it freely. When they partnered, they joined their pieces together to form one. When they had a child of their own, they asked for a sliver for the child. Ishaul gave it freely.

"Before Ishaul died, he gave the statue to his child, to celebrate their love. When Ishaul's child died, his partner returned his sliver of rock back to the statue, where it returned.

"Now we give children a piece of the statue on their name day, as a symbol of their parent's love. Those pieces are joined when they are partnered, and returned to the statue upon their death. It shows us all that we are all loved and all part of the one community."

Margaretta paused, and looked around at the other townspeople who had stopped to listen to the story.

"We have lost pieces over the years, as people have left, but it is so that they may always carry a part of the island with them, and know, no matter where they are, they are always part of us, and they are always loved. This was important yesterday, and important tomorrow, and we must remember this, even with the capital's military on our island."

Margaretta took a drink from her mug. The listening villagers seemed to know that the story was over and returned to their conversation. Cassidy did hear a few mentions of the base and the war in those discussions.

"That last part is new," explained Margaretta. "Stories are not really supposed to change, but when we talk about the morals or reasons for certain stories, we are supposed to try to reflect the current facts of life. The base is a sore spot for many, as you saw yesterday with my grandfather. But people have always left, the base is just making it easier for some."

"That was a wonderful story," said Cassidy. "It still doesn't really say where the statue came from though."

"No," replied Margaretta, "It does not, but it does give hints. Since Ishaul brought it back, people have looked for other pieces, but could not find them. We are not on a very big island, but it seems like Ishaul may have found the only piece. Why are you so interested?"

"Well, I am supposed to look for a mineral with strange magnetic properties, and it seems like your statue might be it."

"I hope not," said Margaretta, a little cautiously. "This statue has been part of our ceremonies for generations. We could possibly part with a sliver, like we give children on name day, but no more. Even that would have to be cleared by the storytellers, and they may not like the idea of more of the statue leaving than has already gone. They seem to like you enough, but they don't trust you."

Cassidy ran her hand through her hair as she thought about it. Gamgee had asked for a fairly large piece, almost half of what was in the statue. A sliver wouldn't be enough, but what if that was all she could get? There was still the matter of the inaccurate compass. There might still be something on the base, and that might be what she needed. Whatever this mineral was, it certainly seemed to have magnetic properties, but not enough to affect the compass like the base.

"I can wait. It might not even be what I'm looking for," Cassidy replied. "What I want might still be on the base; at least that's what my compass suggests."

Margaretta nodded.

"I hope it is. It would be better for you to earn a shard instead. The storytellers would much prefer that."

"But," Cassidy asked, "if the first piece is given at birth, how do the people here earn theirs?"

"No, no, not at birth," explained Margaretta. "It is given at their name day, which is usually when a child is old enough to start walking. Yes, we all get a piece just for being born here, but we do get people who come and stay on the island. We're not that isolated that there is no population movement. We don't like to see people move away, but we also welcome new people. Those people do have to spend time here and decide that it is the right place for them. Then they go through the name day ceremony, and if they want, pick a new name. Most don't, and we accept that."

"Oh, so like a citizenship ceremony? We have those in my world when people move from country to county."

Margaretta clapped, "Yes! Much like that. It's a way of saying that this is your home, where you take your tea."

"Well, that wouldn't work for me, I do have to return

to my side of the portal," Cassidy said solemnly.

"I understand that, but I trust you, and that's why I think the storytellers might let you have your own piece."

"Well, let's not worry about that until after I visit the base." Cassidy hoped she wouldn't have to wait for a naming ceremony or anything similar, but also hoped that what she needed was on the base and could be gotten without worrying about disrupting any of the island culture.

***

After breakfast, Margaretta took Cassidy to the gathering place where the wedding had taken place. In a small shrine sat the statue. Margaretta picked it up and brought it over to Cassidy. Cassidy reached toward it, then looked to Margaretta, who nodded. The statue was cool to the touch and worn smooth. Looking in the harder to touch areas, Cassidy could still see chisel marks around where the arms of the couple embraced. Other parts were significantly less defined, especially around the faces of the loving couple. Looking close, she could see how the quartz-like material was worn thin in certain areas and the darker material was starting to show through. Perhaps in another few generations it would be worn away entirely.

Cassidy took out her compass. Up close, the compass pointed directly at the statue. Cassidy pulled it back a few inches, and the needle started to waver. She took a few steps back, and it returned to bouncing between the two points.

"Your compass, right? What is it doing?" Margaretta asked.

"Something strange. Like I explained, on my world, it would point to the North Pole and I can use it to navigate. Here it keeps wavering between two points, so it wouldn't be easy to use if I were lost in the woods."

"Ah, yes, before yesterday, I had never seen one up close. We use the stars and the sun and the moss on the trees and the flow of the water," Margaretta explained. "They use other things on the base, but we use nature."

"I can understand that. I have used all of those things as well, especially this one time when I was out with just one other archaeologist and I lost my compass in a swamp and he dropped his on a rock, breaking it. That was an interesting day, but we made it out." Cassidy drifted off a little, thinking about that day out exploring with Jameson just a month ago. He threatened to never go off into the woods alone with her again. He didn't follow through, but did make a point of carrying a spare compass in a hard case after that day.

Cassidy shook off her memories and returned to the compass and the statue. After moving the compass forward and back a few more times she asked, "How does it cleave?"

Margaretta turned the statue over to the hole in the back. Cassidy could see that the white rock was thicker around the hole, likely not rubbed as much as on the carved side.

"It doesn't take much to remove a piece. It wants to be together, but at the same time, it seems to push away from itself when it is whole."

Margaretta took a small knife from a fold in her skirt and dug it into the hole. With just a little effort, she brought the knife out with a sliver of the dark stone.

"I will have to put this back. I really shouldn't have taken any out in the first place," she explained.

"I understand. I just want to look and then I will give it back," Cassidy promised.

She looked at the dark material. It was rather smooth, and shiny where it had been removed. Looking closely, she couldn't make out any grains in the rock; it reminded her of a fine-grain chert. She took a few steps back and held the compass out to the fragment. It pointed to it when right next to it, but at even an inch away it ignored the fragment and went back to the other two points. Cassidy walked back to the statue. If the compass was right next to the fragment, it would point to it, but when she brought them both to the statue, the compass pointed to the statue. On a whim, she took the outer casing off of the compass and placed the fragment on the north needle. Suddenly, the compass ignored the statue, and pointed just to the base.

"Wow, I didn't expect that," she breathed.

"Didn't expect what?" Margaretta asked.

"The material is magnetic, and will attract the compass needle. The larger the piece, the more the needle is attracted to it. But that happens for anything metallic. If I held the compass too close to my belt buckle or laid it on the hood of a car, it would throw off the reading."

"Okay..." Margaretta was clearly confused.

"But, if I put the fragment on the compass, it ignores the other points. I can bring it up to the statue and it still points just to the base."

She took a few steps back.

"And from here, it was pointing to the base and what I'm guessing is the northern pole, but with the fragment on it, it just points to the base. It must cancel out the other interference."

Cassidy wondered again if this was the material she needed to bring back. If Margaretta was this protective over a small piece, there's no way she'd be able to bring back even a significant amount without stealing it. Hopefully it wasn't what was needed and what Gamgee wanted was really on the base.

Reluctantly, she removed the piece of the statue from the compass and passed it back to Margaretta. Margaretta took it and brought it back to the statue. As she brought it inside the opening, it seemed to jump from her hand and blend back into the statue. Cassidy peered at it.

"May I?" she asked.

Margaretta nodded and Cassidy reached her hand in. The fragment wasn't just stuck back in, but had reformed back into the original material with no trace that it had ever been removed.

"This is amazing," she whispered.

"Yes, it is why we use it in our ceremonies. While there is so much in the world based in science, this feels like it is outside of that. I am sure it could be explained, but the mystery is a better story. Don't think that we worship it or anything, but it has been a part of our culture for so long that it feels almost mystical."

Margaretta beamed as she put the statue back.

"We navigate with the stars. We look for cues to read the weather. But we also rotate our crops to get the best yield and to make sure the soils stay healthy. We share stories and carry them with us. It is all part of who we are, as is this statue."

She closed the door.

"Now, I have sent word to the base; we should get you on your way," she smiled.

***

Rim led Cassidy to the edge of the village.

"If you follow the road, it will take you to the base. We never had a road here, but the base built it so they could drive their trucks back and forth to the village when they want things," explained Rim.

Cassidy thanked the child, and started along the road. She could see the fence that surrounded the base. It looked much like the older military bases she had seen in her own world; pictures of those from the Second World War. The metal fence was sturdy, but at the same time could be seen through, and she knew she wouldn't be sneaking up on anyone. Not that she wanted to. It seemed like in this world it was better to be forthcoming, if Margaretta and her fellow storytellers were any indication, and that would suit Cassidy just fine. As she came closer to the fence, she could see buildings. It looked like another village, only a short walk from the first, but could have, at the same time, been from different worlds. Margaretta's village had cozy wooden homes, all built a little differently, all with individual character; the base had rows of buildings with multiple doors, like a motel. Each section of each building, in fact each of these buildings, as there were a half dozen of them, all looked exactly the same. There weren't even any distinguishing decorations. Every window had the same curtains, and outside each door, under the window, was a small metal bench. The only difference between each room was the identifying number on the door. As she kept on, she came to larger buildings. These again were very similarly built with what looked like corrugated metal. They were all painted white, and again, hard to distinguish. She could see names painted above some of the doors, or at least what she could assume to be names. She would have to remember the general shape of the signs and hope to match them to their function. . There were some benches outside of some, and Cassidy took those to be the more social buildings, like the mess or a theatre, and guessed the ones without benches had work and maintenance functions.

Beyond the buildings, away from the road and away from the fence, stood the only building that looked different from the rest. It almost looked like a church. It was rectangular and had a spire in the centre. Cassidy squinted at the building. No, not a spire, a tower. It must be the main airfield building and the control tower. They would have to have a high vantage point to be able to see the aircraft.

At that thought, Cassidy noticed a plane taxiing down the runway that seemed to run from the main office along the backside of the residential area. She caught the movement, and still found it strange that the planes made very little noise, especially for propeller planes. She thought back to her flight to Fredericton and how her ears rang for hours after sitting so close to the engines. To be fair, it was a small plane, so everyone was pretty close to the engines. What a joy it would be to fly on a silent plane. Thinking about it, how much money had her world spent on trying to create silent aircraft? Something like this would certainly be in high demand back home.

"Perhaps the magnetic mineral had something to do with silent flight," Cassidy mused quietly.

She continued on toward the base. As she approached the gate, she noticed more activity inside. Most of it seemed to be soldiers running the perimeter of the fence, but others who were just milling around seemed to notice her back. Perhaps she should have asked Margaretta for some clothes, instead of wearing jeans and a button shirt. She certainly didn't look like one of the locals in this outfit, with the women mostly in long skirts.

The people of the base also offered a level of contrast in comparison to the village. The townspeople all wore locally made clothing. Some of the fabric seemed to be machine-made, but many also wore hand-woven cloths. Almost everything was hand-sewn. As she got closer, Cassidy noted that the soldiers all had identical uniforms, and they looked, by her standards, relatively modern. They didn't look like the coarser fabrics of 19th century wars, but the smooth lines of machine-made fabrics.

It was interesting to think that there seemed to be a modern world so very close to the island, but somehow this village kept its traditions, even if that might mean more work. Cassidy had participated in archaeological workshops to give better understanding of how fabrics were made and the traditional tools used, and she couldn't imagine going through the effort if ready-made fabrics were available. Sure, she could understand it from a cultural point of view, and did treasure the hand-woven skirt that she saved for important occasions, and loved her knit hat for the cold weather, but could not understand the want to continue such labour-intensive activities except as a hobby.

She decided to ask Margaretta about the tradition. There was obviously contact to the ominous capital, and people did seem to flow back and forth, but faced with a modern world, they must actively hold on to the traditional ways. From an anthropological point of view, it was fascinating. Not that Cassidy would write a paper on it, but she knew colleagues who would love such a research opportunity. For one, she couldn't publicize the presence of the portals, and second, it's not like she'd really take the time to sit and write a paper to put out for peer-review.

Nearing the gate, the two soldiers on duty stopped her.

"You don't look like you're from the village," one said suspiciously.

"That's just rude," scolded the other. "But he's right, you don't look like you're from the village. Or from anywhere else for that matter. That's a strange outfit."

Cassidy gave them each a quick look. Both were younger than her, with a little of the slouch of youth in their demeanour. Trying to stand at attention seemed like a lot of work, especially for the first one who spoke. His stance seemed better suited for milling around a shopping mall instead of guarding a military base. The other was a little more poised, but not by much. Both wore crisp uniforms, clean, bright boots, and small hats that just barely covered their heads. Other than the hats, which had no rims to keep the sun out of their eyes, but rather seemed to be designed to just cover the tops of their heads and hide their hair, the uniforms were very similar to those Cassidy might have seen on any base. The attitude was more like what she would have seen from teenage cadets when they didn't think supervisors were looking.

"I was told my visit was arranged. My name is Cassidy Cane and Margaretta, one of the storytellers from the village, sent me," Cassidy stated, trying to sound authoritative.

"I don't know nothing about that," said the first soldier.

"Oh, knock it off, tough guy." The second soldier turned to Cassidy. "Yeah, we were told someone from the village but not from the village was coming. Hang on, I'll go call it in."

The second soldier walked away, leaving Cassidy to suffer the glares of the first one.

He must be new to this, she thought.

The first soldier reappeared.

"I'll escort you in. Seems like the director of flight has been waiting for you. I wouldn't want to keep her waiting any longer."

Wonderful, thought Cassidy. *I took my time and enjoyed the walk and have kept this director of flight waiting. No one told me I should have rushed. Oh well, let's hope it doesn't ruin her first impression.*

CHAPTER SEVEN

The soldier was silent during their walk to the large building with the control tower. This didn't really help Cassidy, who was becoming a little more nervous with every step. She thought she might have preferred the glares and snarky remarks from the other one at the gate, instead of the professional silence as soldiers continued to run exercises around them.

Once in the building, the soldier had to buzz an intercom.

"Private Seware with Cassidy Cane to see Director Spear," he called in clipped tones.

Director Spear, Cassidy thought glumly, *that name does not sound like someone who tolerates tardiness.*

The intercom crackled with something indistinguishable, and a click followed by a buzz indicated the door was unlocked. Cassidy's escort opened it and directed her through. The inside of the building was sterile, almost hospital-like, with clean, white walls, long corridors dotted with white doors, and no decorations to be seen.

The soldier led Cassidy through a hallway, turned a corner, down another hall, up a flight of stairs, down another hall, and up another two flights of stairs, down yet another hallway, around a corner, and stopped at a door.

"This is Director Spear's office. Knock and she will let you in," Seware said, before turning and walking away.

I hope I'll be able to find my way out, thought Cassidy as she turned and knocked on the door.

"Enter," said a female voice.

Cassidy did as bade, summoned her courage, and stepped through the door.

As she entered, a woman a little older than herself stood up from her desk and walked toward Cassidy. Her uniform was similar in cut to the two soldiers at the gate, but a little more polished. She wore the green pants and shirt professionally, but also gave a feeling of being comfortable in the uniform. Unlike most of the soldiers Cassidy had seen so far, Director Spear's head was uncovered, and her auburn hair was back in a tight braid. She came around the desk and extended a hand to Cassidy. Cassidy shook it. The director's handshake was firm, but Cassidy no longer felt intimidated by her surroundings.

"Good morning, my name is Sharisan Spear. I am the Director of Flight here at the Vering Island Airbase. You must be Cassidy Cane," stated Director Spear.

"Cassidy is fine; thank you for seeing me."

"Then you can call me Shari. Really, I only expect Director Spear from those who serve under me."

"You know," mused Cassidy, "I have been here two days, and this is the first time I have heard the name of this place. In the village they just call it the village, the town, or 'this place'. It is sort of nice to know the name of the island."

Shari laughed. "I have noticed that as well. It is a strange place, this island. I am from Docknew, on the coast of the mainland of Astrada. It is nowhere near the capital city of Tian, but to most of the islanders here, it might as well all be one place. Except, of course, those who spent some time on the mainland; they have a better understanding of the size of the country. But I digress, let's have a seat and talk. Would you like something to drink?"

Cassidy answered affirmatively, and Shari poured two mugs of warm, golden liquid. It was fruity and spicy, not unlike a mulled cider Cassidy might have at a fall harvest festival.

"So, down to business," Shari directed. "I don't have much information, but you are from through the door in the woods."

Cassidy sputtered a little and choked on her drink.

Shari saw her anguish and tried to calm Cassidy.

"Oh, don't worry. The elders, or storytellers, sent word about you. We, of course, know about the door. That is one of the reasons we have a base here. It is not just a staging centre for aircraft, but a defence base. Your world seems to have many amazing technologies, and we cannot allow that to fall into enemy hands. We may not be able to spend much time in your world, but we can make certain no one else does either."

"I never really thought of it that way," Cassidy responded. "I have been to other worlds, but often no one knows about the portals. It's like it's an open secret here."

"Well, it sort of is. Of course, the general population doesn't know anything about it. Heck, most of the soldiers here don't know that is one of our missions. To most of the world, aeroplanes are our own invention, not something that was taken from another world and adapted to our own."

"I am curious about that. Planes at home are loud and the fuel makes them rather smelly, but yours are quiet and seem to have no environmental impact on the air."

Shari considered this statement before answering.

"Well, we did have to change quite a lot. Frake, the one who brought us back the plans, couldn't figure out how to change the design for use here; that's why he brought it to Tian, to get the help he needed. We couldn't make the aeroplane exactly the same as what is in your world because it would dirty our air. That is why we can no longer use the door, your air is so heavy that we cannot breathe there. Frake, years ago, could only stay for a few hours at a time. According to the storytellers, people moved more freely between worlds, but that was many years and many generations ago."

"Yeah, over the past couple of centuries our technologies have changed drastically, with a reliance on coal then fossil fuels that have changed how we live, but also pollute the world."

"Pollute. Fossil fuel," mused Shari. "Those aren't really words that we have here. We took what Frake gave us and looked for other ways to power it."

"What did you use?" Cassidy really hoped it might be the mineral she was looking for.

"Oh, now, I can't share all of our secrets," Shari smirked a little. "We do use halfstone, which is our main power source, from aeroplanes to lights and everything else. I know aeroplanes came from your world, but I still can't share how we've changed them. Not unless you can share information with us, then my superiors might be more willing to tell you."

Cassidy hesitated. "No, I really don't have anything I could easily share. I don't really know that much about modern technology. I study the past, so most of the technologies I've studied are hundreds, if not thousands of years old."

"That's too bad. But if you are not interested in technology, why do you ask about ours?"

"Two reasons. First, flying on planes at home can be very loud. I flew on one to get to the portal, one that looked a lot like the ones you have with the propellers, and it was so loud that my ears were ringing for hours after. At least the jet engines are much more comfortable. The second reason—"

"One moment, aeroplanes are different in your world?"

Oops, thought Cassidy, *perhaps I need to better watch what I say about technology.*

"Some of them are. They changed since they were first invented." Cassidy paused to try to figure out how to respond. "You see, the earlier planes used propellers, and from what I saw about the airfield that Frake visited, it would have been small prop planes used for a few years. Since then, technology has changed to make planes faster. I have no idea how a jet engine works, just that they can go faster and I think use a different kind of fuel, though I'm not sure about that. They also need much longer runways, so probably couldn't work on that airfield. It was probably one of the reasons why it closed"

Cassidy decided to not tell her that jet engines had greater distance capabilities, or their use in weaponry or space travel. Probably best to not give away those secrets, and if she could, give some of the disadvantages.

"Can you get us the information on how to use those jet engines?"

Yes, with a quick internet search, thought Cassidy, but instead she said, "Probably not. A lot of that technology is classified. State secrets."

"Hmmmm… that is unfortunate. That would really help us in this war," replied Shari with a tinge of disappointment in her voice. "So, what is your other reason for interest in our aeroplanes?"

"Well, you see, I am here to find a mineral with magnetic properties, and while I don't understand all of the principles of magnetism, I figure there might be a way that it could be used to power your silent planes."

"And why do you want it?" Shari was getting a little suspicious of Cassidy, and wondered if she was being entirely truthful about not being able to share information.

"You see, I work for a man who does a lot of good in the world. He sends me places to find things that he uses to help people in my world. He has cured diseases because of what he has found elsewhere. I help because he can't physically visit other worlds anymore."

"Is he sick? Why can't he cure himself?" asked Shari.

"No, just a little too old for it. He says adventure is for young people, so here I am!" Cassidy smiled, momentarily recalling some of her adventures since she met Dr. Gamgee.

"How does he know where to send you?"

Cassidy paused. "I don't know. I have sometimes wondered that myself."

"You don't ask? You are a good soldier, we look for that here."

Cassidy was a little offended at the idea of being a soldier who doesn't question. She questioned a lot, but never really where Gamgee gets his information. If she asked, she might not be sent on these missions anymore, and that would mean less adventure and more work in the lab.

"I have a job already," Cassidy replied a little curtly.

Shari laughed, "I didn't mean to offend. You just don't seem like the type who wouldn't question. I do a lot of recruiting, and your comment would have flagged you as someone I would want. Intelligent, but at the same time, not questioning."

Cassidy still didn't know what to think on the matter. She sat there in silence, thinking about her own actions. Maybe if she had questioned a little more she wouldn't have ended up in some of the more dangerous situations. But then, weren't those situations the ones that made it all worthwhile?

"So I have offended. Okay, let's go back to your question. I will tell you that there is nothing magnetic that fuels our aeroplanes. We do use some magnetic devices for navigation, but not to make the aircraft fly."

Cassidy perked up a little, "Could I maybe see some of the navigational equipment?"

"I don't see why not. It is not a state secret. In fact, it is technology that is so readily available that we give it to kids when they want to go exploring."

That sounded familiar to Cassidy. She reached into her pocket and pulled out her compass. She opened it up and showed it to Shari.

"Is it something like this? Like a pocket compass?" Cassidy asked.

Shari looked at the compass. "Yes, exactly like that. We usually call it nav for navigation."

Cassidy looked down at the compass. It was still wavering between two points, but this time it seemed to be one beyond the base, and off to the side. If the source of the magnetism was at the base, then likely the compass would have been even more erratic, or very still and pointing directly to the source. Cassidy wasn't sure what would happen, but that it would indicate something different.

"I see you get the same interference on yours as we do on ours," Shari observed. "There is something on this island that throws off our instruments. We have to be at least a hundred miles out into the ocean before the navs level out and just point toward the pole."

"From the village, it would point to the base, so that's why I assumed something was here," Cassidy explained.

"Yes, we are on the line to the pole from the village."

So the equivalent to north or south, thought Cassidy. *Then what is the other thing?*

"We have tried to find the source of the interference," Shari continued, "but without any success. We have flown over, but the source seems both large and small at the same time. We have narrowed down a potential area, but even on the ground we cannot find it. Unfortunately, we have lost aeroplanes when they have tried to land here and lost their way."

"That's tragic," Cassidy replied, then added, without thinking, "but easily fixed."

She stopped when she realized what she had said. That wasn't information for her to give. She had reacted to the idea of lives being lost, not what it would mean to Margaretta and her kin.

"You know how to fix the problem?" Shari asked with interest.

"Well, it's not really mine to tell." Cassidy hesitated, "It belongs to the people of Vering."

Shari stood up and leaned toward Cassidy, both hands on her desk.

"We have lost many men and women because of this anomaly. You must tell me how to fix this navigational problem. Lives are at stake," Shari insisted.

Cassidy thought, and spoke carefully, "There is something at the village, but I really cannot say more. It is important to the people there."

"Important enough that they would allow people to die for it?" Shari started to raise her voice. "Important enough that they would risk losing the war?"

Cassidy stood up. She did not appreciate being spoken to in such a way. She was not one of Shari's soldiers.

"Have you met the people in that village? Sure, many serve here, but many more would happily see the war over if it meant this base was gone. Taking the statue would give them even more reason to resent the base, and relations would get even worse," Cassidy argued.

"Statue?"

Cassidy mentally cursed and thought, *My big mouth. I*

need to learn to think before I speak.

"Statue," repeated Shari. "That trinket I have heard they use in ceremonies? We have to fight with soldiers from the village to take off those necklaces that are all part of this statue."

That gave Cassidy an idea.

"Would the soldiers give up their necklaces for the war effort? The mineral in those can fix the compass issue, and they should have plenty for the base to use." Then Cassidy added hopefully, "Then you could leave the statue be."

"That could work, depending on how much we have on base, and how much we need to use. But we have hundreds of planes. No, we need the source. What if it falls into enemy hands?"

"That's asinine!" exclaimed Cassidy. "You know fullwell it won't fall into enemy hands because the whole point in the base being here is to protect the portal. You said so yourself!"

Shari gave Cassidy a serious look.

"Watch yourself. I could arrest you where you stand. This is a military base after all, and I have to put the safety of my troops first. I might feel you are keeping important information from us, and could hold you until I feel you have given me all the information I need."

Cassidy stepped back.

"Please, let me talk to the storytellers at the village and explain the situation. I'm sure they'll be agreeable to help you. If you just take it, you'll ruin whatever goodwill they have."

"Why am I worried about their goodwill when lives

are on the line?" Shari asked.

"What is the point in fighting a war if it only hurts your fellow countrymen?" Cassidy countered.

Shari considered.

"Fine." Shari sat, rested her elbows on the desk and tented her fingers. "Go, talk to the village. Talk to the elders. I will collect what I can on base. Tomorrow morning I expect them to provide enough to fix all of our navigational equipment. I do not do this lightly. If they have something to save lives and help win the war, then we will have it. Make sure you convince them."

"I will do what I can to keep the peace."

"I am not as worried about the peace as I am about winning this war," Shari said, deadly serious.

CHAPTER EIGHT

Cassidy found herself walking back to the village. She was feeling lost, and angry at herself. Once again, she didn't stop to think before she spoke and she may have messed things up. On one side, if Shari could use the stone to save lives, that was a good thing. But on the other side, this statue has been important to the people of the village for generations. They already felt like the base had ruined their way of life, and now it was going to take their sacred object from them. Well, maybe it wouldn't come to that. After all, there were a number of people on the base who had shards of the stone, so maybe there would be more than enough.

Cassidy almost laughed at herself for such a thought. She knew full-well that there were a significant number of planes flying to and from the base. There was no way the military would stop with just the aircraft doing patrols or regular milk runs. They'd want to outfit all of their aircraft with better navigational equipment on the off chance they had to turn back or get diverted to the island. At the very least, they'd want every plane that had even the slightest chance of flying near the island upgraded. Then, after the war, they'd probably want any military, diplomatic, or commercial aircraft outfitted with it. If her home was any indication, there were probably people already discussing the prospect of commercial air travel after the war. In her own history, commercial air travel over the ocean was almost non-existent prior to the Second World War, but with the improvements made during the war, air travel between North America and Europe became much safer and commercial flying became much more common once the war ended. It would be reasonable to guess something similar would happen in this world. After all, they had not really worked to improve aircraft much before this war, but were certainly making a great deal of use of it now that there was a world-wide conflict.

A horrible thought crossed Cassidy's mind. She didn't know anything about this war. Everyone was very friendly, even if Commander Shari was a little intense, but who was the aggressor in this war? If she helped, would she be helping the good guys or the bad guys? Of course they would count themselves as the good guys, so she'd never know by talking to people. If the portal had dropped her into an Axis country in 1944, no one she spoke to would think they would be considered the bad side by the history books, would they? She kind of wished she had paid more attention to modern history.

This mission was turning into more thinking and less action than she was used to. Usually it was so straight forward, and this time she was left wondering about what to do, who she might be hurting, and even who she might be helping.

At the edge of the village, Rim saw her and ran over

to greet her.

"How was the base?" Rim asked. "I never get to go see it. I want to see the aeroplanes and the soldiers. Their buildings are very different from ours, and all boring."

Cassidy laughed at the child's excitement.

"Yes, it was pretty boring. No colour there at all, not like here. And all of the buildings look exactly the same. Even inside, everything looked the same. The soldiers were okay. Some were friendly, some tried to be scary."

"Scary how? Did someone threaten you?"

"Oh no no no. They just tried to make me feel scared, but it didn't work. Most people there were very nice. Do you know where Margaretta is?" Cassidy figured if she didn't head off Rim's questions she'd never get away.

"I think she's in her home," Rim said, paused, and then gave a little jump. "I can take you there!"

Rim led the way, asking questions about the base the entire time. Cassidy knew it was just curiosity on the child's part, but also wondered if relations would be better with the base if they did things like tours for the people of the village. Rim certainly didn't see them as monsters, but, at the same time, Rim also wouldn't understand the fears over losing their culture to the "capital".

Once at the cottage, Rim barged in, announcing that Cassidy was back from the base, and started recounting some of what Cassidy had said. Margaretta listened for a few moments, then shooed Rim away, stating the need to talk to Cassidy. Margaretta invited Cassidy in, brought her to an open room, and sat her down on a cushion. Margaretta sat on another and, before she could say anything, Olisker came in with three mugs of a warm, spiced, berry drink. He handed the mugs around, and Cassidy took a moment to smell the spicy sweet drink and take in the room.

It was certainly the living area of the house. There was a small, low table in the centre of the room, and cushions all around. A nice spot for lounging or for a group of people to gather and comfortably talk. There were a couple of paintings on the wall, both landscapes, and it looked like a mixed media work as there was a sparkle and roughness to the beaches that implied sand was mixed in with the pigments. Margaretta's living room was ringed with bookcases, the paintings sitting over shorter cases. Cassidy couldn't read the script, assuming the decorative scrolling symbols just didn't translate clearly, but could guess that many of these books, especially the older-looking tomes, were probably some of the stories she helped keep, just written down. Overall, Cassidy thought the room was cozy and comfortable, and could almost see herself enjoying the space to do some reading or research. Almost.

After a moment, Margaretta started the conversation. "How did it go at the base?" she asked.

"Honestly, I'm not sure. We seemed to have a pretty good conversation, but then I seemed to just say too much a few times."

Olisker narrowed his eyes at Cassidy. "What does that mean?"

"Well," she continued, sheepishly, "I misspoke about jet engines, a newer kind of engine for planes at home. They're faster and can go further, and I shouldn't have said anything because I think the flight director might want me to bring her information on them. And that had me kind of flustered," Cassidy was rambling now, agitated and worried, "and we started talking about planes crashing because of the funny navigation around the island and I mentioned the compass and the magnetic stone, and she was interested in it and is going to experiment with what the locals on the base have and I'm worried that that's not enough and she's so focused on the war effort that now I'm afraid..."

Margaretta looked panicked, but calmed her features and put a hand on Cassidy's shoulder.

"Breathe. You are saying a lot, but it's coming out mixed up. I think you have to tell us, but just one thing at a time. Take a drink. Breathe."

Cassidy took a long drink from her cup. Her pulse raced, but not in the way she craved. This was agitated and erratic. She took another drink. Cassidy looked at the other two, her anxiety feeding theirs. She took a deep breath and started again.

"I was talking with Flight Director Spear. We were having a nice conversation, but she made me sort of flustered. She knew things I didn't expect, like that I was from the other world, and asked for things. But I should have expected that, given that planes come from my world. Next thing I know, I'm talking about jet engines, which is a newer kind of engine that can go further than the kind of planes you have now. We started talking about navigation and how this island does something strange to compasses. She said people have died because of it. And without thinking, or maybe just thinking about how people have died, I said how the piece from the statue fixed it."

Margaretta and Olisker looked horrified. Cassidy tried

to explain and apologize.

"I didn't mention the statue itself! I just said 'the piece of stone' and she figured it out. She knows a lot about this place, and my place, and I didn't expect that, but I should have expected that because isn't that what militaries are like everywhere? On every world? They always know more than you expect."

She started to panic again, and Margaretta once again put her hand on Cassidy's shoulder. Cassidy ran her hands through her hair, then picked up her cup and took another drink.

"She's going to ask the people from the village who are on the base to give her their fragments of the statue. I don't know if she's just going to ask, or if she's going to take them. And she's asked me to ask for more; enough for their planes. She thinks it's all superstition and your statue doesn't matter when people are dying."

Olisker got up. "I'm going to gather the storytellers. We will have to talk about it and figure out what we have to do."

Margaretta nodded and said, "I'll take care of Cassidy. Can you send someone to get Phia to come and sit with her? I will come when Phia arrives. Please start without me."

Olisker left and Cassidy started to calm a little.

"I have messed everything up," Cassidy sighed. "I'm used to going places where I don't have to think about things like this. It's always so clear, and then here it's all so muddled. The statue is important to you, it's been in your first stories, but it's important to the base because people are dying. I've studied situations like this in my undergrad ethics courses, but I've never had to deal with something myself. And when I find myself involved, I just ruin everything."

"Hush now," Margaretta calmed. "We will work it out. The statue is important, but, like you've said, people are dying. I did not know that. The storytellers didn't know that. We'll talk. We'll figure something out..."

Margaretta didn't sound very confident, but was steady in how she spoke, and that helped calm Cassidy. Moments later, Phia came in. Margaretta asked her to sit with Cassidy, and got up and left, repeating, "We'll figure something out."

***

A few hours later, evening was falling and Phia suggested they get something to eat. Cassidy hadn't eaten since that morning, but was nervous about facing the storytellers. Phia reassured her and they went out. The food was good, but the tension seemed high. There wasn't as much conversation as at other meals. The storytellers were at a table to themselves, with no one near them.

"When they do that, it means they are discussing something important," Phia explained, although Cassidy really didn't need the explanation. She just wished she could have some sort of an indication that things would be okay, but they were all so engrossed in their discussion that none of the storytellers even noticed her and Phia come in. Even Rim was more subdued than usual, not bouncing around, just quietly eating with another group. In fact, all of the kids seemed quiet. Everyone seemed to know something was wrong, and Cassidy wondered if they all knew that she was the one who caused it.

After they ate, Cassidy and Phia went back to Phia's home.

"If Margaretta wants us, she will check here after her own house," Phia explained.

Phia's living room was like Margaretta's in that it had a short table surrounded by cushions. Cassidy was surprised that Phia's home was not nearly as colourful, and most of the cushions were dark colours, deep purples and blacks. There weren't as many bookcases, but there were a few shelves with a few books, and a lot of knick-knacks. Cassidy took a closer look and recognized some things. There was a green glass cola bottle, some red bricks stamped with English lettering, a railroad spike, what looked to be musket balls, and a very old hafted scraper and bone needle. The scraper was a small stone tool used by the Indigenous people who used to live along the Wolastoq River, renamed the Saint John by Europeans, to prepare hides. It was wrapped in some very dry, very brittle sinew. Cassidy longed to touch it, but knew it must be at least a few hundred years old and would probably crumble if she touched it. But to find such a thing intact was any archaeologist's dream.

Phia caught her looking at the treasures.

"My family has used the door for many years. It used to be that we were the ones who would go through and see what we could find. It was one of the women of my family who found the door when out collecting plants. Margaretta would tell it better – she's the storyteller after all – but it was our family responsibility to collect things. We used to trade with people on the other side of the door, but then new people came, and the trade changed.

It became less about sharing food and more about sharing things. Then it got harder and harder to travel through the door, and my family stopped going."

Phia looked at the items, a hint of sadness in her features.

"Have you ever gone through the door?" Cassidy asked.

"I tried once, but the air was so thick and heavy that I could only stay there for a minute. It was nice to look around, though, and feel a different sun, even if it was just for a moment."

Silence weighed heavy in the room.

"It's a strange thing," Phia continued, "having a role, a responsibility, passed down through the generations, only to have it taken away through no fault of your own. It is something I've had trouble reconciling. I even left for a while, trying to find a new role, but I haven't found what is right. I more end up taking care of the people who come through the door, rather than getting to go through to meet them."

She indicated the objects around the room. "We still trade, but it isn't the same because it's whatever people have on them when they come through, and many seem to have very little, so we would rather give than trade. It's not easy for us, though. We don't have a lot here, although we could if we opened up more to the capital..."

Phia faded off again.

"What sort of things did you trade for?" Cassidy prompted.

"Interesting foods, and you do many wonderful things with different kinds of metals on your side of the door. We have traded for pots and pans, and tools to fish with. We have such things here, of course, but some of yours work differently. When your people started using nets made out of different material, and the thin line to fish with, it was so much more durable than us growing plants to make the rope to make the nets. And sometimes we could get the fire rocks, and those we could keep for long, hard winters when the dry wood gets low."

Plastic, nylon, and coal. *Interesting and practical trades*, thought Cassidy as she looked at an empty soda can.

"I don't think they fish on that river a whole lot anymore, it seems mostly like a city. And not many people use coal to heat their homes anymore." Cassidy brightened. "I will have to repay everyone's kindness, so maybe I will be able to get some of those things to bring back through. I can't promise anything, but I can try." She wondered if she would be able to talk to anyone in the homeless community about such trade, but, like Phia said, chances are they had very little to start with anyway.

"Oh," Phia brightened, "that would be wonderful! I don't suppose you live near the door, do you?"

"No. Once I leave after this, it would be difficult for me to get back."

"Well, at least it would be something. Many thanks."

"Don't thank me until I see if I can do it." Cassidy gave a little smile, worried about what was going to happen with the statue.

With that, a child younger than Rim popped into the room.

"Hello Tor," Phia introduced. "Are you here to collect Cassidy?"

The child nodded and said shyly, "The storytellers need her."

CHAPTER NINE

Cassidy quickly said goodbye to Phia and rushed after Tor. The child was nearly running and Cassidy struggled to keep up. Tor brought her to another house, a few lit lamps flickering through the window to stave off the first hints of twilight.

"They want to talk to you; I said I'd get you," Tor said quietly but proudly, and brought Cassidy to the door before running off again. Cassidy kind of wanted to run away as well.

"Come in Cassidy," came Margaretta's voice from inside.

Cassidy took a deep breath, and entered. All of the storytellers were standing around a kitchen, each holding mugs. Margaretta took a mug from the table and offered it to Cassidy. She took it and wrapped her hands around its warmth, taking comfort in the feeling and smelling the spicy liquid. She didn't take a drink, she was too nervous for that.

Sasamuel cleared his throat and started. "Cassidy." His voice was stern, but not intimidating. Cassidy relaxed just a little. "In talking to the flight director at the base, you have put us in a difficult situation. We know the idol has no magical properties and is just a symbol of a long-ago story that connects us to this place. But you are saying that if we give some of it to the flight director it could save lives. We have decided that we will give a large piece from inside of the statue to help the fighters, because that is what we do, we help." This last bit wasn't said for Cassidy, as Sasamuel shot Carlson a hard look, who in turn, muttered something about "people through the door should keep their stuff on their own side."

The rest of the storytellers, Margaretta included, glared at him. Sasamuel continued, "Not everyone is in agreement, but we have been helping the people who have come to our island for generations. Many of our stories involve helping people, so we're not going to stop now. Plus," again he glared at Carlson, "the people through the door are not the ones who gave us the aeroplanes; that was our own people going through and learning new technologies." Looking back to Cassidy, his features softened. "We help. Sometimes we'd trade with the other side of the door, but we never ask for anything. If people are dying, it is our responsibility to help. Tomorrow, we will bring some of the statue to the base, and hopefully they will let our people keep their personal fragments of the statue."

Margaretta stepped around the table and over to Cassidy. She took Cassidy's mug, still full, and laid it on the table. She took both of Cassidy's hands in her own.

"We know you didn't mean to say anything to the flight director, but in a way, we are happy that you did. We did not know that people were dying trying to get to our island. Don't despair, just, if something like this comes up again, maybe talk to us first," she said with a kind smile.

"I will. Thank you. And I am still very sorry for all of it," Cassidy replied. Margaretta looked at Cassidy once more before wrapping her arms around her and giving her a big hug.

***

Cassidy awoke the next morning to general commotion. She could hear people yelling and running around. She threw off her blanket and grabbed her bag, pulled out some clothes and hauled them on. She quickly tied her hair back and walked out the door.

Soldiers were marching past her building. She looked toward the centre of town and saw villagers running around and soldiers moving toward the gathering hall. She started moving that way, trying to find out what was happening. She found Director Spear walking out of the building holding the statue. Margaretta followed close on her heels.

"Please, don't take it," Margaretta begged. "We are happy to share it, but please, don't take the whole thing! It's important to our community."

Shari turned to face Margaretta.

"We need this. We need all of this. This will save lives. This will help win the war." She looked at the idol then back to Margaretta. "It is your duty to help your countrymen and women to help win the war." Shari turned on her heels and marched away, barking orders to her soldiers as she went.

Sasamuel came up next to Cassidy.

"She took the idol. All of it. The rest of the storytellers are not happy, and when word gets around the village that you told them about it, well," Sasamuel paused, then said, very seriously, "we're a giving people, but it might be best if you leave for a little while until things calm down somewhat."

Cassidy just looked at him for a moment and said, "I didn't mean to cause this."

"I know," he replied, "but it will take everyone else a while to know that as well."

Cassidy turned back to the guest house, threw her stuff in her bag and quickly went to the border of the village. Just past the last house, Phia and Rim caught up with her.

"Are you leaving Cassidy?" Rim asked.

"I think it's for the best right now," Cassidy replied.

"What happened? Why are the soldiers here?"

"I made a mistake and the soldiers took your idol. But I am going to go away to try to make it right." Cassidy knelt down to talk to Rim face-to-face. "I will fix this." She looked up at Phia. "I will."

Phia took Cassidy's hand and pulled her back to her feet. "We know, Cassidy. You are a good person."

Cassidy smiled, and left the village.

***

She wasn't sure what she should do. She walked into the woods and just walked for a while. She couldn't go back to the village, but she did have to try to get the idol back. She also didn't want to go back to her own world yet, not when she had found the mineral she needed, but lost it. She wandered for a while, not really knowing which way she was going, until the trees thinned and she could see the base.

If nothing else, she thought, *perhaps I could talk to someone about it.*

Cassidy approached the gate and saw the same soldiers as before. She approached Private Seware, not really looking for the aggression of the other soldier.

"Hello. I am wondering if I might be able to meet with the flight director. Please." Cassidy tried to sound confident, but her nerves were getting the better of her.

"One moment, and I will call in," replied Private Seware.

The private walked away, leaving Cassidy once again with the other soldier.

"Um, my name is Cassidy, by the way," she tried being friendly, but only received a grunt in reply.

Better than being rude like last time, Cassidy thought.

Private Seware came back. "Flight Director Spear is not available right now, but has invited you to stay here for the time being. She will find you when she is ready."

That solves that problem, thought Cassidy as she allowed herself to once again be led on base.

Private Seware brought Cassidy to a barracks and gave her a key to one of the rooms.

"You can leave your bag here. This is your room for the time being. The flight director said she might not see you today."

Cassidy opened the door to a spartan room containing a small bed, desk, and chair. She stepped in and laid her bag on the bed. Turning back to Private Seware at the door, she noted the door to a bathroom and a small wardrobe. Basic, but comfortable.

Locking the door behind her and pocketing the key, Cassidy followed Private Seware to the mess hall.

"You can move freely within the two buildings, but nowhere else on the base. Meals are available for an hour after dawn, an hour at high sun, and for two hours before dusk. When she wants you, Flight Director Spear will send for you."

With that, Private Seware turned and walked away, leaving Cassidy in the empty mess hall. Cassidy wandered outside, looking at the sun, thinking that there might be another hour or so before the sun was at its zenith, so she went back to her room and unpacked her small bag and washed herself and some of her clothes in the small sink. Not that the village was unclean, and as the only person in the guest house the bath was private, but Cassidy was a little uncomfortable with the communal space and that people didn't seem to knock at the village.

Refreshed, but still unsure of what to do, Cassidy went back to the mess hall to find food. With all of the confusion of the morning, she had not eaten, but still was not really hungry, but thought it was best to do something. She could smell the food as soon as she passed through the door, and her stomach did give a little grumble. The hall was much more active than before, with thirty or forty people in the room. Some were sitting, while others were in line, holding plates. Cassidy picked up a plate and took her place at the end of the line. Within moments, some soldiers got in line behind her.

"Hi!" one young man said to her, "you must be the one from through the door. I'm Breen, this is Aline," indicating the woman next to him, "and behind her is Trice." The other two nodded in acknowledgement.

"Does everyone know about the door?" Cassidy asked.

"At this point, just about. Half of us here are from the village; myself and Aline were born there. Trice is from a small town on the other side of the channel, so is almost from the island." Aline elbowed Trice, and he grinned at the gentle teasing. "So we've always known about the door, but news got around the base pretty quick, both from talking to our families and from the on-base rumour-mill, that there was someone from the other side who could talk to us."

Trice piped up with, "Thanks for finding out about the compass. I lost my brother a couple of months ago, and they figure he just got lost. So, thanks." Trice blushed a little, but put out his hand. Cassidy took his hand and he shook hers briefly before dropping her hand and letting his fall back to his side. Cassidy felt like she was blushing a little herself.

Before she could say anything, Cassidy found herself far enough in the line to be at a small counter. Following the person in front of her, she placed her plate on the counter, and the person behind the counter put some food on it. She pushed the plate along the counter, and other staff put more food on her plate. When it was full, she took the plate, walked toward the long tables and hesitated. Breen came up behind her.

"Drinks are over this way." He led her to a variety of

juices in jugs. They each poured up a glass, and he invited her to sit with them.

The four of them sat at the end of one of the long tables, and Cassidy started to pick at her mountain of food. Once again, she couldn't recognize anything and really wanted the comfort of something she knew. The other three asked her a few questions, but then started to talk about their own lives on the base.

"So, do you think they're going to put the new nav equipment on all the aeros? Even the little ones? Or is it just for the big ones?"

"Oh, I hope it's the little ones, too. I have a supply run coming up and want to give it a try."

"Did you hear Thulu got reprimanded for trying to sneak off base? Seems he's got a bit of a thing for one of the guys in the village."

"I didn't hear that one, but it sounds like Celia might have had a secret date with Amer."

"Wait, Celia on the gate? And I hear it was Amer in the village that Thulu liked!"

"Sounds like a love triangle!"

Cassidy wasn't really listening while the three discussed base and village gossip. They all seemed friendly enough, and that 'thank you' from Trice had sent her back into her thought spiral. Meeting people who were so grateful about the discovery made her feel even more confused. And she still had to figure out how to get some of the statue back to Gamgee.

Cassidy was pulled out of her thoughts as the other three tried to engage her a little.

"So, what can you tell us about the other side of the

door?" Aline asked.

"And what are the aeros like?" Trice leaned forward, waiting for an answer.

Cassidy considered. "First, I can't tell you much about the planes. That's what we call them. Airplane, or planes for short. I have flown in them, but only as a passenger."

"A passenger? Like on a supply run?"

"Not really. We use planes for military runs, sure, but most air travel is commercial, meaning people pay to be flown from one place to another, often to go on business or holiday."

The trio were shocked. Aline wanted to know more. "So, not just supplies, but for leisure? We don't have enough for something like that!"

"We didn't either, at first, but after our last worldwide war people started using planes instead of boats to get around the world."

It was Breen's turn to question. "You had a whole world war like ours? Did the good guys win?"

"We did. Two of them, wars that is, but planes were used more in the second one. But that was 70 years ago. When the technology for planes was brought through the door that was during or just after the war. And from what I can tell, that airfield was mostly used for leisure flying and as a flight school. It didn't get big airplanes."

"What about who won?" pressed Trice.

"Our side won. But there were heavy losses on both sides, and a lot of civilians killed in horrible ways." She didn't know how to bring up the atrocities of the Second World War with these people from another world that she had just met.

"So the side with the aeros won!" crowed Trice.

"Both sides had planes," Cassidy explained. "In fact, it could be argued that the other side had better engines in some cases."

Breen said quietly, "They keep telling us we'll win because of the aeros."

"I can't really predict anything like that. I'm not an expert in planes or the wars of my world. I wouldn't be able to say anything on battle strategies and why one side won and one side didn't. There have been other wars, but nothing on the same scale."

The three considered this and Breen commented, "I hope we win."

That seemed to end the conversation, and all four of them started to pick up their dishes. Cassidy figured it was best if she just headed back to her room. She had caused enough trouble and didn't want to cause more problems. If she did, they might march her back to the portal and she'd never finish her mission. Bored, she laid on her bed and eventually drifted off to sleep.

CHAPTER TEN

For the next two days, Cassidy heard nothing from Shari. She was starting to worry that the flight director had forgotten about her. She would go to the mess hall at meal times, usually lingering over a hot drink or slowly picking at her food. Sometimes someone would sit with her, and they would have some idle chit chat. She wasn't feeling the same connection she had with Margaretta and Phia, or perhaps she was purposefully keeping herself distant. Trice would often make a point to sit with her and chat. At first, she thought there might be some sort of attraction, but really, it seemed that he was just grateful for her role in making flights around the island safer. They would talk, but he often wanted to talk about airplanes in greater detail than Cassidy was familiar with, and she was often lost in his questions and explanations.

At supper on the second day, Cassidy had arrived at the mess hall early, as she was wont to do with nothing else to occupy her time, and as she was trying yet another mystery food, Trice almost bounded over to her.

"Cassidy! I have amazing news!"

His smile was huge. She noticed he hadn't even picked

up his food before coming to talk to her. She looked up at him, and he pulled out the chair opposite to her.

"Flight Director Spear said I can take you on a flight around the island!"

Cassidy was shocked, "She said what? Why?"

"I was given the assignment to test the new nav equipment and fly around the island. I don't know, maybe they hope we can start to map this place or something. But I have the most flight hours of anyone currently on crew, and most of those are supply runs to and from the island, so she figured I should get to test it. And she suggested I take you. As a reward! Isn't that amazing?!"

He was thrilled with the idea. So was Cassidy. She was tired of being cooped up with nothing to do. At least when she was stuck on an archaeological site she was finding artifacts or fixing equipment or something. Laying around, literally, was torture.

"So I'll get to see the island?" she asked.

"Yeah! We'll go tomorrow just after first light. Grab some extra food to take back to your room so you can eat in the morning. It's not regulation, but it's what we all do. We should be back before lunch, but I'll get meal kits just in case." He beamed at her again. "I can't wait!"

With that, he dashed off to get in line for food. A few minutes later he was back with Breen, talking to him just as excitedly about the flight.

"So, it's not like it's top secret; they wouldn't tell me that beforehand," Trice was explaining as he sat down. "I'm to test the new nav equipment and see if there is the probability that we might be able to map this island." He turned to Cassidy. "There isn't even a map to this island.

How absolutely ridiculous is that? But we've never had the equipment to do it."

Cassidy listened and wondered why a magnetic compass was their only option. She thought about the time she was on a site and they didn't have a working compass. A bunch of archaeologists and not one working compass between them was a story in itself, but they had a geometry set for drawing maps and used the protractor to create a map. It was painfully slow, but it was an isolated dig and a two day drive to the nearest shop. The biggest problem was that they couldn't orient the map in the real world. That was easily fixed on the next supply run, but without a compass, there was no way to do it right. She could only imagine the difficulty of flying, where navigation was so important.

"Alright, Cassidy," Trice declared. "Get that extra food and head off. We'll be up early."

With that, he shoved back his chair, walked to the desserts, picked up a few things, and left. Cassidy liked his idea of breakfast, and followed his lead.

***

The next morning, Cassidy stood outside of her quarters, unsure where to go. The sky was starting to lighten and she was worried about missing the flight. Next thing, Breen was running toward her, carrying a small bag.

"I figured Trice forgot you didn't know your way around. While he's a great pilot, he sometimes gets a little too focused on the flight and forgets about silly things like that. It's a good thing someone else has to worry about his logistics..." Breen handed her the bag. "Here's a lunch, in case he forgot one for you. I doubt it, he might forget everything else, but not food. Come on."

Breen led the way across the base to the airfield. The doors to the second hangar were open, and a crew were bringing out an aircraft. Trice was watching, holding a clipboard and directing the crew.

"Trice!" Breen called. "You forgot about Cassidy!"

Trice turned and waved. "What? Really? Well, thanks for bringing her. Hey Cassidy. I picked up your lunch."

Cassidy and Breen shared a smile.

"Hi. Thanks, Breen, for showing me where to go."

"No trouble. Be safe, don't let him show off too much."

"I won't," Cassidy said as Breen turned and ran off, probably to head off to wherever he was supposed to actually be.

Cassidy turned to Trice. "So, what can I do?"

Trice glanced at his clipboard, the airplane, then at her. "I think maybe see if one of the flying suits fit you. You'll be more comfortable. Just haul it over your regular clothes."

Cassidy found a number of dull, grey coveralls hung on pegs along a back wall. She sorted through them, looking for one in her size. After trying on two, the third fit comfortably enough. She was buttoning the suit as she walked back to Trice.

"That looks like it fits well," he said. "The aeroplane is ready to go, and I have all of the outside safety checks done. Let's climb in and I'll start the next batch of checks."

"I am glad to see that there are a lot of safety checks. That makes me much more comfortable."

"Why? Do they not do safety checks where you are from?"

Cassidy laughed a little. "Oh, I am sure they do, just I only fly commercial, so it's rare that I see them do it. I only saw the full rigmarole of checks when I was in a heli…" Cassidy cut herself off. It was bad enough she had mentioned jet engines; she didn't want to have to explain helicopters! "When I was flying with military craft. On commercial flights, the passengers aren't really privy to the safety checks, except for what we should do in case of emergency."

"In case of emergency? I think if the planes goes down we just need to hold on and hope for the best."

"I think that's the same basic idea as the emergency briefings on commercial flights, but if people are told what they should do, it makes them feel less helpless, and maybe bracing for an impact will help some people sur-vive. I really think it's more about the oxygen masks and emergency exits."

Trice considered this. "Well, we're not going high enough to need air, but there will be a canister and mask next to your seat. As for emergency exits," he indicated the plane itself, "wherever and however you can get out, I guess."

Cassidy wanted to ask about parachutes, but guessed if they had them she would have been told.

They walked over to the airplane and Trice directed Cassidy to get in first.

"You'll sit in the second seat, and I'll be in the front with the controls. You have some controls, but don't touch them." He handed her a compass. "Here's some nav for you. The flight director thinks you'll be a good second set of eyes. You know how to use this?"

Cassidy was surprised that Trice's nav equipment just looked like a simple compass. But, then again, magnetic compasses had not really changed in her own world in thousands of years, so why would they really be any different here? She pulled out her own compass to compare. Hers was wavering back and forth, as it had been since she arrived, but the one from Trice was focused on a single point.

"Oh, you have an old one? Looks a little different, and it's doing that strange thing. So, our plan is to circumnavigate the island, then fly in both of those directions," he indicated Cassidy's compass, "and see what the difference is."

Cassidy nodded, and started to work on strapping herself into her seat. Trice pulled himself into the cockpit, strapped himself in and tapped a few dials.

"I'm going to start the engines. It will be a bit loud so we won't be able to talk. Are you ready?"

"Ready as ever," Cassidy replied. She thought back to the din from the prop plane to Fredericton as she pulled a small waterproof notebook out her bag and pencil. She figured she might as well take some notes while in the air.

"Here we go!" Trice whooped and the engines roared to life. Cassidy listened as he revved one, then the other, then left both running with a steady hum. She chuckled to herself at how quiet they were, though Trice thought of them as loud. With a jerk, the plane started forward, slowly at first, then picking up speed. After a few little bumps, the aircraft started to lift off. Cassidy looked out the window and watched as they climbed. A straight run from the airfield took them out over the water. After another minute or so of climbing, Trice banked the aircraft to the left. He circled back over the base. Cassidy had not realized how close to the water it was, but it was almost on the shore. In Cassidy's opinion, the plane still felt very low, but Trice seemed to be keeping it steady. They flew along the coast and within minutes were over the village. Cassidy felt like if they were just a little closer she would be able to identify people. Funny how moments ago she felt too low, and now found that flying so close to the ground was exhilarating! She held two fingers on her pulse. It was certainly up a little. Once the initial thrill passed, she glanced down at the compasses she had in front of her. The one Trice had given her was still pointing true, and she guessed that it must be the pole for this world; whether that was north or what, she did not know as the arm for the compass that was pointing in that direction was painted black and the other half was unpainted and was a light silver. There wasn't a handy little N like on the tip of her compass to say north, but then again, with the translation, it's not like she actually knew the word they might use for north. The little circle on the end of the black tip she could be seeing as an "O" or it could just be a random symbol; she couldn't be certain. Her compass was still wavering back and forth, but she noted that one side of that arc was in the same direction as the fixed compass. So hers was obviously trying to point to the pole, but something on the island was keeping it from staying true to the pole. She wondered if it was something that would interact with the mineral from the statue and that's why it would interfere, or, if she was really lucky, perhaps it was more of the mineral. If it were, if nothing else, she would have to make sure she got a sample to bring back to Gamgee.

The flight was wonderful. Trice kept them close to the coastline, which was amazing to watch. The island was so diverse. Sometimes there would be a luxurious-looking beach, dotted with small boats and people out with fishing nets, casting them into the water. Then the coast would get a bit rocky and change to forest, with trees almost hanging out over the water, reaching for the sunshine. In the interior, the island seemed to be mostly forest, with thick trees covering most of the land, except for a few breaks in the trees that opened up to bodies of water. Trice took the plane up, and Cassidy could see that the island was not very big at all, likely hardly a day's walk to cross it, and two rivers created a large, meandering X through the island, meeting in almost the middle in a large pond. She wished she had a camera as it was beautiful. Instead, she used the compass to do a rough sketch in her notebook and made a few notes to possibly be able to do a better sketch later on. If only Jameson could see her, voluntarily drawing a map without any complaints at all! Then she thought about how she would probably have to make a copy of it for the base, and realized it would be a heck of a lot of work and she would make sure she didn't tell Jameson at all. Next dig he might expect her to keep the site plan, and that was just too much fine work and small measurements for her liking.

As promised, Trice took them for a flight around the

outside of the island. He changed altitude a couple of times, and Cassidy could not figure out exactly what the reason for the change was, but it was nice to get the different perspectives. She noted that her compass kept trying to point to one spot that seemed like it was relatively central to the island, but from the air she could not see what that might be. It all just looked like forest. She wondered where, in all of the trees, would she find the door.

Back over the base again, Trice flew in low and, for a moment, Cassidy thought they were going to land, but, no, he just waggled his wings and took off again, this time to the centre of the island. They flew straight across, not quite following one of the rivers, but as it wandered, the river did pass under them a couple of times. It looked like the river ultimately came out next to the village, which made sense from a settlement point of view as it would be a good source of fresh water. They crossed the entire island and Cassidy worked with her rough map and the two compasses to try to get an even better idea of the source of the interference. She narrowed it down to a fairly broad area just off from the central pond, away from any of the major branches of rivers.

Once they passed the island, Trice brought the plane higher, and they crossed the water and they flew over the mainland a little. Cassidy was again shocked at how little water separated the island from the mainland, for such an independent attitude. She thought it would be like Hawaii relative to the continental United States, but in fact, she guessed, on a clear day, one would be able to see the mainland from the coast. Now, the village was on the opposite side from the mainland, as far away as possible, which likely led to some of that feeling of isolation.

Along the coast, they passed over a small town. It was about twice the size of the island village, but still not very big at all. Trice again went in low and waggled his wings over the town. She guessed there was a good chance that he was from the area. Cassidy also wondered for a moment if it was the same village that Shari was from, remembering that she said she was from a small town herself. But then again, depending on how large the country was, there could be countless small towns and villages all along the coast, let alone the ones that would be further inland.

Once past the village, Trice turned back, circling over the continent until they lined up almost exactly with one of the major rivers on the island. He kept his altitude low, crossed the water, and came back over the island.

Suddenly, there was a loud pop and the entire plane shook. Cassidy looked out the side of the aircraft just in time to hear the rip of metal and see a large piece of the engine cowling fly away. A bright light seemed to almost slither out of the engine and the propeller slowed and then stopped turning. She looked to the other side, and the propeller was still turning, but stuttering, and she assumed it must be struggling as the only one working. The damaged engine was glowing brightly and licks of fire were coming out of the engine. They were falling, and fast.

CHAPTER ELEVEN

Cassidy's pulse roared in her ears. She could feel the rush of adrenaline and tingled all over. She savoured it for a millisecond before she checked her straps and wondered about all of the safety demonstrations she had seen in airplanes. She had even read the information cards from time to time, when a flight was particularly boring and she had run out of absolutely everything else to do. Should she brace herself? Her seat was further back from Trice's than in a commercial plane. Would it help? At the same time, she found she kept wanting to watch what was happening outside. The other engine seemed to be fighting to keep turning, but just could not keep the plane in the air. That light was just starting around the propeller, and she could see as the smooth circle of the propeller would occasionally stutter. Not that it mattered, the one propeller could not keep them in the air. Trice was fighting with the plane, trying, with some success, to keep it from spiralling toward the ground. As the other propeller stopped, they stopped spinning toward the earth, and Trice managed to tilt the aircraft a little forward, so it wasn't barrelling nose-first at the ground. The trees came up to meet them just as Trice straightened up the plane, and Cassidy heard the tops of the trees break against the metal as she felt the aircraft shudder. She saw part of a tree lodged in the broken engine, the flame licking at its branches. The plane continued to push forward, and now the trees were at eye level, reaching for the metal intruder. It seemed they were grabbing at the plane, each branch slowing the bird as it wanted to land. Cassidy was thrown in her seat as a wing collided with a large tree. The wing ripped off with such ease that it reminded Cassidy of ripping a piece of aluminum foil. The plane continued on, leaving the wing behind. As another tree grabbed the other wing, the airplane turned, circling around the tree until they were turned completely around before they escaped the tree and the airplane continued to fly, but backward. Cassidy bent over, thinking about the brace position, now not knowing what might be coming, and put her arms out to just barely touch Trice's chair ahead of her. She did it just in time, as the plane came to a sudden and violent stop and she was thrown forward. She was thankful that she had just put her hands forward, as they protected her head somewhat as she was pushed forward. The harness did grab her, and she knew she would be bruised.

Finally, the airplane stopped. Cassidy stayed still for a few breaths and felt her blood rush before she sat up and called Trice.

"Are you okay?" she asked.

Trice moaned and Cassidy knew he was alive but was afraid for how hurt he might be.

"I'm fine. I struck the dashboard, I think I'm bleeding, and I am going to have a lot of bruises."

"Yeah, me too," Cassidy replied.

"Cassidy, I am so sorry."

"I'm bruised, but otherwise okay. Nothing to be sorry about. Unless you crashed the plane on purpose, and that engine makes me think you didn't," Cassidy replied, trying for joking, but coming off a little tersely.

Trice was a little cowed, then defensive. "I would never try to crash a plane. I don't know what happened. Something must have gotten into the engine, or it was faulty. I've flown this one before, and all the checks were fine."

Cassidy took a deep breath. "Yes, I know it's not your fault. I meant that as a joke. I guess it's hard to joke after a plane crash."

They both looked at each other, then untangled themselves from their straps and clamored out of the plane. They each took a few steps out of the aircraft before turning around and examining the wreckage.

"So I guess we walk?" Cassidy asked.

Without answering, Trice went back to the plane. The engines were still bright, but they didn't seem to be flaming anymore. Cassidy walked back toward the aircraft while Trice rummaged around in the aircraft for a moment. She bent down and picked up a small sliver of glowing stone, its light fading quickly. She pocketed it just before Trice emerged from the wreckage with Cassidy's bag, and three bags of lunch.

"First, we eat!" he declared. "And thanks to Breen, we have an extra lunch to share!"

"Maybe we should save that one in case the walk out is more difficult?" Cassidy asked.

Trice started spreading out the contents of the bags.

"Let's eat the buns first, they're filled with cream that could go bad."

Cassidy doubted they were actually called buns, or, given that nothing she'd had in this place tasted like dairy, cream, but the offered food looked like a steamed bun, so she guessed her translator decided that was the best fit. At least it had an easier time with the military folks who seemed to use fewer colloquialisms; even those from the island. Whatever it was, Cassidy took the offered food and enjoyed the softness of it, and the creamy meat and vegetable filled inside. She thought it was almost like a chicken pot pie in a potato crust. Almost.

They went through the rest of the food. There were some soft pieces of fruit that they also ate, and some harder fruit that they put back in a sack and put in Cassidy's bag. There were canteens of juice, and they took one each and Trice attached the third to his belt. The sun was hot, so they agreed that it would be wise to follow the river and refill the canteens as needed. Trice assured her that the river water was fine to drink, and likely she had been drinking it the entire time as there was no sort of water treatment on the island.

"We don't have any in my town either, but when you get to the bigger towns and cities, they can't drink river water, it's too dirty," he explained.

"I think in some areas it can still be like that where I'm from, but there is a lot of pollution and so a lot of smaller, more isolated places have a lot of trouble getting clean water."

"We have some places like that too. It is sad."

Finally, they each took a sort of cookie, and wrapped

the others in a different sack to put in Cassidy's bag. Sweet treats in hand, they consulted the compasses.

"Mine doesn't seem to be wavering as much from here, so whatever is causing the interference must be in the same direction as the magnetic pole," Cassidy deduced.

"If that's the case, we can do better on our mission and maybe find out what's causing the problem. Especially if it's on the way. They're not expecting us for a bit, but they might have heard the crash. It's not a big island, but we are pretty far off from the base. Search missions aren't easy here, with whatever the problem is, and if they think it made the plane crash, they might hesitate about a fly over. But, just in case..."

Trice jumped to his feet and ran back to the downed plane. He rummaged in the wreckage, around Cassidy's seat, and came back with a small pot.

"Standard on all planes is a pot of paint so we can say which way we're going!" He called to Cassidy.

Cassidy wandered over as Trice unscrewed the top and climbed up on the wreckage.

"If I paint our direction here, it will let them know where we're going. Which way are we going?"

Cassidy pointed along the angle her compass would sometimes point to, thinking they'd go that way then follow the pole. Trice, on the aircraft, was talking partly to himself and partly to Cassidy.

"So this means we're going that way. And this means we're uninjured, relatively speaking of course, and this means two people... There!" He hopped down. "Ready to go!"

Trice's excitement was catching. They had just survived a plane crash and now were going to discover the great mystery of the island. While she was a bit sore, and expected to be very sore tomorrow, for right now there were things to do. This was the most excitement she'd had in days. Weeks even, as finding artifacts was nowhere as exhilarating as surviving a plane crash! They picked up their supplies, and, with Cassidy and her compass leading the way, they set off into the trees.

The crash had obviously done a fair bit of damage, creating a bit of a clearing with the impact, and breaking trees as it came in to land. Most of that was in the opposite direction, but newly broken pieces of trees could be seen clinging in the forest ahead of them. Flying debris had further damaged some of the trees. It looked like part of the tail must have whipped forward when the aircraft turned when it went around that one large tree, and Cassidy saw the piece had ripped through the branches of two trees, cutting the branches away, before embedding itself into the trunk of a third. She took a moment to just stare at it, and really contemplate how lucky they were to be alive. Her heart beat a little faster and her fingertips tingled just thinking of the crash again.

Once out of the debris field, the trees were close together, but far enough apart that they could easily walk through the forest. There was a slight bit of leaf litter, surprising for the number of leafy trees, but Cassidy supposed it was the equivalent to summer. In the fall, it would be much more difficult to navigate the trees if all these leaves were to fall. They both watched their footing, and even so would still stumble over the odd branch.

After about an hour of easy walking, the foliage

changed, and they found themselves faced with a tangle of bushes about the height of themselves. It was thick and difficult to pass through, and they each tried to fight their way through the branches. Any gentle conversation they were having stopped as now communication consisted of grunts of effort, and the occasional "Watch your eyes!" when someone would let go of a branch and it would fly back toward the other person. Cassidy wished for a machete or some other tool to be able to cut through the thick, wooden plants that tugged at her boots and tangled in her hair.

"Stop!" Cassidy called suddenly.

"What? Are you okay?" Trice asked with concern.

"I dropped the compass! I was trying to check it"

"It's okay, we'll find it. Somehow," Trice sighed.

They both crouched down as best they could in the brambles and started to search through the plants. The branches tore at their hands, and they tore back, ripping at the branches. Cassidy produced a pocket knife and started cutting at some of the smaller branches, trying to throw them away, but often just managing to get the branches tangled in others nearby.

"Got it!" Cassidy cried, pulling her hand up from the tangle. She opened her hand, to find a round rock. With a sigh, they kept searching.

"I think I actually have it this time," Trice chided as he stretched his fingers into a small opening near the base of one plant, and pulled out the compass!

Cassidy thanked him, and took it back. She carefully checked it, then put it in her pocket. "I think I'll keep this in my pocket until we get out of this mess. But it looks like we've been going in a pretty straight line, so let's keep going this way." She pointed, and went back to fighting through the bushes.

Suddenly, Cassidy burst out of the tangled shrubs. They stopped suddenly just a few steps from the bank of a river. With a struggle, Trice pushed his way out, stumbled, and caught himself before he fell into the river.

"Those bushes are crazy! I have never had to push my way through something like those before! I hope no one else at the base ever finds them, because they might bring them into training!"

"I've had to deal with something similar before, when I was working in a boreal forest, but those were even worse and more tangled than anything I have ever dealt with." Cassidy took a moment to catch her breath, then decided to just sit and take a proper rest.

"Good idea," declared Trice as he unhooked his canteen and drank deep. Cassidy did the same, and within a few minutes, both had drained their containers and crawled to the stream to refill them. The water was refreshing and cool against Cassidy's hand, so once her canteen was filled, she reached both hands into the clear water, pooled them, and splashed some on her face. She reached down, pooled her hands again, and lifted the water, drinking some. It was refreshing inside and out.

She wasn't sure if she had ever seen water so clear in a deep stream. Certainly she had seen clear streams before, where you could see the bottom and see fish swimming past, but this seemed even clearer, like the water was almost magnifying what she could see. It was magical to watch a snail slowly crawl along a rock. After a few minutes she felt rested, and turned to Trice.

"Ready to go again?"

"After you hand me a plum."

"A what?" she thought she heard right, but nothing in the bag looked like plum. Another mistranslation.

"The fruit you have in your bag," he explained.

"Oh," Cassidy responded as she brought her bag in front of her and searched for the fruit. "I haven't figured out the names for many of the fruits or vegetables here. Everyone just assumes I know what everything is."

Trice took the piece of fruit and bit into it. "That's understandable," he said in between bites. "You're speaking the same language, so it's easy to forget that you're not from here. You just have a different dialect, so it sounds like you're from another part of the country, not a whole other world."

"Hmmm... yeah, fair. I sometimes forget I'm speaking a different language, because I only hear my native tongue."

"Weird," Trice said as he gave her a considering look.

Cassidy looked away and picked up her own plum and started to eat. When he was done, Trice threw the stone from his fruit back into the tangle of branches. Cassidy decided to put hers back in the sack and back in her bag. While she didn't like the mess of branches, she also didn't want to be the one to introduce a potentially invasive species to the island. She had seen enough climatological devastation; she didn't want to be the cause of it. It was probably a wasted effort though, as who knows what the base was doing with their food. Plus, for all she knew, plums, or whatever they were, grew on the island.

"Ready to go?" Trice asked.

"Sure." Cassidy pulled out the two compasses. Her was wavering more than back at the plane crash, so they had obviously veered from the pole, and thus from the base because the base seemed to be in that direction. From her aerial view, they could just follow the river and come out around the village. Her compass said they had to cross the river to find whatever it was.

"Ready to get wet?" Cassidy asked.

Trice looked down at his boots. "Guess so," he said.

They both bent down and took off their boots and rolled up their pants. Boots in hand, Cassidy sucked in air as her feet touched the cold water. The river wasn't very wide, maybe fifteen meters at most, but each step had to be taken carefully on the slippery rocks. As she walked across, the water kept rising until it was licking at her pants, rolled up to her knees. She started to bend down to further roll up her pants, but as she bent, her bag shifted and she worried about losing it or her balance, so she straightened up and kept going, even if it meant wet pants.

They both splashed along and made it across the river without incident. Cassidy rolled her pants back down and laughed quietly to herself, looking at the stripes of water across her legs. At least it was a warm day, and her pants should dry quickly. She put on her socks and boots and finished tying her laces as Trice finished his. She checked the compass again, pointed the direction, and they both set off again.

This side of the river was even easier to navigate than before, without a tangle of bushes. The area was very open, with only a few trees with large canopies shading them as they walked. Colourful flowers with long, teardrop petals hugged the trees. Cassidy thought the area looked like a park it was so beautiful. Looking up through the canopy, the sun was high, around its apex, telling them half the day had passed, but they still had hours of light left. She was thankful for the light covering of leaves, especially because she didn't have a hat with her to help protect her fair skin.

The two almost strolled through the grove, not wanting to rush, but at the same time taking advantage of the easy walking conditions. About a half hour in, they came across a small stream, flowing toward the river. Cassidy checked the compass again, and noticed they had gone off course. The leisurely walk was a little too much so, she guessed. The compass pointed along the tributary, and so they walked upstream. The stream started to widen, but was still narrow enough that Cassidy guessed she could jump across it if she wanted. Still, it was an easy walk. After some time, more flowers started to appear along the shore, leafy green plants with soft pink flowers clung to the bank of the stream.

Cassidy noticed a noise and looked up from the flowers, and saw that the little stream flowed from a small pond surrounded by flowers and flowing trees, and soft white blossoms dropped from the trees to float in the pond. At the head of the pond was a cascading waterfall that was still far enough away to barely be heard. It was a beautiful sight, a little piece of paradise.

CHAPTER TWELVE

Cassidy had seen some beautiful places in her life, on her world and others, but this small oasis was perhaps one of the most amazing. The small pond was crystal clear. She could see the red, blue, green, purple, and black rocks right on the bottom. Bright green plants stood between some of the rocks, waving gently as orange, red, and yellow fish darted among them. The pond itself wasn't very big, maybe ten meters across, if that, and almost perfectly round. The coloured rocks extended on to the shore, expanding outward until they were blanketed by a bright green, thick, moss-like plant with small pink flowers. The moss gave way to a variety of brightly coloured flowers of every colour and shape, which in turn, gave way to lush, flowering trees. The large white blossoms weighed heavily on the branches, and fallen flowers floated on the pond's surface. At the head of the pond was a waterfall, which created a small basin of churning water.

The crash of the waterfall was not loud by the river, in fact, she could still hear the burble of the stream along with the waterfall. The sheet of water was falling from a high peak, a small mountain that created a shear wall just behind the pond. The cliff seemed to extend back into the forest, and out of view. Cassidy sat at the edge of the pond. The moss was soft and the rocks smooth. She took out her notebook and started sketching the area. Trice came and sat next to her, watching her draw, occasionally pointing out a detail she missed. The drawing wasn't to scale, but she had to record the spot. Then they worked together to draw a rough map of where they crashed, the larger river, and this small pond. Cassidy used the changes in the compass headings to estimate the meanderings of the bodies of water, and the corrected compass to estimate the direction of the village and the base.

"Looks like your nav is pointing right at the waterfall. It's hardly even moving toward the pole now," Trice observed.

"Hopefully whatever is causing the pull is near or even behind the waterfall. If it's up the hill, I don't think we'll be able to find it. Do you think we'd be able to come back with climbing gear?" Cassidy liked the idea of climbing that rock face and seeing the island from up high. That would be a thrill. Not that from the airplane wasn't up high, but from the top of the hill she would be able to potentially see more landmarks that she would have missed from the plane.

"Don't see why not. Well, if we get permission that is."

"Oh, yeah. Permission," mused Cassidy as she wondered if she could come back without the base's blessing. "Anyway, it might be a moot question anyway. Let's see what's at the waterfall."

Cassidy closed her notebook and tossed it in her bag.

She stood up, brushed the moss from her pants and started around the pond. Trice followed a step behind.

The rock wall made only a small ledge between itself and the pond, and the two had to pick across carefully. The pond looked fairly deep at this end, but with the water so clear, it was difficult to guess how deep it might be. Twice Cassidy's foot slid off the ledge and she got a little wet. The water was frigid, and the cold shocked her each time, but she kept her balance and managed to find secure enough hand holds to not fall in. Trice had a little more trouble and came close to falling, splashing up to one of his knees before he managed to find somewhere to grab on and pull himself back up. He cursed the cold of the water. Not that it would have been a huge concern had they gotten wet, but it was cold enough that it would take some time to warm up after.

The entire effort to stay dry was wasted when the waterfall was so close to the rock that they both had to go through it to see if there was something behind it. Cassidy got through to find a small opening, just big enough to walk through if she turned sideways. She went through, and Trice followed moments later.

"Given how wet we ended up getting, we should have just swum across the pond!" Cassidy exclaimed as she twisted her hair, trying to get some of the water out.

"Guess we'll just save ourselves the trouble and swim out," Trice decided. "Now, where are we?"

They looked around the small cave. They had no light source, but the waterfall was thin enough that the light could get in. They waited a moment for their eyes to adjust. It took Cassidy a moment to realize that her eyes weren't failing to adjust, but the cave was full of black rocks. She walked forward and touched one of the rocks. It was smooth, almost glassy. She tried to pick up a rock, but it resisted. She pulled harder, until it came away and she could hold it in her hand. It was like pulling two magnets apart! She brought the rock back down to where it had been, and could feel the pull. She opened her hand, flattening her palm, and tilted it just a little, not enough that gravity should take the rock, but it still rolled off her hand and stuck fast to the other rocks again. Cassidy picked up the piece again, and walked back toward the light of the waterfall. It was black, just like the rock inside of the statue!

Meanwhile, Trice had wandered further into the cave. Cassidy could not see where he went, but also wasn't really paying attention. She was wondering just how much of the rock was there. She guessed this was the source of the interference. She pulled out her compass and stood in the middle of the rocks. The light was poor, but she could just see the white of the compass point. It was still. She turned. And it still didn't move. She moved around in a circle. Nothing. She must be right in the centre of all of the magnetic rock. For it to have caused such a problem on the island, it must be a huge source of it! Perhaps more than enough for the flight director to fix all of the aircraft, and give the statue back to the village! Cassidy remembered her mission and took a few chunks of rock and put them in her pockets for herself. She put two smaller pieces in one pocket, and, when she reached back in that pocket, found they had fused together.

"What amazing properties to this rock," she muttered

to herself. "There are pebbles and small stones around that haven't fused, but the two pieces I just put in my pocket fused."

She picked up another two pieces, and when she brought them together, they too fused. She thought how she wished her geology were better, but then she doubted anything like this existed on her world.

"Cassidy, come check this out," Trice called from deep in the cavern.

Cassidy carefully picked her way through the cave. As she went further, she really wanted some sort of lantern, but theirs had been destroyed in the crash and the batteries for her small flashlight were dead. The cave grew darker, the black stones seeming to consume the light. When she moved too close to a pile of rocks, she could feel the stones in her pocket pull toward them. She considered removing them and getting some later, but given how things went so unpredictably with the village and the base before, she thought it best to get her sample for Dr. Gamgee now. The cave had become so dark that she could not see in front of her. Just to check, she waved a hand in front of her face, and, knowing it was there, could not see it. She wasn't sure what Trice could be showing her in the pitch black, but she shuffled on, trying to stick to the path that seemed to flow through the rocks.

Moments later, she noticed that she could see again. Just the barest outline of the rocks ahead of her, but she could see. She brought her hand up, and sure enough, she could see it. She kept moving forward, and as the light increased, so did the confidence in her steps. The rocks were changing too. Some of them had what looked like snowflakes on them. She looked closer, and they were small occlusions of a white rock. As she kept going, the white became more prominent until the rocks were covered in it, just like the quartz-like material on the outside of the statue from the village! She found Trice at a wide entrance, standing in the sunshine.

"Don't get too close," he said and pointed downward.

Cassidy looked, and it seemed that the hill they were in did not end gradually, but rather was a sheer cliff. She wondered if the ground had dropped away, or if they had gradually climbed while inside the cave. Either way, they were well above the tree tops. Cassidy stepped back from the ledge, and took out her compass again. Hers was pointing directly behind her, at the stones. No surprise there, she thought. The other compass, the one from the base, seemed to not quite be corrected enough, because it seemed to be struggling to point away from the rocks.

"I wonder how far we've gone; it didn't seem that far through the mountain," Cassidy mused.

"I doubt it is very far because I've never noticed this from the air, and you'd think a big line of rock like this would be noticeable. I am still curious about the source of that waterfall, even more now that I know the hill is so narrow."

"Yeah, it would almost have to be a very deep pond to create it, or, I don't know." In all honesty, Cassidy had forgotten about the waterfall, she was so absorbed in finding a source of these rocks.

"The story!" she exclaimed.

"What?" Trice looked at her, confused.

"The story about the idol. The statue. Margaretta told it to me about their ancestor who found the statue. He must have stopped somewhere under here to rest when he was hunting. I bet there is a giant rock down there that looks like a sleeping beast. Down there must be the spot where he found the stone, and no one has found any since because they're behind the waterfall and up this cliff. The one he found must have fallen down from in here."

"So this is the same stuff as the statue? The same stuff used to fix the nav equipment?" Trice asked.

"It is! This solves everything! There's so much of it that all the planes can be fixed, and the village can get their statue back!" Cassidy was thrilled.

Trice picked up one of the white stones. "Do you have much room in your bag? Maybe we should bring some of this back?"

Cassidy agreed and picked a couple of fist-sized rocks that could easily fit in her bag. She had a bandana with her and wrapped a few in it to make it easier to carry. Trice picked up his own rock.

"I'll take some from the other side of the cavern as well. Well, I guess I'll take one, because if I put in a few, they'll just turn into one if they come into contact with each other."

Trice looked confused again and Cassidy explained the strange magnetism of the rocks, and how that seemed to be the thing that fixed the compass to negate the interference caused by the mineral. Trice seemed to understand, or at least understood as much as Cassidy did, as she still couldn't quite explain the physics behind the phenomenon. She'd leave that for Dr. Gamgee to understand.

Cassidy regretted leaving her bag back by the pond. It would have been nice to have been able to sketch the view from the opening, but she would just have to try to remember it to do a basic drawing. What she really wanted was a camera because no drawing she could do would do it justice. They both sat at the edge of the cliff for a little while, just enjoying the view.

It was Trice who decided they should start making their way back.

"We know where this is now, we can show people the way, but we should get moving if we want to make it back before dark."

Cassidy agreed, and they made their way back through the tunnel. Cassidy picked up another of the black stones and put it in her clutch, and Trice played with some of the smaller ones, examining how they pull towards each other before putting a piece in his own pocket. Even though they had both thought it easier to swim, they opted for the more difficult route out of the cave, and again picked their way across the lip of the pond. Once safely on solid ground again, and only a little wet this time, Cassidy looked back at the pond. Now that she was looking for it, she could see, in amongst the red and purple rocks, the black magnetic rocks. They were so distinct, she wondered how she missed them in the first place.

Back at her bag, they had a quick snack and Cassidy went to transfer her bandana full of stones to her bag. The ones covered in the quartz-like material didn't fuse, the outer shell likely blocking some of the magnetism. She took out one covered stone, and one uncovered one, and placed them in front of her, at about 10 and 2 on a clock. She took out her compass and brought it closer to them.

While the needle was certainly still being pulled by the massive amount of material behind the waterfall, it did seem to be a little more attracted to the uncovered mineral instead of the covered one. She found this interesting, and put both of the rocks back in her bag and pocketed her compass.

Everything packed up, they decided to follow the stream. It would lead back to the river, which in turn, would lead to the village. Certainly they could use the fixed compass to walk in a straight line, but walking along the river bank seemed like it would be much easier than trying to sort through anything like that mess of woody shrubs that they had encountered on their way from the crash.

The walk out was uneventful, almost peaceful, if not a little rushed. Trice, even knowing there was still food left in Cassidy's bag, was pushing to get back to the base before the mess closed that evening. Cassidy reminded him that he would likely be called in to be debriefed and might still miss supper, which only made him hike faster. He set a rigorous pace and all conversation ceased as Cassidy tried to keep up. She was fit, but wasn't doing regular military drills like he was. At one point, while walking back along the main river, Cassidy recognized an area and thought the door might be close by. For a moment, she debated just leaving with her samples and putting this world and its complications behind her, but decided against it. It would be wrong to leave the village, especially after the kindness they showed her. Leaving would be easy, but not right.

That also meant they were close to the village, and back to safety. Maybe even in time to eat.

CHAPTER THIRTEEN

As predicted, they came out of the woods on the other side of the village from the base.

It was Rim who saw them first, and the child rushed over.

"Cassidy! You're back!" Rim exclaimed.

"No, not really. We were just lost in the woods. But I found the most amazing thing!" Cassidy started to explain until Trice cut in.

"Cassidy, we were on a military mission and what we found is a military matter." He was all authority, very different from the Trice she had been talking to over the past few days. "I must forbid you to talk about our mission and what was found."

"But this will fix everything."

"That is not for you to decide. If you do not come to the base now, I will tell the flight director and you will be removed to the base."

Cassidy saw how serious he was, and how he was scaring Rim. She leaned down and gave Rim a comforting hug and whispered, "Give this to Margaretta," and slipped a small quartz-covered stone from her pocket to the child's hand. More loudly she said, "I'm sorry Rim. We didn't mean to scare you. I have to go," and got up.

She turned to Trice, "I'm sorry, I'm not used to military protocol."

He nodded in agreement and they turned and walked across the village, Cassidy careful to not make eye contact with anyone lest they try to talk and Trice scare them again. Once they were away from the village, Trice turned to her.

"I'm sorry for that, too. I know you're not military, but we do have to follow orders."

"I understand," she lied.

Once at the base, Cassidy and Trice were sent directly to Flight Director Spear's office.

"Good, you made it back. Now, report." Flight Director Spear looked at Trice.

"We departed just after first light, all checks were accomplished and everything was normal. Takeoff was normal."

As Trice spoke, Cassidy heard a clicking noise, and looked to see a stenographer behind her, taking down Trice's words. The young man would have been hidden by the door as they came in. The man was typing on a strange contraption. It was certainly similar to a typewriter, but larger. Almost like an old style typewriter for Cantonese or Japanese, complete with paper scroll at the top. Cassidy wondered if the writing style might be logographic instead of alphabetic, and she wished she could turn off the translator because watching the stenographer type seemed out of sync with what Trice was saying. Instead, she turned back to look at Trice and Shari.

"As we turned back toward the island, things were normal for a minute or two, but then the right engine shuddered. Moments later, it caught fire, the halfstone going into overglow, before the cowling ripped away. The other engine, overtaxed, gave out. We crashed, catching on trees, but landing with minimal injuries. Once assessed, we determined that the source of the interference was likely nearby, and followed the flawed navigational equipment to find the source. It was located, and we followed the main river back to the Vering Island village, passing through the village to return to the base."

"Good," responded Shari, "and the source of the interference?"

Trice produced the stones from his pocket.

"A large collection of these stones in a cave. Some are covered in a white material."

Shari examined the rocks.

"These are just like the stuff in the statue," she mused.

"Yes," Cassidy interjected. "There's a lot of it too, so you can get that and give the statue back to the village."

"Hmmm... we would have to verify it, of course, but yes, if we have another source of it, I don't see why we can't give the statue back."

Cassidy let out a sign of relief. "That's good, I thought you might have destroyed it."

"Oh, no no. We haven't destroyed it. We haven't even used any of it yet. What we have we were given by villagers who now serve. We were still only testing the material yet."

"Then why did you take it?" Cassidy exclaimed.

"Because I assumed that you telling them would not actually work. The village here is so overprotective of their superstitions and stories that they probably wouldn't have let me have it anyway."

Cassidy levelled her gaze on Flight Director Spear. "You are wrong about that," she said coldly, "they talked about it and were going to give you the statue. Instead you took it. You destroyed any goodwill that might have been left. You have made it much more difficult for you to coexist in this place because you couldn't have any faith that they would do the right thing. The villagers are good, intelligent people, and you treat them like they are clueless about the world. If you ever want to have good relations with the village again, you had better do something to make it up to them."

"I'll give back the statue. It will be fine," said Shari, a little dismissively.

"No, it won't," Cassidy responded, still very serious. "These are a people of storytellers, and if I have learned anything in my travels and studies it is that storytellers don't forget and storytellers can hold a grudge because they don't forget. You will need to make things better with them."

Shari considered this. "And how do you propose I do that?"

Cassidy paused for a moment then replied, "By bringing them in on the discovery of the cavern. No, hear me out. There is a huge source of these stones, both the covered and uncovered ones. I already know you need very little to fix the navigation equipment, and with the amount there it would take generations to use it all. Look at the statue. Yes, they put the stone back in when people die, but they lose the pieces of people who leave or die at sea, and the statue is still almost full. You need less than what they give to their own people. And this cavern is full. Trice took small samples, not the large boulders that are there. But it's also in a beautiful place. It's in a pristine environment that could be used by the people. As long as you don't destroy the place, the villagers might even help you quarry some of the stone."

"Why do you think they would help?"

"Because I have spent time with them, and they are good people who, while not looking to partake in the war, and not even completely understanding it, don't want to see people hurt," Cassidy was pleading a little now.

Shari considered Cassidy's words. "So, what you are suggesting is that I bring them to this place, and they get the place, and you think they will freely give the material we need."

"Yes," Cassidy was suddenly feeling hopeful, "approach the storytellers, the elders of the community. Take one or two of them with you, Margaretta for instance, and she will bring them around. You will all be able to work together."

"That's not really how we do things."

"Are you sure? Aren't you, as part of the defence of this place and this country, supposed to also instill a sense of patriotism in the outlying places?" Cassidy was pulling out everything she could think of from dealing with other militaries and a thesis defence she had once attended that discussed just this. "Showing cooperation will make these outlying places remember that they are part of the country, and, without that goodwill, it is much harder to recruit. If you do this right, the village will tell stories of how you impacted one of their oldest stories by finding the lost location and giving it back to the people, and they will be less afraid of the capital and more willing to volunteer. If you help them with this, you will be a hero in their stories for generations to come. Otherwise you will just be coming in with might and taking from their stories. They just want respect as the residents of this place."

Cassidy was proud of her speech and wasn't entirely certain where it came from. While she wanted to smile, she kept her face serious, but celebrated a little internally and waited for Shari's response.

Shari again considered before answering, "I... I wouldn't have thought of it that way. The biggest problem with this place is how resistant they've been."

"And it's not like you plan on leaving after the war, what with the door here," Cassidy cut in.

Shari eyed her suspiciously. "How would you know a thing like that?"

"You're not the first military I've dealt with, and the history of my own world says it has happened time and time again. So earning favour can only help you."

"You really didn't come off as this knowledgeable when we first met."

Cassidy took it in stride, "I'm aware. I don't try to cultivate it, but it usually takes me a while to figure a place out."

"Interesting... But you are right, now that the base is established, it will be permanent, and having a good working relationship with the locals will be an asset for the future." Shari paused. "And we will follow your suggestions. I will reach out to the community elders and make it a joint mission."

"May I approach Margaretta for this? She might not be receptive to you returning, and I had convinced her to let you take the statue in the first place."

Cassidy knew she was pushing it a little with that jab, but wanted to be the one to make it up to the town and to Rim, Phia, and Margaretta.

"Fine. Saves me the trouble. Get something to eat, get some sleep. Meet here at daybreak and we will make the plan, then you can go back to the village. If we're efficient, we can leave before midday. Leave the map sketches and I'll have them copied."

Cassidy handed Shari the pages from her notebook. The maps would be useful to them, but not her written notes seeing as they wouldn't be able to read them.

"Is there anything else in there I need?" Shari asked, eyeing the book.

"No, mostly notes to myself, and the last archaeological site I worked on. That last bit honestly has nothing to do with here and I need to give the notes back to my friend."

"Fine," she turned to Trice who had been so quiet Cassidy had almost forgotten about him. "Say nothing. Report here at daybreak. Dismissed."

Trice said nothing, but turned and walked out of the room.

"You too. Dismissed."

Cassidy pocketed her notebook and walked out of the room. Trice was by the door, waiting.

"Ready to eat?"

Cassidy laughed a little, even though she was disappointed that Trice had nothing to say about her speech.

"Sure, I'd love to eat."

She walked with him to the mess hall, where they just got in before the kitchen closed.

CHAPTER FOURTEEN

Cassidy felt good on her way to Shari's office. The meeting was pretty quick, mostly just to discuss the map and how long it would potentially take to get to the pond. Shari asked pointed questions about the location, how much material was present, and how difficult it would be to remove it. Cassidy and Trice answered as best they could before being dismissed. Shari and Trice would meet Cassidy and representatives from the village at the river so they could go together. Shari and Trice would collect more of the rocks, but would also start negotiations. If Cassidy was right, they could negotiate the use of the place for the villagers and the removal of the minerals for the aircraft.

Not surprisingly, Rim greeted Cassidy at the edge of the village.

"Cassidy! I gave what you gave me to Margaretta. What is it? Did it come out of the statue?"

Oh no! Cassidy thought, *I didn't think they'd assume it came out of the statue!*

"Or did it come from somewhere else? Where did it come from?" Rim prattled on.

Cassidy was a little relieved that these might just be the questions of a child.

"Rim," she asked, "could you bring me to Margaretta please?"

"Yeah, sure, of course!"

Rim led the way to Margaretta's house, telling Cassidy all about the past couple of days, especially focusing on the dessert they had for supper the night before. Cassidy had to laugh; after all of her worry over the situation, here was Rim, just worried about food. Much like Trice.

At Margaretta's house, Rim walked in and shouted, "Cassidy's here!" and ran off again.

Moments later, Margaretta and Phia appeared, and welcomed her in. The rock she had given Rim was on the living room table.

"Cassidy! Where did you find that stone? All Rim would say was that it was from you!" Margaretta asked.

"That's all I had time to say," Cassidy replied. "I was with one of the guys from the base, and he wouldn't let me say more. I had to sneak it to Rim and hoped you'd know I found a solution."

"A solution?" asked Margaretta. "Oh, to the base taking the statue. Yes, it was a shock, but in the end, it's just a statue. I understand why you left, Phia explained it, but you are welcome back here. You might get some foul looks from Carlson or Sasamuel, but that's expected. They're like that to just about everyone. So, what's this solution?"

Cassidy told them about the plane wreck and finding the beautiful pond with the waterfall and the cave behind the waterfall and how it led to a cliff. She explained how she thought that maybe they were missing a key part of the story and that this place was where Ishaul found the stone, but no one else had found one because they had never gone through the waterfall.

"We do know of that place; it's a common spot for couples to go and court, although the water is always very cold and I never heard of anyone trying to go in. There are better swimming areas."

"Well, the base wants to go and access the rocks, but they want to do it with a storyteller or two present so you can work together and maintain the area."

Margaretta paused before responding. "So, they know of this place, and instead of just taking what they want, they want to work with us? That's... that's very different from before. Cassidy? Did you say something to them?"

"I just explained how it would be good for them to work with you instead of against you. That way there might be a little more trust, and it would be easier for the villagers who work on base to face their families."

Phia cut it, "That is a good thing. We have, as a whole, not been very good to those who choose to work on the base. Not everyone wants to fish or tell stories. And we've never been that way to anyone who has left and come back."

"True as the tide," Margaretta said solemnly. "We should work together. If we work together on this, then maybe we can work together on other things."

Margaretta got up and walked to the door.

"Rim!" she called, and within moments the child appeared.

That kid has a talent, or is just really nosy, Cassidy thought.

"Please go and get the storytellers. Tell them to come here as quickly as possible," Margaretta ordered.

A few minutes later, the storytellers started coming in. True to his character, Carlson gave Cassidy a sour look. Once everyone was in, Margaretta got started.

"I had Rim send you all here because Cassidy has brought some amazing news," she started.

There was some muttering, until Margaretta produced the stone that Cassidy had given Rim the day before.

"Cassidy brought us this."

Suddenly, they were all quiet and listening. Margaretta continued.

"Yesterday, Cassidy was with someone from the base in that aeroplane that flew overhead. We didn't see it come back because it crashed."

Gertrand and Olisker shot Cassidy concerned looks.

"For those of you worried," Margaretta glared at Carlson, "Cassidy is okay, as is the one who was flying the aeroplane. One their way back, they found a cave filled with the same stones that the idol is made of. Cassidy brought one back, against the wishes of the base."

Cassidy was about to interject, but then realized that Margaretta was right, even if she didn't quite think of it that way.

"The cave is behind the waterfall at the pool, and it extends through the cliff. There's a huge chance that this is where Ishaul first found the stone we use. Speaking of which, the base is going to give back the idol. They haven't touched it yet, and want to work with us when collecting more stones."

There was some grumbling to this, from Carlson in

particular, but Gertrand shushed him and nodded for Margaretta to continue.

"They want to collect some of the stone. Cassidy says there is a lot of it behind the waterfall. But they want a couple of us to go with them to the area to make sure they also protect it so we can keep using it."

Carlson cut in. "It's our place, they have no right—"

Margaretta cut him off in turn. "We know full well if they wanted it, they would take it. They want to work together on this. Cassidy has convinced Flight Director Spear that she should work with us instead of demanding things of us, and it starts with this."

Margaretta was very firm, leaving no room for Carlson to argue, although it was obvious he wanted to.

"Myself, Cassidy, and one other – I suggest Olisker or Sasamuel – will go with members of the base to the pool and develop a plan for how they can recover the stone they need. Which one of you will go with us to help speak on behalf of the village?"

Olisker looked less than confident, but that was not unusual as he was still trying to get used to being a storyteller. Sasamuel was about to say something when Gertrand cut in.

"I think Olisker should go. Then he can help develop the story of this. This is a pivotal moment and will need to be told." She looked at Sasamuel. "You have created a few stories already, of course."

Sasamuel responded to the elder, "I was going to recommend Olisker. My days of going to the pool, I think, are over. It is time for the young people to create."

Gertrand smiled at him, and at Carlson, who looked

even sourer that he was not part of the decision making. Margaretta snickered a little and mumbled something about the pool creating many things.

***

The hike to the pool was uneventful. Margaretta and Olisker led as they already knew a better route as compared to the one Cassidy and Trice took. There was actually a nice, well-worn path to the area, used by generations of villagers to sneak away when courting.

Margaretta was still amazed. "I can't believe no one ever thought to go behind the waterfall! I know the water is icy all year round, but no one would ever swim in it?!"

Olisker joked. "Really Margaretta? If you ever came out here, were you really thinking of swimming? In the cold?"

Margaretta blushed and Trice laughed. "Sounds like the water is cold enough to destroy any chance of affection!"

Shari, shot them a look and rolled her eyes, but was happy to have the easy route.

Once at the pool, Trice once again confirmed just how cold the water was by sticking his hand in. Then he suggested they sidle along the cliff-face the way he and Cassidy had. They each followed, trying to balance small lanterns so they would be able to see. Inside, Shari was thrilled with the amount of material available, and Margaretta and Olisker were amazed to look down on the other side of the cavern and see where Ishaul must have found the first large stone. They tossed a couple of stones out of the cave to try to find later and finally know where the story took place.

Once out by the pool again, Shari conferred with Margaretta and Olisker.

"We will need to build a walkway to get to the waterfall. If we are going to take out a substantial amount, we will need to be able to carry it safely," explained Shari.

"I agree, and that is agreeable, but what is a substantial amount?" Margaretta asked.

"For now, let's say two of the large boulders in the front of the cavern," Shari said.

"Instead," Margaretta countered, "let's leave the boulders in the very front. There are others just behind by a few large steps. Take from there first and work back. That should maintain the way the waterfall cascades."

Shari considered. "I would never have thought of that, but there's no reason why we can't approach it that way."

Olisker broke in, "And when you say for now, what does that mean?"

Shari looked to him. "It would mean that we see how many aeroplanes we can alter, and how much nav equipment we can change with that much before taking any more. So far, we have altered six aeroplanes and a dozen or so handheld navs with just what people from your village gave you."

"So two boulders is a significant amount?" asked Olisker.

"It is, but should last a very long time," responded Shari.

Margaretta asked, "Could we draw up some form of contract for the future that says we have to be consulted before the removal of more material, but that we won't counter the request without cause?"

"Sounds fair," said Shari.

Cassidy knew this was something for them to work out, but also knew that such a contract could be difficult to enforce in the future. But it was not her place to negotiate. She had done enough damage, and Margaretta, Olisker, and Shari seemed happy to mend that for the time being.

Once everyone was in agreement about the place and how it would be used, the group went back to the village. In a surprising move, Margaretta invited Shari to the evening meal, and she accepted. It was the first time she had spent any significant time among the villagers, and conversation was slow at first, but soon the villagers were as welcoming to Shari as they had been to Cassidy when she first arrived.

***

"I am sorry to see you leave. It was lovely to speak to someone from the other side of the door."

Phia pulled Cassidy into a hug. When she let go, it was Margaretta's turn for a hug.

"The storytellers asked me to give you something," she said and handed Cassidy a small fragment of stone on a cord. "I know you have pieces of the stone to bring back, but this one is for you."

Cassidy put it on.

"Thank you so much, you have all been very friendly." Cassidy turned to Phia. "Do you have the note I gave you?"

"Yes, of course. I will use this as an introduction for

when people come through."

"Remember, there is always a chance that not everyone who comes through will be able to read, or be able to read that language. Most do, but this area of the world has a few different languages."

"I understand, but this should help quite a bit."

Cassidy had written out a note of greeting, explaining that the village would offer a place of comfort when it was needed and share their food. It also asked, if people were willing or able, for things they couldn't get, such as charcoal. It also asked that they tell a villager when they are leaving, so they could be given a care package of food and other supplies before they go.

"Are you sure it isn't unkind to ask for these wonderful items that you have in your world?" Phia asked.

"There's no harm in asking, as long as you're not demanding. Many of the people who come through are ones who have very little, but will likely be generous with what they do have," Cassidy explained. "And I will drop some things through the door before I go back to my own home."

"I thank you again, Cassidy. Are you certain you don't want your own package of food to take with you?" asked Margaretta.

"No, thank you. Save that for someone else."

In all honesty, Cassidy was looking forward to stopping at the convenience store for some chocolate and familiar food.

"Please say goodbye to Rim for me, and the storytellers."

"We will," Phia smiled. "Have a safe journey."

With that, Cassidy turned and walked through the space in the woods that was just a little different, and was greeted with the chill of the September air. Time was a little different, and in her week in the village, August had passed to September and the air had lost that last trace of summer. The air caught in Cassidy's lungs, making her breathe a little deeper. She felt like she had to suck the oxygen out of the air, and not just breathe casually. Cassidy walked to the corner store and bought herself a snack. She was a little out of breath from the walk, and guessed it would take her a little while to get used to the heaviness of the air again. She could better understand why the people from the village couldn't come through anymore as she felt like she could taste the exhaust and pollution on the wind after being in such a pristine place. Perhaps some of their knowledge of energy supplies would be more helpful for this planet, but Gamgee wanted a magnetic rock. She did think of the small sliver of halfstone in her bag.

She asked the clerk at the convenience store to call a taxi, which took her to an outdoor shop where she bought some camping gear, including a couple of bags of charcoal. She took another taxi back to the door and passed most of the items through. She had picked up a sleeping bag, which she left in the lean-to near the door for whoever was using it. From there, she walked up the road to a motel and checked in for the night.

Once in the room, she plugged in her phone to get her messages, sent a quick email to Dr. Gamgee, and called her family to check in. They were used to her disappearing, and were surprised when she called so soon after a field season. To be fair, they thought she was just back in service range from her excavation.

She laid the two samples of the mineral on the hotel desk, one covered in the white quartz-like layer, and the other just black. She put the piece of halfstone on the desk next to them. Tomorrow she would book a flight home, and deliver these to Dr. Gamgee. For tonight, she would catch up on emails and social media, and head down to the motel restaurant for a pile of fried foods she could name.

EPILOGUE

Margaretta writes in one of her books. The nib of her pen slows across the page, pausing only to collect more ink to continue the story. She is the keeper of the tales. While stories are told, and are meant to be told, they are also recorded in the library. Over the years, as stories change, they are recorded again, and again. The library has new stories, old stories, and how stories evolve over the generations. She inherited the library from Gertrand, and one day she will pass the library on to a new storyteller. Right now, she writes Olisker's story of the woman who came through the door.

One day, a woman came through the door. It was the wrong time of year. People come through the door in the warm season, but it was just after the rainy season. The woman, Cassidy, who came through the door could speak our language thanks to science from another world. She said she was looking for something to bring back to her world. We welcomed her, as we welcome all visitors who come through the door. We gave her shelter, a place to sleep, and food. She was different, because we gave her conversation and she gave us knowledge. She was welcomed, and we showed her the village and could tell how things are done in the village. It was a pleasure to talk to someone from through the door. She told us about her world.

The woman, Cassidy, came through the door during the Great Conflict, when the world was fighting. Cassidy spoke to the village, and to the military base. She shared information between the two groups. She shared that our idol, carved by Ishaul and brought to the village from somewhere unknown on the island, could help stop the aeroplanes from crashing on the island. She tried to bring the village and the base together, but the leader of the base stole the idol to help protect the soldiers and the aeroplanes.

The woman, Cassidy, left the village to talk to the leader of the base. In her time trying to retrieve the idol, she was taken around the island in an aeroplane, but like many others, the aeroplane crashed. Cassidy and the pilot survived an aeroplane crash and as they walked back to the village from deep in the forest, they came to the pool. The people of the village knew the pool, they would spend time there in the warm months, enjoying each other's company on the bank of the cold pond. Cassidy explored the pool, and went behind the waterfall. Behind the waterfall were stones like that found by Ishaul many generations ago.

The woman, Cassidy, brought a stone back to the village, and brought the leader of the base to the village. Together, the storytellers and the leader of the base shared the pool and the stones. The aeroplanes could fly safely, and the village gained the knowledge of where Ishaul found the idol. Cassidy, having brought the village and the base together, left, back through the door.

Margaretta knew there was more to the story, but stories didn't always need all of the details. This one was good, for Olisker's first story. More would come, and they would get better. And this story would change, but they would always remember the woman who came through the door and found Ishaul's secret place.

FLOWERS FOR ALBATROSS

MATTHEW DANIELS & JD RYOT

CHAPTER ONE

Sky, horizon, treetops.

In that order.

There was a lurch as the plane went over the edge. It was a Cessna 140, fourth or fifth-hand. Old, well-maintained, sturdy, cheap. Cassidy had some bush piloting in her background. It was about the same as swimming: up good, down bad, and don't let your gas run out. Here she was, though, coming out of a hole in the sky and facing oh so much down. She was laughing.

Just as the engine began to build, she'd had people in the cave in her world push her out of the hole in the sky in the other world.

Most of the strapping of her outfit was for the pouches and tools she brought for her adventures. There was the seat belt, for what it was worth. The canopy filled her whole vision now that she was nosediving. Even so, at this height there should be a break in it. She'd seen mountains in the distance, before all that green. She could even smell it. Not a pine green. More lush.

Wind.

Everything leaned behind her. Behind was up. This

kind of freefall wasn't a zero-G experience. There were plenty of G's, and they were in a mad dash for the ground. She thrived in the adrenaline, even as part of her ran through possible maintenance oversights.

Hey, there are fruits above the canopy. Reddish-orange? How about that.

Eyes on the prize, guys. Time for the engine to do its thing. ...Now would be great.

Sputter.

Okay, okay. She's got this.

"Up and at 'em!" she shouted. She kicked hard at the floor and under the dash while she cursed, and her hands danced with the controls for the flaps and slats of the wings.

Eureka!

She wasn't sure if it was the wind or just this particular Cessna, but the engine roaring completely to life reminded her almost of the metallic teething of a chainsaw. Except the sound had been recorded and sped up, like a person speaking after inhaling helium.

Now the plane was adding even more acceleration to its nose-versus-ground race.

She pulled up so hard she felt it in her molars.

The sky was an earthquake. As the plane rattled like bushes in the wind, she righted her view so that now she could again see far and wide. "Ha! And they wanted me to take a pilot," Cassidy laughed at the clouds. "Can you imagine...?"

She banked. She didn't have to, but it felt great. Banking a plane was like surfing, just with a fuel tank and much higher stakes. Now she was parallel with the canopy, which was the closest thing to ground she could see until she made most of a circle in order to face roughly the direction she'd come from. Just how much she'd descended really struck home as she had to lean forward over the dash and crane her neck up to see the horizontal, ovaloid hole in the sky. From here, she couldn't see any of the people or equipment in the dig site on the other side of the portal. Just earthy red-brown in a vault of blue.

But then, it was much smaller from down here. Directly below the portal, a bizarre mountain stood at something like three or four thousand feet. It looked like a fault-block mountain, but also a fortress. If she could have seen through the front of the plane on her way down, she'd have noticed it then.

It was a ruined fortress. And to see it below the portal, it almost looked like it had coughed up the hole in the sky. Or maybe the rock had leaked down. She'd have to get closer to—

One of the "fruits" flew by her left wing and made a sound like a scream travelling through a tube!

"Whoa!" Cassidy spat out as she tilted the plane. More of the surreal shrieks sounded from different places. With the wind and the noise of the engine, she couldn't make out how many or where they were. "Let's drag, then!" she shouted. "Show me what you can do, baby," she said to the dashboard.

She went full throttle.

"Ha!" she cried out as some of the shrieks sounded farther away. But there was a metallic squeal and an organic, cawing shriek of primal rage above her. Unable to help herself, she looked up, but could see nothing from inside.

It was like the canopy was a carnival, letting up a flo-tilla of balloons which, now that she was getting a better look, were not fruit. Going faster didn't help when they were making a collision course. Other than blurs of black, blue, and brown, though, it was hard to get more than the sounds they made. She did her best duck-and-weave fly-ing and shouted over her shoulder, "Take that!"

She thought she was winning.

The mountain was closer. It was like an empty set of torso armour standing out of the forest. If she didn't know any better, she'd have sworn that the material for the walls had come from the heights of the mountain. If that was true, though a ruin now…

One of the screaming things slap-landed full-body over the windows of the cockpit. Cassidy couldn't see the eyes because she was looking up at the underside of the neck and jaw. But the beak, comically short legs, and fanned-out membrane left no room for doubt:

It was a pterodactyl!

CHAPTER TWO

"Gamgee!" she burst out. Whenever she had mixed feelings, between gratitude for the ended boredom and blame for impending doom, she thought of the scientist who got her into all this portal rigmarole. The Cessna jarred, her fingers tingled, and her heartbeat soared between the lobes of her ears and the ravaging of the open air by predatory wings.

She pulled up, hoping the wind would tear the beast from her vision.

Cassidy Cane, an archaeologist thirsting for adventure, had gotten into many scrapes over the years. Young by the standards of her faculty — most of them men half again her age — she'd nonetheless run the gamut from the mundane to the exotic.

Crashes were like that. Part thrill, part everyday, and yet a shockingly alien experience. One of the things they don't talk about in the movies is how the senses all suddenly go down different timelines. Her vision had slowed. Everything was almost boring from what she could see. What they wouldn't give back home to see a live pterodactyl! But right now she was just seeing a cockpit and a lizard-bird.

The engine spiralled in an awkward parody of the Doppler effect: that here-and-gone of passing cars. Wind and predators screamed. Her stomach was a centrifuge, and she was glad of her seat — she could feel the spin. Rainforest air, even so high up, was fresh and wild in its scents and even flavours.

The sound of the wing colliding with a flying blade of meat, and the distinct ring of the wing divorcing the plane, came last. It was like seeing a truck go by, looking at a sedan without the front of the car, and then hearing the metallic rending after.

The good news was that the blockage was now free of the window.

Cassidy unbuckled herself from the seat and made a leaning, weaving, bucking series of dashes to the gear nailed and strapped to the back of the plane. Green and blue alternated in the tiny side window she passed. Was the plane careening to the ground like a wheel? She found herself lifting slightly from the floor and ceiling, and "down" became one of those far away, big-picture ideas.

She got to the parachute and had to wedge her hands and feet into the surrounding straps because there was so much spinning in so many directions — punctuated by skrees and meaty thuds — that she climbed more than stood. But this made it difficult to work the straps to get the parachute out. Cursing, she brandished a flip knife and took a steadying breath. Then she cut the straps holding it down, hugged the bundle tight to her left side, and focused on getting the knife re-folded.

Some of the baggage came undone with this hasty unstrapping, and she had to catch a box with her now-free hand — which meant the knife (folded at least) joined the floating dance of bags, bundles, and boxes. She threw the box at the escape hatch, hoping to hit the opening lever and smash out of the plane in a badass dive.

Instead, the box bounced back and bruised her arm before flying off as she slammed into the hatch. "C'mon, you budget bucket of..." She got it open, hung from the edge of the opening because the plane spun again, and slowly hauled herself up with the bruised arm. The spin brought her more and more sidelong to the entrance, and she kicked off the wall to get the last momentum she needed.

She was free!

CHAPTER THREE

She was free!

Her one consolation was that the pterodactyls weren't nipping at her heels. She couldn't tell up from down, though, and didn't know if she had full clearance from the plane. Yet the amount of green she was seeing in her spin meant she was too close to the trees to risk delay. As soon as she had the braces and straps in place, she pulled the cord and the parachute did its thing.

There was so much tearing of branches that all she could do was yell incoherently as she got jerked around even more. So swift and brutal was the swing on breaking through the canopy that the parachute must have caught more tree than air! All the ripping sounds were sickening, and she was so dizzy at this point that she'd have been spinning even if she were lying on the ground.

Dangle.

Breathe.

Wait for the glowing tree trunks to stop orbiting her like a solar system.

Hold up.

"Whoa…" she muttered as soon as she trusted her gut

to stay where it was. How long had she been up here? She couldn't even remember the plane crashing. You'd think a forest would have something to say about a plane crash.

But never mind that.

Many of the trees were glowing! Light was limning intricate slivers through the bark. They reminded her of overhead photographs of highways, slow-exposed so that the headlights smeared into a steady stream of activity. A clear, precise delivery system slowly emerged as she studied them. Absently scratching, she realized she was not in as good repair as the trees.

Blinking a few times, she began a head-to-toe examination. Many twigs were extracted, as well as leaves and some kind of mossy vine. She brushed off some critters and tried not to think about why they were that high in the trees. Lots of cuts. Looking up, the canopy was so thick that her penetration didn't even leave a clear hole. It would have been gloomy, if it weren't for the trees. The light was earthy hues, mostly browns, yellows, and oranges.

It was a warm, honeyed glow. The parachute was hopelessly shredded, and she saw that the ropes were so entangled in the tracery of branches that nothing would be gained from trying to climb them. Her flip knife was lost, but she had others on her person. Never go to other countries, the wilderness, or unexplored portal-dimension-things without multiple knives.

That said, at this height she was going to need a better option than dropping. Beneath her were many extremely large, oddly-shaped bundles of rocks. They looked small from here only because few places on Earth had trees to rival the ones she hung among. The rocks all had spikes, one or two as far as she could see, but rarely in the same place. She took a few moments to rest and prepare herself, through the aching of muscles and lurking emotions (*How am I getting home?*), and swept her gaze around for options.

Plenty of animals, many plants that a botanist would love to see, and nothing she could use. "Okay, um...hello?" she called out.

"Anybody there?"

Despite everything, she was excited. She realized that the portal she'd taken here was roughly pie-shaped, and that her goals were a pie in the sky. She giggled and registered that she had the internal static of being roughed up. Nevertheless, she was all about taking samples home to Gamgee. Real pterodactyls! And trees so large that, even from their lower branches, they went down far enough to look like they were tapering up toward her.

"Huh..." she said with wonder.

Ick!

She managed some awkward fumbling to retrieve from the back of her neck a...bone dart? She drooled out words and all the colours went away.

When she woke up, she felt wonderful. Not goodnight's-sleep wonderful, but finished-a-marathon wonderful. She moved to get in a joyous stretch and instantly cut her luxury short. Her senses flashed open. "Where am I? Why am I tied up?"

"Let the rest do its work," came an odd but soothing voice.

Cassidy looked for its source and laughed. "Oh, I see,

I'm dreaming."

"They say that most times," said the person to her right. "Usually to the humans, though," added the same voice but from an identical body on her left.

The body of a troodon. It looked a little like the Jurassic Park movie version of the velociraptor. Small forearms, the same forward lean and long tail. Even the length and shape of the jaw were similar, though the whole body looked more bird-like than the movie monsters.

She hoped they hadn't taken her phone. There were going to be so many pictures!

"Please do not be alarmed," said one of the troodons. "I am responsible for your treatment."

Cassidy was actually enjoying the feeling of being overwhelmed. It was so rare. "Like a doctor?"

"Most u-halbu have strange words or ways of thinking. But if I understand you rightly, yes," said the other troodon. She was alone with this doctor (for lack of a better word) on a large platform made of intricate and clever weaving techniques. She felt as stable as though she were on flat ground, but the platform was a diamond shape roped with an elaborate suspension system to four dinosaurs — one to a side. All of them were a type she knew little about, called deinocheirus. It was like the super-lizard version of a turkey, but with the arms of a gym enthusiast.

"We tried to give you the usual ear resin," one of the troodons said, "but found that it would not take. Yet we can understand one another. Do you have some illness of the brain?"

"Can you untie me now?" Her brain was digesting

myriads of information on the fly, which was fine, but... "I figure you'd have killed me already if that's what you wanted."

As one of the troodons complied, the other replied: "We were worried about you attacking us. There is little threat from us, most of the time."

Once her bonds were undone, she was careful not to startle her host with any sudden moves. He...it...they... seemed quite calm and collected, but they also felt the need to tie her down. "Most of the time?"

"There is much for you to learn if you are friendly to anybody in our community," answered the one that was tidying up her recent bedding. "We expect, of course, that you'll connect with the other humans first. They have the same strange body you do."

Cassidy stared. "You think *I'm* strange?"

The tails of the troodons made a shivering motion. "I mean no disrespect," they answered together. Cassidy shivered at the effect.

She kept her eyes firmly on the two troodons, her back to the edge of the platform. It was like a hovering elevator. Content to go on carrying it, the deinocheirus showed no apparent interest in her. "You two talk like you're one person," she remarked, pointing at each of them in turn.

"They call us the Twin," one of them answered. "About thirty years ago, our kinds — that is, dinos and humans — tried an experiment that produced many unusual people and unexpected results. I'm one of them."

She cast a glance at the wider forest and gasped, only partly in response to the troodons' unusual medical history. It left her with countless questions that she knew would be inappropriate to ask, such as what it would mean for the personalities of each of the individual troodons who had entered the experiment. Each of them, she noticed, had an amber headpiece vaguely resembling a headset, but built into the skull.

Though she'd been looking for relief by looking at the forest, it only dominated her calm with its massiveness. The trees were so monumentally large that they needed huge spans of space between the trunks. Yet their branches and leaves intertwined to the point that daylight was more an ambience than a set of rays. There was plenty of space for the mobile platform she rode, and the light came as much from the resonance of amber materials in its construction as it did from the ambience of the surrounding natural world.

The deinocheirus must have each weighed as much as one or two buses, and the four of them had a hip height somewhere between fifteen and twenty feet. The platform she was on could have easily held two dozen patients like how she'd been set up. And the forest was going by at a surreal, sliding pace, far faster than she'd have thought such large beasts of burden could accomplish.

Various quick things scurried between stems, roots, and the legs of the great beasts around her. It was hard to get a good look. Other than that, she never saw much beyond what looked like massive trees and typical wildlife. Yet she hadn't forgotten the bone dart. "Is that why you have those headpieces? I thought they were jewellery." She made conversation. What else could she do?

"What is jewellery?"

Her jaw dropped just a little, but she regained herself.

"They look like amber."

"I suppose they would. And, to an extent, they are. My kind and the humans have worked together for many fires. These," the other troodon used its tail to point at the headpiece of the one speaking, "are how I can be one individual. We're sharing brain matter as one mind."

Frantically, she searched herself.

"Easy now," the Twin said.

Once she found that her tools and weapons were where she'd left them, she swept her eyes over the platform again. Other patients, some human and some dino, occupied the curiously pod-like structures throughout. If there were security measures beyond tying her down, she saw no evidence of them. "You asked about why the work you tried to do on me wouldn't take. What were you trying to do?"

"I see we still have much to discuss," came the reply. "Not long now and we'll be arriving at the nearest gathering. Be at ease. I was trying to give you a temporary translation bulb. Your body would have absorbed it within three days. We do nothing without consent except for the preservation of life and speech."

She began walking all around the platform, her archaeology degree and profession performing parkour in her head. There was cuneiform script on the wooden equipment and even painted onto the dinosaurs. They were about to meet up with the community, as she understood it. "So you would have enabled me to understand you. Is that how you communicate with other dinosaurs and humans?"

"Differences thrive everywhere. Even among my fellow troodons, there are those of us who use different words, think differently, believe at variance." The dip of its head suggested a kind of sadness to her. She had no idea how to read their body language, what messages might be in their eyes or faces. "We do our best to bridge the gaps and survive."

"Do I look like the other humans?"

"No."

"What about my clothes, tools, and such?"

"Not much is obvious to us. We have knives, but generally made of glass or stone. I confess I am feverishly curious. Even your skin looks different. Yet you are unmistakably human."

"You've been awfully patient with my questions," she remarked, "and I'm grateful. But why haven't you asked much, if you're so curious?"

The Twin's troodon arms extended from the chest, with short feathery frills. They weren't as tiny as a T-Rex's in proportion, but they were small enough that much of the rigging of this...facility was in place to assist unusual body types. Nevertheless, the Twin pointed ahead. "There is a process for such things. We'll all have our answers soon enough."

She was sure he — they? — meant that as reassurance and not a threat.

Well, mostly sure.

Cassidy turned to follow the Twin's indication and sure enough, even from where she was, there was obvious evidence of a gathering. The humans were so small that at first she took them for bits of rigging or equipment from this distance. The dinosaurs, of course, were less subtle. She took advantage of the remaining time to rest and collect herself. She'd love to know how they achieved so much strength and stability in what looked to her like ropes and a platform similar to a log cabin. There should have been swaying, at the least.

Easily ten to fifteen feet separated her from the forest floor, but it was patchy. Rocks, holes, knotted roots or dismembered trunks, and even smaller dinosaurs littered her potential landing zones. Occasional rustles and flurries from above – shadows she couldn't place, or caught out of the corner of the eye — told her that the doctor had more security than they were letting on.

On arrival, it took more than an hour for her court session (if that's what this was) to get underway. She finally got a good look at the humans of this arrangement. They all had a Middle-Eastern air, neither Iraqi nor Iranian but more related to those groups than, say, the Saudis. She recalled the mountain below the portal she entered and the wedge-shaped writing. Babylonian?

"She does not have an ear resin," remarked a woman across from Cassidy. Her clothes were similar to robed pictures and paintings Cassidy had seen of Sumerian and Akkadian descent. The legs were distinct, the robes having been redesigned to have pants. They were shortened at the hem and sleeve, with clever weaving for preventing loose folds. Dress was not what set the judges before her apart from anyone else, except that some had specialized tools, straps, belts, and the like for whatever their roles were.

"No, but if I understand this 'Twin,' I don't need it," Cassidy answered with as much poise as she could manage. She was surrounded by dinosaurs big and small, though most were separated by the ring of small fires that had been set up around her and the judges. They hadn't bothered tying her hands or taking her weapons. Their confidence excited her.

The other woman raised a brow. She seemed...impressed? A nod from the troodons confirmed Cassidy's words. The woman pursed her lips as though considering this information, but proceeded. "I am Abnir. I shall be your guide."

"Then you are not a judge?" Cassidy asked. A palpable tension danced along the body language of the humans present.

"We do not know this idea you ask about," Abnir replied, "but be warned: you are to make an account of yourself, not speak with me as an equal."

Cassidy suppressed the urge to grind her teeth at that. Stones had been rolled forth and worked with large plants found nearby. Apparently, the resulting seats suited the three "guides" well enough. Cassidy had been left standing. So she stood. Without further comment.

Abnir's features softened. "Excellent. We have an understanding. Now, tell us about the Deep of the triceratops."

"The what?" Cassidy answered.

"The triceratops are the bulky four-legged—" Abnir began.

"I know them," Cassidy said, "but I d— I apologize for interrupting." Hairs had raised on the back of her neck; she wondered if another dart was aimed at her.

"Then what is the problem?" Abnir prodded with

barely-bridled patience.

"I don't understand what you're asking," Cassidy said, struggling not to study too much of her surroundings. It was obvious that she should have her attention solely on the ju...guides. But she was as afraid as she was intrigued by the dinosaurs and (honestly) wanted more to talk to them. "Some of these..." What should she call them? She gestured at a few of them, making sure to point at a different type every time. "...Are known in my...um... where I'm from."

Abnir seemed skeptical. Her two partners, one male and one female, remained silent and impassive. There were a few snorts, shuffling sounds, mutters, and even a fart from one of the corythosaurus behind her. So little was made of that last noise that Cassidy had to conclude that cultural norms about body sounds were different here. Or maybe some dinos were people while others were beasts?

They waited for her to elaborate.

How could she proceed without asking questions? Surely they'd allow clarification? "What is the Deep?"

Everyone looked at one another — dino and human alike — in consternation. "Just finish her off!" someone shouted.

"I will have the tongue of the next person who says such a thing," Abnir said. Her eyes never left Cassidy's. Cassidy never doubted it. Abnir went on: "The Deep is—" a chorus of roars broke out in the distance. Abnir nodded in that direction. First came the stiff vibrato of a splintering tree, then there was a sound unlike any Cassidy had heard before. It was a blend of Chernobyl and ghost stories.

CHAPTER FOUR

"What was—?" she began.

Abnir held up her hand in a gesture that transcended culture.

Cassidy frowned so hard she almost felt it in her feet.

"Many of us want you dead," Abnir resumed.

Cassidy stared.

"Fortunately for you, I believe as few believe," the leader continued. "Hope must come from elsewhere, delivered from earth or sky."

Crashing sounds, and the unmistakable fleshy thumping of large beasts in combat, sounded from afar. But they grew farther still. Cassidy jerked a thumb in the direction of the noise. "I'm not a lot of reinforcement against whatever that is." Already dim from the canopy, the rainforest was darkening into dusk. It seemed the mood was matching the shadows.

"It grieves us, but this shall have to be cut short," said the man on Abnir's side.

"I will consult the Twin," added the woman opposite him.

"It is planted," Abnir said. Cassidy had to think

through what her translator was not converting: there were metaphors and cultural assumptions at play here. Things that are planted have been fixed in place, and will create their consequences. That, at least, was what Cassidy assumed. Abnir continued: "To the tips of the branches, then — we have witnesses who say you arrived with the shine-wood bird."

Shine-wood? "Do you mean my plane?"

"We do not know this word. We found it dead, but without innards. It was surrounded by wounded and dead dactyls," Abnir added. "Why did it bring you here?"

There were still crashes in the distance. Various wildlife figures screeched or shrieked. It was hard to tell what the sounds belonged to, but they didn't seem to frighten Cassidy's current company. With darkness falling and a surrounding circle of burning mistrust, she was ready to move the process along. "Do you recall the wooden platform that brought me here?" No response. "Well, my machine of 'shine-wood,' as you put it, is like that. It carries people above the ground."

"Much higher than our works," Abnir pointed out. "It flies true."

"Yes," Cassidy replied. "So you see, it doesn't have innards because it's a device. I used it to arrive…" Should she explain what portals were? "…in these lands."

"The Twin told you, I assume, that we have a policy for placing temporary amber on u-halbu so that they can follow our speech?"

"He…er, they…"

Abnir's cohorts shifted in their seats. Their foreheads had a downward tension, and their mouths were thin lines. Abnir, however, was a born leader — graceful (in a hardened way) and concise. "Speak to one of their pair at a time, use 'he.' The Twin is not the only one among us so equipped, but we are not without sympathy for your... misplacement of step."

Beyond the fires, it was hard to see much because of the contrast between struggling light and looming dark. It was sound more than the flow and flight of shadow. The larger dinosaurs either reflected light through scales or hides, or had mounted bundles of luminescent amber. Soon, as though a constellation had come to the ground and become the community, the group was alight with earthy or honeyed glows. Like the trees she'd seen when she (for lack of a better word) landed.

Cassidy nervously watched the proceedings as she fitted words and plans together. There were bundles and platforms, people wrapping themselves in sheets of woven plant, managed fur, and measured hide. They were going to sleep on the move! "Thank you," Cassidy said awkwardly. While the whole settlement tore down or repackaged their set-ups with staggering efficiency, she hoped to sneak in a question: "What do you mean by u-halbu? I don't think I know anything quite like it."

There were people leaping and swinging on vines and ropes above her. Many humans scrambled up rope ladders, got lifted by the dinos, or jumped from trees to get to the backs, saddles, platforms, and other strategies for leveraging the dinosaurs as a means of travel. "It wasn't the triceratops!" someone called from above.

Abnir put her thumb and index finger to her mouth and whistled. Instantly, people and smaller dinos like oviraptors and compsognathus skittered and flitted about. There were corythosaurus, roughly twice the size of Clydesdales, acting like squadron leaders for both humans and the smaller dino groups. Cassidy just took it all in. She noticed that, when they came near her, human hands dwelled on the handles of obsidian knives or whips of a material that might have been leather. When groups of compsognathus, about the size of house cats, flooded by her, it wasn't just a tiny flood of feet. The ones nearest her kept their attention on her. The individuals on the outer edges of their groups watched for other community members or changes in their surroundings. With subtle changes in their tails or how they held their backs, slight changes in their steps or small sounds they made, each sub-group of these clusters communicated to the others.

No one got tripped or stepped on. All items were accounted for. Articles and individuals were secured and organized in remarkable feats of speed and coordination. Cassidy was constantly watched. "It refers to people who are not from the forest," Abnir said amidst the apparent tumult.

The other woman was not escorted. A casual observer might have thought that she and Cassidy were alone amidst a flurry of activity. "Is all the world a forest?" she asked, and it was a multi-pronged question: did they believe so religiously? Had the portal taken her to a forested planet? Were they nomadic, trapped in a prison made of impossible arborous towers and things that screamed when the sun went down?

Abnir's answer came in measured tones and matched her pace. To Cassidy's surprise, the two of them were mounted upon a deinocheirus with the assistance of two human men and a nearby corythosaurus. The latter was chatting with another of its kind at a distance uncomfortable for human conversation. Though she could understand them, she had to concentrate on her co-rider.

"Not all the world is known," Abnir began, "at least not to any one tribe." In a fraction of a second, Cassidy's brain launched fireworks of questions about the organization that Abnir meant by a tribe. Were humans and dinos separate tribes? Was this whole group one tribe? How much meeting and cooperation — or competition — was there? Member transplantation? Territory? But she could not interrupt her guide/ judge, who didn't miss a beat: "Yet there is the forest as a physical thing, and then there is the forest as greater truth. But none of this is your question," she remarked, looking over her shoulder to smile at Cassidy.

The archaeologist was reminded of intelligentsia and investors she'd met in numerous circles of power. Hunting for grant money, university conferences that were really thinly-veiled recruitment strategies, festivals of ego and threat arranged by the bigwigs for no other purpose than to have lips applied to their hindquarters. Abnir would have appeared to them as primitive because they wouldn't have looked at her properly, but this woman was the sort of figure who could sharpen her tongue on the mirror of Helen of Troy.

Cassidy smiled back.

Abnir elaborated without any obvious acknowledgement of the exchange, but a shift had occurred. "You must be thinking that if we were going to kill you, we'd have done so." Cassidy felt the question in her fingertips, but didn't need to respond. "I figure much the same. You will notice we relieved you only of your damaged harness."

Blinking, Cassidy quickly checked herself. She'd been so focused on physical injury, possible violence, and social dangers that her clothes only mattered for comfort. The contents of her pockets and pouches mattered more. "Many are the strange things about you," Abnir continued, "but as you see: we know a harness when we see one."

It was time to risk a question. Cassidy asked, "Did you train the dinosaurs? Many of them seem quite clever. How many of them are people?"

She didn't get an immediate opportunity to ask Abnir about the other woman's tension because their mount stopped and swivelled her neck around. Cassidy was looking the massive creature in the eye, and it felt like sliding down the pebbled side of a mountain. "Why would any of us not be people?" This was a deep-chested being with singular muscles larger than everything Cassidy was. It was like the angry moan of a bull, turned into a reptile's piping force and enlarged many times over.

Cassidy was a soda can that had been stepped on.

"I...I'm sorry," she stammered.

"Never mind the offence," the lumbering being replied. "I want to know."

Cassidy processed that for a moment. The rest of the community (tribe?) continued about their business. No one was worried for Abnir, it seemed, and none of them were going to wait. "What's your name?" asked the archaeologist, in the hopes that it would help somehow.

"Belessunu," the deinocheirus replied. She still hadn't resumed walking.

It occurred to Cassidy that she didn't have to go into explanations about other worlds, dimensions, or portals. They'd seen her plane, perhaps even the "battle" (to put it generously). But did they see her come out of the earthy hole in the sky? "Where I'm from," she started carefully, "the only evidence of dinosaurs are remains. Bones, mostly." Well, fossils, but she wasn't getting into that. She wondered absently if they lumped the dinosaurs together wholesale; if she was just misunderstanding the terms they used based on her assumptions, and where their marks of separation might be. But she didn't lose verbal stride: "The bones were far larger than most — if not all — of the animals any of my people had ever heard of. But still, they were more like in shape to animals than to pe... humans. So you see…"

"Humans are the only ones with intelligence where you're from," Belessunu finished for Cassidy. She started walking again. They were now closer to the end of the line of the group. Abnir, in front of Cassidy, kept her gaze straight ahead and made no comment.

Striving to hide her concern, Cassidy took up the conversation. "I meant no disrespect."

"I understand," the deinocheirus replied. "We must be frightfully new to you, then."

You have no idea.

"And big," Cassidy said. Belessunu nodded. With the size of her head and the relative haste of her stride — she was gradually inching her way back up the line — the deinocheirus moved both ponderously and quickly. It was as surreal as encountering a blizzard the very first time one has seen snow. After a pause, she risked another question: "Where are we going?"

"We're moving," Belessunu answered, as though this were the most obvious thing in the world.

"Yes, but where?"

Belessunu sharply turned her head so she could regard Cassidy as though the human was daft, but set her gaze forward and focused on navigating the group, the trees, and the terrain. They entered a span of trees like the ones Cassidy had seen on first arrival, with the limning bronze-ish light. Abnir turned around and said, "Let me teach you."

They spent some time moving and re-working the (to give it a name) saddle-like contraption that occupied so much of the back of the deinocheirus. It could have easily seated a dozen humans, with other accommodations clearly intended for smaller dino varieties as well. Yet the two of them were the only occupants, made all the more conspicuous by Belessunu's sheer size.

Cassidy spoke little because the guide was keeping up the conversation to show her how everything worked and why, and to help her move back a bit and re-adjust so that both of them could be secured. They now faced one another. Some of the adjustments involved clever interwoven ropework so studiously arranged that it acted solid, like a bamboo vine. Working with them, despite her youth and athleticism, took enough effort that Cassidy was breathing heavily at several points throughout their lesson.

Only when they were restored to proper and secure seating, and Belessunu had returned them to the front of the line, could they readily resume conversation. At which point Abnir still had to coordinate the activities of the group and field questions. Food and water were passed along. Cassidy accepted what she was given with gratitude and hoped that there weren't any germs or parasites to which she might be vulnerable. It wasn't like Gamgee and the rest of the team back home could prepare vaccines for a new dimension!

While she waited for Abnir to be able to pick up where they'd left off, she watched everyone's efforts, roles, tools, techniques, and behaviours. She had to be quick — it didn't look like they'd finished with her little tribunal earlier. In the back of her mind, other questions were bouncing around. Dinosaurs lived in conditions very different from the modern human Earth she knew. Oxygen, temperature, possibly even pressure, moisture, and the kinds of gases in the air were all different in their day. She couldn't recall anyone showing fossil evidence that dinosaurs had anything resembling speech, and certainly not the brainpower for culture, names, and language!

She watched and she wondered. Many people were smoking. None of them were close enough for her to smell it or engage with them, but it didn't look like any cigarette or cigar she'd ever seen. In fact, they were green tubes and reminded her of the veins of a leaf. Abnir finally returned her attention to the archaeologist. "I didn't understand your question earlier." They reached the visual edge of the towering, lighted trees and turned. It wasn't quite a reversal, but more like they were keeping a respectable distance from the dark.

Cassidy pointed. "Are we staying in the lighted areas

during the night?"

"Of course. You cannot see danger in the shadows."

"Where is your community?"

Blank stare.

Cassidy rolled her hands as she tried to find a way to express her question. "I see that you've built beds for people on the move." Abnir nodded slowly, her eyes darting from one side to another. She clearly didn't see where the archaeologist was going with this. "So where are your still beds?"

"Are you asking how we deal with our dead?"

"Heavens, no!" Cassidy sat up straighter. "Where do you lie down for the night?"

As though the other woman were an idiot, Abnir again pointed at the bed platforms and saddles with rigging for the smaller dinosaurs.

A conclusion was tugging at Cassidy's brain like a child urgently pulling on a sleeve. "Where do the larger dinosaurs sleep?"

"In groups, guarded by other dinos and humans. We are attentive, we stay well-armed. The lazy cannot contribute." Cassidy knew the word as "lazy" because of the effects of her translator, but she thought she caught something and refused to believe it. "Say that bit about dealing with your dead again."

Abnir's expression was dangerous.

"It's not what you think!" Cassidy quickly clarified, holding up her hands in self-defence. "Please, humour me."

"Are you asking how we deal with our dead?"

"No, the other part — about contribution." Cassidy

wasn't blinking. She must have sounded delirious. But after a moment's hesitation...

"The lazy cannot contribute."

It was true: the words for lazy and dead were the same in their language!

Cassidy wiped the sweat from her brow. She was lightly dressed for travel, but thoroughly covered. She hadn't expected the night to be this warm. Despite their colossal size, the trees felt close and crowded. There was a whistle from somewhere along the line, but it couldn't have been made with human lips. The archaeologist witnessed a changing of the guard. They were moving in shifts!

She turned her attention back to Abnir. "You never stop."

"Is that a question?"

"More or less."

"We meet up with other tribes from time to time. There is trade. We've been sundered from others of our group because of the last Deepening. You found the triceratops sleeping it off. And we have work platforms, though those are repurposed for medicine or sleep depending on need or time of day. I hope you won't judge us harshly; you've crossed our path where it is well mucked."

Why would she care what I think of her? Cassidy was taken aback. She was also exhausted. "So then..."

"You should rest," Abnir interrupted.

"No, but..." Cassidy had been feeling the fatigue for hours already. Adrenaline, fascination, and the awareness of some obscure danger they weren't talking about kept her going. "How long was I with the Twin?"

"Since early yesterday. He worked on you overnight.

We had to compel him to rest when he arrived at the council with you. He was the only true healer to survive the last Deepening."

Cassidy slept, and didn't even know it was coming.

She leapt up, sleep still in her eyes, and blinked rapidly while she turned to and fro.

"Are you well?" There were a few other humans on the platform, but the speaker got her attention.

"The Twin!"

Both troodons tilted their heads. "Yes?" they said together. Then again, "Are you all right?"

"I…" she started, and checked herself. "I think so." She then spent some time on the cricks and stiffness in her muscles and joints. "It's been a while since I've been that tired."

"Is that why you slept so long? Are you prone to that?"

She didn't stop limbering up. At this point, Cassidy had accepted that feeling normal wasn't in the cards. "Same as most people, eight-ish hours."

"You must have a relaxed world," the Twin said. One of the troodons had sat back, plopping down with his tail and two legs spreading out equally. Cassidy giggled, as it looked ridiculous. Only the standing troodon spoke, but he did so with such awe that Cassidy forgot the antics of the Twin's other half and stared at him.

"What do you mean?" she asked.

"More than four hours at a rest seems an awful lot. We have guarded you so long only because the revered Abnir has high hopes for you."

She turned and regarded Abnir, who was at the other

end of the platform, in what appeared to be a small meeting with the two other guides from the circle of fire. "Wait, how did I get onto this platform? We were on the...I mean, we were riding...we were with Belessunu."

"When you passed your fifth hour with no sign of waking," the Twin explained, "you were sent to me."

CHAPTER FIVE

Part of Cassidy's mind, accustomed as she was to taking in all her surroundings and processing many details at once, registered that many of the humans in the group were smoking again. Daylight was as strong as it was likely to get. None of this stretch looked the same as the rainforest of last night, though it all sort of looked the same and different times of day could change a surprising amount of the landscape. She never missed a beat: "You never sleep more than four hours?"

"Some of the large dinos do, but triceratops don't have as many weaknesses and predators as you humans do. That is, after all, one of the things you gain from us. Now that you mention it, humans do generally get six to ten hours throughout a given day. But all at once? No chance."

That made sense. Well, as much as anything made sense in a place where humans and dinosaurs could talk and breathe the same air. "It seems," she started, trying to find the right words, "that you and I come from very different communities. I'm used to places where we can settle long enough to build. Not just tools and things like this platform," she spread her hands out to indicate where they were, and noticed a strange cluster of indentations in one corner that never much registered before, "...but whole buildings." When she saw the uncomprehending light in the Twin's eyes, she tried a different take on the concept. "We built containers, like solid pouches or boxes, big enough for people to live in."

Abnir had rejoined them, but did not interrupt. Her wonderment at Cassidy's wild tale of houses and sleeping in one spot was as complete as the Twin's. "Even in your sleep," she continued, "you have to keep moving?" Abnir nodded. Cassidy registered that the trees were starting to show signs of that telltale glow again. She pointed. "Why do they do that?"

"The glow?" the Twin clarified. At Cassidy's nod, Abnir took up the explanation: "The dinos have helped us humans with all manner of ideas, as well as their physical work. Our size and body type comes with its own advantages. We work together in all things, and building a resin network is one of them. Most of our tools, materials, and abilities come from our studies of the ambers and resins."

"That must mean that you alter as many trees as you can, whenever you have the luxury of stopping long enough to work on the trees," Cassidy remarked.

Abnir shook her head. "We have to begin the process straight from the seeds," the Twin said. "The amount of work to change a tree already grown is well past any hope of safety."

Cassidy was fascinated. "Some of these trees are huge! They'd have needed centuries to grow!"

"Yes," the Twin said.

Abnir added, "We have not learned how to alter the seeds past their own generations, though."

Cassidy frowned. She'd registered that she needed to relieve herself. She also noticed that humans were using the strange indentations every once in a while to do just that. She supposed it was logical: the dinosaurs acted like horses when it came to nature's call. Why would the humans feel any shame, and how would it be practical to keep moving if they did? While she mustered the courage to go about her business in full view of everyone, she continued the conversation: "Do you mean you can't get the new trees to keep making seeds that will produce the light?"

"We cannot get them to produce seeds at all," Abnir answered.

"You'll notice that even the most densely lighted patches still have unlit trees," the Twin said.

Cassidy, unable to hold it any longer, went about her business. Abnir and the Twin began conversing about their various responsibilities and plans. She had to wait to rejoin them while they concluded their management. Then she picked up again: "How long has it been since you could create such wondrous uses for the sap?"

"Countless generations," Abnir answered easily.

"Why do you ask?" the Twin said.

"I just…" she pointed in various directions. "I see a lot of rainforest that goes for many…" she faltered while she tried to phrase distance, "…days without the glowing resin. Shouldn't all of it be covered by now?"

Again, one of the bodies of the Twin seemed to fall in

a child-like exhibition of shock. Abnir, equally astounded, was the one to find her voice: "You expected even more? That any have survived — never mind whole groves of light — is a source of great pride to us."

"Forgive me," Cassidy said, trying to match their gravity. "I see that I am accustomed to much more safety than you are." Both of the others offered a solemn bow, and she mimicked it — if only in an attempt to show respect. "We also have different takes on space," she reflected aloud, "and I don't quite follow some of your reasoning. You all keep together as though you have a purpose or destination, but you just sort of...keep going."

"The only stillness we understand for the living is to be a plant or be dead," the Twin said.

"That's our next 'purpose,' if I understand how you're using the word," Abnir rejoined. "We call it utuki, and mostly we smoke it. We want it because we enjoy it, but we must also destroy it."

"There's a lot to that," Cassidy mused aloud.

"There is," the Twin confirmed. "We dinos dislike the plants, though we don't know why. There are slate outcroppings we've encountered where our young will scrape their claws. The sound has a similar feeling." Cassidy resisted the urge to laugh: nails on a chalkboard was a strange cultural bonding point! He answered before she could ask: "It isn't just that the humans like the flower. Utuki make the glow-trees sick, and much of our toolery comes from glow-tree sap."

Toolery? She knew he meant technology. This translation phenomenon was strange. It got across what they meant, despite having nothing in common in terms of the roots of the languages. It's not like there was any Greek or Latin influence in these people. In fact, they reminded her of stories of ancient Babylon. It was like the jumping of the language barrier used her knowledge as a frame of reference.

She also realized there were no trees with the telltale luminous resin lines. And that the people around her were arming up far more than they had against her.

"What's going on?" she asked.

"We've shared a great deal with you, given that you're the one under suspicion," Abnir said. She stood casually, relaxed, as though her role in the proceedings was over and others were taking up the operations. Cassidy wondered at the odd friendly-hostile dynamic here. Abnir went on: "Many of us, Belessunu included, wanted to end you straight off because you came to us amid a flight of dactyls."

Cassidy let her jaw drop at that.

"Abnir believes we need outside help to win the wars we wage," the Twin said. Each troodon was operating independently, speaking with compsognathus and humans alike as he coordinated the rigging for a mobile battle-hospital arrangement.

There was so much to learn! Before Cassidy could form a question, though, Abnir's commanding but calm tones demanded attention: "You built your wings, or someone from your community did so. My scouts heard you before they saw you. They saw there was smoke. Your wings and your clothes, and even your tools and equipment, are made of materials we've never seen. Your toolery is strange. How came you among the dactyls?"

Her pride chafing at this shift in handling her, Cassidy said, "I'm not a bucking stallion, and we're going in the same direction — at least for now. Pick a stance already." Abnir's eyes had an almost visible sheen of indignation and outrage shimmer through them. Cassidy made no apology for her mouth getting ahead of her, and didn't even lose stride. "I wasn't among them. They attacked me as soon as I was within reach of them. It all happened so fast, I wasn't sure what to make of it. They did a lot of what I thought was screaming. Were they angry? Did I do something wrong, just going about my business in the air?"

"We're not used to humans having business in the air," the Twin remarked. The troodon that hadn't spoken made a scaly barking noise that eventually registered as laughter. She realized he was trying to cut the tension in the air.

The human leader was ambaric. Such was the stillness in her poise and the feeling, like static electricity, of her sheer presence. Her silence was on the cusp of long before she decided to pick a stance — for now. "That does sound like the dactyls. We've long ago come to the conclusion that they have a kind of intelligence, though they are not people by any measure we know," Abnir said with some disgust. Cassidy was vaguely reminded of stories she'd heard in her homeworld of dragons. "Dactyls are beasts, destroyers from the skies. They mostly stay above the canopy, because the forest protects the people who learn to love and protect it in turn."

Cassidy had her doubts about that conclusion, but didn't voice them. In fact, she didn't get much chance to voice anything: she realized that the darkness had thickened here. The canopy was denser, the air here close and tight, and a cacophony of lungs, feet, and wings lunged at them from beyond their sight.

Many of the larger dinos spread out and lowered the platforms they were carrying. All this time Cassidy thought they were for tools and resources: it looked like rock, bark, possibly obsidian or other forms of volcanic glass. Instead, many of those "stones" stood up as the platform lowered! Humans around her laboured alongside smaller dinos to leverage massive wooden contraptions. They were too odd to have been obvious to her while she was occupied in discussion, but these were arbalests and dino-mounted ballistae!

Some of the platforms also featured things made largely out of wood and amber, and she had no idea what they were. The dinos who'd stood away from these contraptions — the same ones she thought were boulders — turned out to be ankylosaurus. These were like the dino equivalent of badgers. Though bulky, they stayed low on all fours and seemed resolute and immovable. Unlike badgers, these bony-shelled living tanks had sizeable tails that ended in a wrecking ball. They marched forward, and not a moment too soon.

Stegoceras rampaged and stampeded out of the dark!

They were two-legged and most of their size was in their length. They weren't as low as alligators, and not much shaped like the more familiar creature, but they were big when compared to humans. Their heads had natural bone helmets, which they used for ramming. Though any one of them were no match for the deinocheirus and other larger dinos in this group, the stegoceras were a flood of dry carnage. They ran, they rammed, and they wrought.

Several corythosaurus went down.

Even as they fell, human and dino fought together. Human tools and contraptions fired bundles of fire and some — once they burst — appeared to be acid. Spears and other shaft-like weapons were launched from ballistae and the like. Dactyls joined the fray, throwing everything into chaos. Humans were plucked up to be eaten or dropped, devices were rent asunder, dinos were attacked in the eyes or pulled off the backs of larger dinos. It was then that the amber "toolery" was put to use.

Cassidy fell to the platform, each of the troodons of the Twin working to protect her and Abnir. The amber weapons launched sonic blasts! Waves of sound, dense enough to be briefly visible, passed through the dactyls. For a fraction of a second, Cassidy thought there was no resistance, but then she registered that every one of them lost flight from the wave. Additional amber blasts, flattened and widened when aimed downward, tossed the stampeding stegoceras like toys lined up in front of a newly activated industrial fan.

"We should be quick," someone said as he landed on the platform next to the trio.

"What? Why?" asked Cassidy. She was the first to regain herself.

The man was not alone. He and the others, along with some oviraptors, were carrying sacks and backpacks. They were using some kind of gliding getup made with a membrane Cassidy didn't immediately recognize. And rope. Lots of rope. Abnir was up quickly, and the Twin focused upon incoming wounded. "They're harvesting utuki before we set it all alight," Abnir explained. "You should—"

"Let me go with them!" Cassidy wasn't passing up this opportunity.

Doubt bounced between Abnir and the collectors, but there wasn't much time. "I'll want a report, Eshkar," she told the man.

He nodded once, tossed Cassidy an extra sack, and his team set to work. They didn't waste words. Cassidy kept up with them to a point that seemed to surprise them. They leapt and swung down the lengths of rope and elaborate dino harnesses with almost superhuman ease, whereas she kept it simple and not quite as graceful. Still, she'd done enough adventuring that ropes and ladders and the like — no matter how oddly configured — were like a second home to her.

It was like the running of the bulls.

The trees were so large that, now they were away from their larger dinosaur friends, the humans had to dodge using the massive roots. A tree trunk isn't a quick go-around when it's more than forty feet wide. Blasts of fire quickly caught with the underbrush, so there was a slithering black-orange contrast that made details harder to catch. Some of the stegoceras came and went so quickly that it was like the darkness itself gave and took their forms.

"Watch your left!" Cassidy called out to one of them as she jumped for the cover of a mushroom the size of a pickup truck.

He didn't even look: the man dove into a roll to his right, and a stegoceras foot clomped on the ground where he'd stood a fraction of a second earlier. He didn't bother calling out thanks, and she didn't wait for it. A blast, wide and loud, raked the ground ahead of them as one of the amber guns took out a wave of the rogue dinos.

CHAPTER SIX

Eshkar ducked. Cassidy poked her head out enough to watch him, lit by a nearby fire, as he gathered a four-pointed flower. His cohorts had spread out, avoiding the fire, and the ones most in the smoke held something to their faces. A cluster of compsognathus wove between the hardheaded stegoceras and had nowhere else to go but to flow over the next patch of flowers.

The ground urged as though it would throw up with all the shifting and stamping of the larger dinos. A deinocheirus, its leg broken by a group of reckless and determined stegoceras, crashed hard into a tree. Cassidy heard a sound she couldn't believe: the breaking of a bone. A bone the size of a cement mixer. Unforgettable, the sound was somewhere between the sharp crack of a splitting glacier and the wet smack of a massive tree hitting something hard.

Colours swarmed Cassidy's vision, and for an instant she thought the bones were hers.

"U-halbu!" she heard Eshkar cry out. Shaking her head, she ran forward again, following the curve of the mushroom. "Don't!" he shouted, but it was too late: she slid to a stop in front of the compsognathus.

They were like angry, cat-sized lizards. They'd been helping the community not ten minutes ago. But now they looked at her with a primal cross of hunger and revenge. Thinking quickly, she dug a magnesium flare out of her leg pouch, watched the creatures eye-to-eye as the little dinos stepped in clumsy unison toward her, and lit the flare with her free hand. They screamed when its vicious light took hold. Cassidy took a certain satisfaction from the impressed and frightened sounds of the human collectors behind her, and flung the flare into the mushroom next to her.

It was slobbering flame and spores even as she turned.

She ran.

A wooden stake slammed into the ground to her right, a skewered dactyl still twitching at its end. Her legs wrestled with the acidic tension of weight and haste. A fleshy landing thumped on her left. People cried out in pain, triumph, fear. Dinos let out roars and vibratos, shrieks and gulps and snarls.

Cassidy saw a patch of the flowers sheltered between two roots of a massive tree that was being ignored several large dinos away. Smoke billowed and stegoceras bellowed. She jogged, and did her best to sway in imitation of the dark plant stalks that sprouted up here and there. A dactyl crashed and slid by her, but the teeth marks in it suggested that it had been tossed — not that it was diving at her.

She filled her pouch, but didn't do any harm to the remaining flowers. Several of them blossomed so quickly that she did a double-take, but they didn't seem to do anything else. Her stomach leapt as though there'd been a big G-force change in an odd direction, but she managed to lurch back the way she came without too much issue. It was getting harder to tell foe from lesser foe. In the back of her mind, she wondered if the dactyls were some kind of albatross. Had they goaded the stegoceras into attacking?

Cries and shouts rang out above. Shattered amber landed a good hard run ahead of her, but she made no effort in that direction. Instead, she pivoted, heading for what would be the rear of the dino-human caravan that had taken her here. She climbed a mound of something she couldn't make out in the confusing darkness and firelight, but it felt fleshy and she thought it might have been green if she could have seen it.

It was too late to stop when she went far enough over the mound to practically land on a stegoceras. So she embraced the situation and straight-up landed on the bipedal ramming beast. It wasted no time running for all it was worth. Her arms were wrapped around the base of its neck. Wind held her legs aloft with the dino's momentum. Had she startled it? Was it trying to shake her off, escape the melee, or hunt something down?

A huge foot thumped nearby, hard enough for the stegoceras to lose its footing. Cassidy pulled and let go for all she was worth so that her momentum carried her well past the stumbling beast. She rolled into the landing on what turned out to be a slight upward slope of the ground. To her surprise, she was able to roll out of it running. A rope dangled from a corythosaurus and she managed to clamber her way up.

"Hi!" she said, once she was mounted. "I'm Cass."

"Mashda," the corythosaurus replied. "Did you get your flowers?"

"Yep; got separated."

"Clearly."

"Do you think you could get me back to Abnir?"

"Possibly," Mashda said. "But first: did you see any resin toolery? Some of it fell."

"Yes," Cassidy answered, a little nonplussed. "It's up there, past the burning mushroom. Why?"

"We'll need to get what we can. Hold on." And she was off.

Cassidy ran with it. Questions later.

Once Mashda brought her abreast of the crumble of amber, Cassidy had to jump off to help two of the humans from the collection group and another corythosaurus gather it together and bundle it into a kind of dumbwaiter setup attached to the side of a deinocheirus. "Where's Eshkar?" Cassidy called to one of the humans while she worked.

"Had to regroup," he answered. "He's with the dactyl fighters now. I saw him fend them away from…" he was cut off as three more ramming skulls came their way. A wooden battering ram swung down sidelong and took them all out at once. Shocked, Cassidy turned and looked up. It had been mounted on a second deinocheirus, a rope and pulley system working it from the side of what she now realized was Belessunu. "Nice shot!" she waved up.

"Thank you," Belessunu said with a shuffle of her head.

Cassidy was being helped up the length of the

deinocheirus before she knew what was happening. Soon she stood beside Abnir again, the other woman limping on a bandaged leg. A flurry of dactyls went up beyond the canopy. As the monstrous trunks of the trees swung in the extremes of Cassidy's vision, she realized they were on a turn.

"We're retreating?" she asked no one in particular.

Eshkar was by her side. He looked vaguely Iranian — like the others — and his hair was kept short. Between their appearances and the wedged writing system they used, it occurred to Cassidy that they might even be Sumerian. The site where they'd found the portal was, some argued, the place of the Tower of Babel in ancient days. But surely her mind was running on without her. She pulled herself back to the tasks at hand.

Blood, dirt, and a telltale gleam of a varnish over Eshkar's skin told her there was more to him and his team than she first thought. In the vanishing firelight, she noticed that several people were coated in this resin. Eshkar answered her: "The dactyls seek reinforcements. We want to be well out of thought by the time they arrive. We got a good supply. Your eye is sharp: you picked good samples."

"Thanks," she said.

And without another word, she set about working on the rest of the platform. At first she helped with some basic debriefing and cleanup tasks, and she spread what food she'd had from her rations among the group. They sniffed at it at first, but ate soon enough. The rest of her work was with the Twin. Medical wasn't her field, but she took every opportunity to help with triage, field dressings, moving people, and using some of the tech. The troodons explained to her whenever the Twin had a mouth or some hands free. She wasn't exactly an X-ray tech, but they did have (and showed her how to use) a strange bathing device made of worked amber parts that glistened and shivered.

She was reminded of a cat purring. "It uses a sound that helps with healing," the Twin explained.

Abnir was in and out to receive reports and give instructions, but largely congregated with Eshkar and his team of what Cassidy thought were some kind of scouts. Once the humans were sorted out, she wasted no time in requesting and receiving assistance getting to the platforms used for the dinos. The Twin came with her, leaving his assistants to keep an eye on the patients. Cassidy laboured for their aid because she didn't really know what was happening, but she knew this: pain and loss bring everyone together.

Hands drifted away from obsidian knives as the night went on. Dinos stopped watching her for danger and started watching her methods, her state of exhaustion, her attempts to learn their ways.

She took a turn of her own in the resin healing pool. She could have sworn she'd only blinked, but the darkening night was now so punctured by slivers of white sunlight that she had to accept that it was daytime. "Is it noon?" she asked. She couldn't believe the brightness. She was also surprised by how much her tongue stuck to the roof of her mouth while she spoke.

"Ah, yes, well risen," the Twin replied. One of him was adjusting the settings of her pool while the other troodon was holding a discussion with Abnir a few feet away. If Cassidy cared to pick out the words, she could have, but it took more focus than she could muster right now.

"Uh, well risen to you," she said. "How long was I out?"

"I was told you had gotten in about an hour before dawn," he answered. "So at a guess: six hours or so. How do you feel?"

"Wonderful," she answered, and caught herself off-guard with just how true that was. "It's like I've had all the benefits of a hard workout, full rest, stretching, massage, and yoga," she finished. "I'll need one of these for my bedroom."

"You are using many terms I do not know," the Twin said.

Right.

"Never mind," she said, and she was halfway through dressing before she realized that she'd fallen into this culture's attitudes about nudity. Extra warmth made its way to her face, but her glances didn't uncover any unusual (or untoward) attention. "Wait: did you leave me in that all night?"

"Clearly."

"Isn't that well in excess of...I mean, you have so many others..."

The Twin let out that laugh-bark. "Usually, yes, but you've done much to ingratiate yourself. And you had a somewhat chafing welcome."

She shrugged. "Trust me, I've dealt with much worse."

"I don't doubt it," he replied confidently.

Cassidy tugged at and smoothed out her clothes some more, and focused on them. "Hey," she said, "why do my clothes feel funny?"

"We did what we could," Abnir answered. Cassidy stood straighter and faced the other woman, who was still dirty. She'd had sleep, but little else; her eyes were tight, sharp, and edged with premature wrinkles. She studied Cassidy as she spoke: "Your hides and fabrics are strange to us. But we are grateful for your help."

"Of course," Cassidy responded. She looked around as the caravan came to a halt. There was no sign of dactyls, and she was surprised to see several stegoceras being treated on a different platform. One of the troodons was talking with someone who'd just swung over from there, while the other was still with Abnir and Cassidy. She registered absently that the troodons never went beyond ten feet of each other if they could help it, and often kept less than five.

"I brought you this," Abnir said. Most of the others in the caravan, as far as Cassidy could tell at a glance, were resting. Abnir was holding out one of the tubes the others had been smoking. Many of the ones resting — the humans, at least — were preparing to do just that.

Though most were trying to play it cool, Cassidy could tell that everyone felt a certain awe but a pressure not to pay too much attention. She wasn't surprised: having a leader personally present a gift, regardless of its scale, was considered a great honour in many cultures. She didn't smoke, but this also was clearly not tobacco. "I...I'm touched by your generosity," she managed. She accepted it gingerly.

She'd noticed that there were no ankylosaurus in evidence, but couldn't remark on that just yet. She turned the stalk about this way and that, making no effort to hide her inspection. Abnir said, "We make it entirely using the utuki. Even the stalk is made by an art of the utuki stem." Sure enough, Cassidy recognized seams and portions in the tube-shaped object: it was an unusual weaving technique.

As she spoke, Abnir retrieved something that looked like a small coconut from one of her aides. There was a hole in it, continuously producing a tiny column of flame. "How…?" Cassidy asked as Abnir lit her flower-stalk and passed the coco-flame to her.

Abnir's lips quirked on one side as Cassidy accepted the flame and availed herself. "Even were I to pass you to each of my people and the dinos in turn, for a year apiece, I doubt we could teach you all there is to be said for our ways, tools, plants, and animals. Could you teach me everything, even just about your wings, if I came to your home?"

Cassidy smirked in turn. "Not a chance. And thank you." She took her first puff of the utuki.

And sat down hard.

A chorus of laughter washed over her. Oddly, she could taste the laughter. It was like macaroni and cheese, if each noodle carried a different flavour. Steak, french fries, oregano, blueberries, kale. She smelled colours. Her whole body awareness got blended in with her surroundings. Then everything snapped back. She was woozy, but somehow back on her feet, and there was nothing in her hands.

"I'm sorry," Abnir said without being sorry at all, "I couldn't resist. Most of us have been smoking whenever we could since we were old enough for moonblood. An adult who'd never tried it…"

Cassidy coughed. Her eyes watered. She felt like a five-year-old who'd taken a shot of something that was whiskey mixed with something that was not. Charges would have been laid where she was from, and for good reason, but those laws she knew were no good here. At least this meant they accepted her? "Don't worry about it," she rasped.

The Twin shuffled nervously. It was a little surreal seeing the same emotion play out in the same way between two different bodies, especially knowing that they had the same mind. It dawned on her to ask, but Belessunu, striding nearby, lowered her head enough to join the conversation: "Smoking is a human thing. The utuki works differently for you. We don't understand how you could enjoy it."

Cassidy stopped herself from agreeing with the deinocheirus. "None of the dinos smoke?"

"None."

"Never?"

"Never. Just being around those plants gives us the shivers." Belessunu watched as a cluster of ankylosaurus crested a small embankment. "They're here."

Abnir went to the edge of the platform, near the body of one of the deinocheirus carrying it, and got some assistance from some of the other humans as she made her way down an elaborate rope ladder setup. "She's expected to greet lost members of the group when they come in big numbers or belong to the same spines," the Twin re-marked for Cassidy's benefit. "Should it come up in song, I do not care for this smoking practice."

She tried to parse that.

"Our different kinds have different backbones," Beles-sunu answered the confused human's expression. "Your idea of lumping all dinos and all humans into two groups is a little unnatural, though perhaps not so much. Humans are, after all, very strange."

"I won't deny that," Cassidy smirked. The others laughed, or made sounds that she now knew were laugh-ter. But she had more questions. "Why do you seek out the plants at all?"

"They harm the glow-trees," Belessunu said. "A sick-ness spreads from them. It does nothing to the normal trees, but it's a threat to our way of life."

Cassidy saw more benefit from the resinous technol-ogy for the humans than for the dinos, but wouldn't risk coming across as arguing the point. Besides, she was hu-man herself — she was likely privileged or otherwise bi-ased. It made sense to her to wait for the ankylosaurus to catch up, but... "How did the ankylosaurus get left be-hind?"

"They're rearguard," the Twin explained. Cassidy watched as they were examined, information was ex-changed, and the process began in earnest to bring them up with the platforms. Witnessing this slow and careful procedure, and remembering the chaos of the double at-tack of the dactyls and the stegoceras, everything fit into place for her. Besides, it's not like anybody could harm the heavily-armoured dinos. They were simply too slow to catch up. When lined up and well-placed, though, they were an impenetrable wall.

"How many did we lose?" Cassidy berated herself for not thinking to ask about that earlier.

Silence.

She looked at the other two. Neither would meet her gaze. Eventually, she said, "Forgive me."

Both nodded. Neither spoke.

Eshkar joined them. Belessunu, called upon as a deinocheirus to assist with the caravan responsibilities, said, "To the march," and turned away.

"We'll be ready to move once the ankylosaurus are secured," Eshkar said. "Abnir sends her congratulations: it was a successful weeding."

Cassidy stared. People and dinos died in order to kill some flowers? What was going on?

"Have there been any signs?" the Twin asked.

"None," said Eshkar. "One of the ankylosaurus Deepened in the midst of battle, but she was far from the others, so we…"

We what?

Cassidy didn't risk asking, but the Twin and some of his nearby assistants who were in earshot all nodded in grim understanding. She had a different insight: "Do the dactyls get the Deep?"

The Twin turned to his duties. She wondered if she'd offended him, or if he was just overburdened. Eshkar took on her guidance: "I'd never thought to ask that myself. Our myths and legends tell us of a sap that came from the sea and split apart, some of it becoming amber. The rest became song. Some say that music is a part of the world, and was there before us. It will be there when we are gone. There are many stories that connect the dactyls with these histories, but each tribe sings differently about this."

Cassidy digested all of that. "I would be grateful if I could learn your stories sometime. Maybe after I've figured out how I'll get home, I could come back. If you'd let me?"

"It is not for me to make such a ruling," Eshkar said. "But I do love the resinfire."

"The what?"

"A festival of story between tribes. It's too big a discussion to get into right now, but later..." he said.

"Later," she agreed. "Do humans get nothing like the Deep?" she asked, careful to keep her voice too low for any nearby dinos to hear.

He studied her for an uncomfortably long time. Was he wrestling with something internally? Making decisions about her? Considering social or cultural implications? She was about to retract her question or change the subject when he said, "Not exactly. With the dinos, it seems to be random. Once there is Deepening, it's important to get them away from the others, because sometimes they seem to catch it from the ones in the Deep. But there's never been a pattern that we could congeal." She realized he meant there was nothing they could nail down, but their culture and technology was based upon resins, saps, ambers, wood, and strange methods of sound. Even structures she'd have expected would use nails or cleverly-worked sticks were made with either some kind of paste or glue, or very interesting rope work. Eshkar's speech continued while she processed all of this. "But we do have our own kinds of Deep, usually when we get older. It can happen in fever, from head injuries, or love sickness."

She had to ask about that last one. They spent some back-and-forth on clarification before she realized that he meant diseases like syphilis. At first, the idea of love causing illness seemed off-putting, but she recalled that her own culture has written many songs driven by heartbreak or cynical takes on romance. All's fair. The fact that the dinos and the humans clearly had very different kinds of intelligence, but recognized and respected each other's minds and ways, was incredibly interesting to her.

She still had no idea how she was getting home. Nonetheless, she pressed the conversation on this Deepening phenomenon: "I take it that the different tribes of humans and dinos have different ideas about where the Deep comes from, and why it happens?"

He nodded. "It is why we must keep moving. Stillness might last for some time before there is any Deepening, but if we fall into it and we're not moving, it takes all the dinos, and the humans won't survive that. The dinos, for that matter, would either die from the chaos or...see to the matter once they've come back to their senses."

"But they can come back?"

He shifted his weight several times. Eshkar's expression had varied patches of tension and ticks, and he lulled his head back and forth. It seemed equal parts important and uncomfortable to him to talk about this. "Sort of. No one who has been in the Deep is the same after. Most of the time, the dinos feel great shame from it. Humans have tried to remind them that it's not their fault, but..."

"It's hard to shake the guilt," Cassidy finished for him.

"I get that." He frowned. "Where I'm from, life is plenty complicated, even without dinos and the Deep. Well, not the Deep like this, anyway. The humans I'm a part of can still have fevers and hurts and all the rest." Eshkar's chin slowly dipped and lifted again as he took this in. She was picturing everything she'd seen to this point: the (seeming?) violence of the dactyls, the triceratops when she'd crashed, the way they tried to stamp out this utuki and keep up their glow-trees, the stampede of stegoceras. "It seems like the utuki are never far off when the Deep is threatening," she mused to him. She still kept her voice low.

He looked at her like she was an idiot. "We try to wipe it out, it is bad for our amber toolery. But it is everywhere, and we are always moving. Besides, we smoke it. Wouldn't the smoke, or keeping samples of the flowers around, bring the Deep about right away?"

She scratched behind her ear. They were tingling from the sheer electric joy she was feeling to be in such an incredibly new situation. But she was also wrestling with many questions. "Are there always dactyls about when you find groves of the flower?"

"Not always," he said, "but often. And sometimes they come after us once we've set fire to the groves, if we're not quick enough in leaving."

"And the dactyls are violent, right?" she reasoned.

"They do not get the Deep," he said, with growing frustration. He struggled to keep that in check, and she could see that he was wrestling with his own questions. "Unless they are just always in the Deep."

"The common part here is the flowers," she pointed

out.

"But that's just as true of the trees, the soil, the air," he said. She had to acknowledge that his thinking made a kind of sense. Besides, if it were the flowers, that would raise an awful lot of questions — many of them intensely uncomfortable, given the smoking culture.

Cassidy phrased her thinking delicately. "Suppose the flowers only do this when they're still in the ground, alive and able to do their...usual thing?"

He looked around anxiously. The caravan was in full swing at this point. Medical platforms were organized and more populated than Cassidy would have liked. The Twin was on a different one than hers. Abnir was also elsewhere at this point, and the archaeologist couldn't find the leader among the crowd. Belessunu was part of the next platform over, and glanced Cassidy's way occasionally. She wondered if the dino wanted to talk more with her new human friend of the odd skin colour. Eshkar returned her to the conversation: "If that were true, it would explain why the smoking and keeping them in pouches makes no difference. But they are flowers. They have no magic for causing things around them."

"What about something like pheromones, pollen, or other signal systems?" she proposed.

"We have no words for what you're trying to say," he answered.

Interesting.

CHAPTER SEVEN

Cassidy looked around. "Do you have anything like magnifying glasses?"

"I don't understand the question. We use glass when we find it, usually for knives and other times when we need something sharp. The healers use it for surgery."

She'd noticed obsidian among their tools. Somewhat like the aztecs in that way, but not really; they still seemed to her like Babylonians or some other older Middle-Eastern civilization who didn't have metal and went down a very different road because of the resins and other unusual organic material here. "How do your scouts improve what they can see?" she asked.

"Some of our best healers have ways of making the eyes be the best they can be," he answered. "Why?"

"So you don't use glass for any tricks with light?" she pressed.

"Oh! That's what you've been getting at," he said. "Yes, we usually combine it with the amber toolery. Sometimes light levels are important for energy, and our builders have some interesting techniques. But what does this have to do with the Deep?"

"I have some ideas I want to try," she said. "Can you gather some of your friends for me? I'm looking for your tech— toolery, and research." He blinked at that. "Um," she tried again, "Your people who study. The ones who examine things, and come up with ideas for new toolery?"

"Ah, dreamers and believers," he said. "Belessunu leads some of them."

Human and dino science was shared. She supposed that made sense. "Please. I know I ask a lot, but if I could meet your idea leaders," she doubted they had a concept of science as she understood it, "then I might be able to help. I can add some of the things that my people know."

"I'll pass the message along now," he said, and he appeared to be oddly excited and relieved. "Abnir already speaks much about finding outside help for lasting problems, and I admit that I'm curious myself. So are many of the others. Now that things are settling down, it might not even take all that long. Until the march," and he set off.

Did that phrase mean goodbye?

"Thank you," she said as he set out. This left her some time to reflect. She had very serious doubts and concerns about sharing knowledge and technology. Her background in archaeology and anthropology addressed this concept many times. True, they were on the move and there were things about that which seemed pitiable to her. They didn't have any settled-down methods of study. They didn't seem to stop to smell the roses, including knowledge like pheromones, or signal systems like pollen. Though that could have been that he was a scout and not representative of all his people. She'd find that out soon enough.

But what about the risks of cultural interference? Did she have the right to meddle with their ways and beliefs just so she could get home? But if she didn't, she'd never get back! It wasn't like she could climb those trees, and even if she got above the canopy without falling or getting eaten by a pterodactyl, what was she to do? Jump to the portal? Not that she had much hope this way as it was. Even if she gave them new ways of dealing with this "Deep," it didn't help her climb out of her situation.

She'd have to adapt. She might be here for the rest of her life. It would be nice not to have to spend that time fending off random attacks. She also had to admit that she was fiercely curious. Not just about this amber technology — so many questions! — but also the dinos, the dactyls, and the whole environment. How high could the dactyls fly? What could she build, combining her knowledge with theirs? She wasn't in aviation, but everyone talks about lift and drag and all that at some point in high school or undergrad. Could she give them flight? Should she? If the dinos are people, just in bodies she usually associated with great beasts, why were the dactyls so wild and violent? Was this a cultural divide? Did she have the right or ability to bridge that divide?

She was left to her own devices for longer than she'd have liked. Minor activities blurred the day: dashes, swings, and dives of the scouts among the enormous trees; bursts of discussion and odd glances among the deinocheirus; shifts in the positions of the platforms; many of the running and jumping dinos coming and going. She couldn't help but note the greatly reduced numbers of compsognathus after those scuttling dinos turned or fell during the Deepening of the stegoceras.

None of the influential people she'd spoken to — like Abnir or the Twin — came back her way.

An escort of scouts landed all about her. They moved with such acrobatic grace that even watching one of them coming for her still felt like it came out of nowhere. Their movements were hard to predict. She doubted this was accidental. "They've decided to hear you," one of the scouts said.

"Wonderful," Cassidy replied. "How do I...?" One of them bent in a gesture she knew from her own culture: piggyback riding. "Oh," she said, and climbed on the other woman's back. At first, she felt somewhat insulted, but it didn't last: dismounting a large dino was one thing, but she could never have kept up with the swinging, gliding, and ropework that these people were accomplishing. Before she knew it, she was up in the trees.

The caravan was stopping. Platforms were lowered and unstrapped from the deinocheirus, and they were afforded the opportunity to rest. With punctuated brevity, the group disembarked and unmounted their people and supplies, the dinos shifting in their conversations and responsibilities. Meshed and lashed branches and fibres; all manner of wooden components; some resinous structures and tools whose purposes were less obvious; bridges, shelters, and rope wizardry; all quickly turned the patch of treebound and hole-pocked ground into an ad hoc village.

There were no circles of fire this time. She was tossed about as the scouts did their work, and didn't actually realize right away that she was on her own feet on the ground again. "What's going on?" she asked some nearby oviraptors who were performing minor errands.

"Heartwood Council," one of them said. "That's where you'll come in."

One of its fellows added, pointing with her tail, "Over yonder, you'll be in that amber circle. Big rumble, this. Not a lot of councils."

"Ah. Well, thank you."

"Don't mention it."

Before long, the intelligentsia of the tribe were collected with her inside a circle of sap technologies she didn't recognize and some wood-and-amber guns whose purpose was clearer. They were all aimed up, toward the canopy. A slow rotation of dino guards roved outside the circle.

"Many of us think you might be a threat," said an oviraptor who clearly held some position of command. The council was one quarter human and the other three quarters were different varieties of dino: small runners like the oviraptor, armoured ones like an ankylosaurus, and bulkier ones including a tyrannosaurus. The latter was far from the biggest dino of the tribe, but probably the largest they could manage for keeping in a meeting. Of course, there was no guarantee that size was the actual guiding principle here.

"Others believe you are an adorable curiosity, but no help to us," said one of the armoured dinos. "We've survived thus far, and shall continue."

"Still others," Abnir said pointedly, "have more hope than that."

The tyrannosaurus said, "It is time we heard your plans, u-halbu. We will help you and answer what questions we can, and we are confident you will contribute to us fairly." This one was so calm that Cassidy had to remind herself that the movies got a little excited about their predators.

Cassidy tapped her chin. "I am glad to have met you all," she began carefully, "and have learned much. But I didn't come here to visit. I was just doing a fly-by." To their various glances and mutterings she answered, "I was taking in some of the sights, getting a sense for what's around. It was supposed to be quicker than this. I'm probably missed back home."

"So you wish to return," Abnir surmised. She remained stiff-backed and proud, but Cassidy thought she caught a note of disappointment.

"Not without giving you all my gratitude," Cassidy quickly clarified, "but yes." She thought it just as well to start from the beginning. Not quite from the dig in Iran where Gamgee had located the portal. Nor after that, when they found a deep cavern and a wall that had clearly been built with great effort to withstand the test of time. Certainly not when the team drilled through the wall into — impossibly — the sky. She skipped the part about being supplied a Cessna as well. "I have to fly to get back home. It would take too long to explain why. But I think I can help you. I believe the dactyls have intelligence. They might even be people."

Outrage. Grumbling, yelling, argument.

A dino with a longer neck, not actively part of the council, let out a shriek that could have sent the sap back into the trees. This was a magyarosaurus: much smaller than the well-known brontosaurus, it had some bony armour on its back but otherwise bore out the comparison. This one appeared to be a moderator or facilitator of some kind. Grudgingly, the various leaders collected themselves. The oviraptor said, "What you say is heresy. Gliding is sometimes necessary, but true flight is evil — that is why some of us distrust you. More than that, dactyls are violent, chaotic, and merciless. They are no more people than a landslide. And they come — many sing it — from the Ear."

"What's the Ear?" Cassidy had to ask.

"A hole in the sky," answered the magyarosaurus. "We can tell little about it from so far below it, but it always stays above the Temple of Hearkening. You must have seen it, if you were flying?"

She'd come from it. "Yes, I have — and thank you," she answered the moderator. She turned back to the oviraptor. "And I believe the dactyls showed tactics and intelligence when we fought them last, by the mushrooms," Cassidy pressed.

"Only we had tactics," said the ankylosaurus spokesperson.

This was the problem, Cassidy reflected, with always being on — always on the move, always rushing, always pushing the grind. You never stopped to look at things another way. As an adrenaline junkie, she struggled with it herself. She addressed the armoured ones: "They went for the amber weapons," she started.

"Hardly conclusive," the tyrannosaurus cut in. "If something were striking even an animal, they'd run or they'd attack it back, right?"

"A fair point," she had to acknowledge, "but it doesn't stop there. They didn't really come in much other than to go for those weapons — yes, I know, but let me finish. They plucked humans up, didn't they?"

"They eat us," Abnir said, "and they've long done so. You are not from the forest, it seems, so you wouldn't know that there's little food to be had up there."

"Has anyone been up there to see what they eat?" Cassidy asked the entire group.

They radiated pride. They were angry, insulted. But they looked at one another. "It is known…" the oviraptor started.

"Common sense is dangerous," Cassidy warned. "I'm sure you have your climbers," she softened, "and your explorers and the like." Numerous nods. "I saw an awful lot of those dactyls up above the forest, before my plane was wrecked," she pointed out. "So, how is it that they don't hunt you more? Why are they always around utuki when they do attack you, and why didn't they keep after you once we backed off?"

"Too dangerous."

"They're not that bright."

"There are many humans, not just our tribe."

"Some sing that dactyls eat each other."

"Who is this u-halbu to spill her thinking all over us like mushroom flow?"

"I thought we were here about the utuki."

"If you know so much, go talk to them."

"I plan to," Cassidy Cane said to the ankylosaurus.

Their hubbub came to an abrupt halt. They stared at

her incredulously.

"You can't be serious," Abnir said.

Humans, it seemed, were wonderfully different every-where — and yet always human. Cassidy wondered, not for the first or last time, how these dinosaurs could look even remotely similar to the ones she knew of from her world. The brain power for true intelligence, and the ability to speak, would surely have led to seriously obvious differences in their bodies. But that was beside the point.

"I can and I am. I think the dactyls cherry-picked their targets, and that they do the people-eating thing as a scare tactic," said the archaeologist from another world.

The human leader responded, "It certainly works!"

Unbelievably, this garnered general amusement through little sniffs, snorts, and dino gestures that Cassidy was learning were the equivalent of a chuckle. They used body language somewhat differently than humans did, but that made sense: they weren't the same as the humans. Cassidy flashed Abnir a glimpse of gratitude.

"We have often witnessed dactyls and utuki together," the oviraptor remarked, "but they are both evil. It is to be expected."

"You must hope to reach the dactyls through the utuki, then?" asked the tyrannosaur.

"Just so," Cassidy confirmed.

"Dino religion forbids it," said the ankylosaurus. "The glow-trees, sown from the holy seeds of knowledge, must be protected. The utuki, destroyed. There could be no communion with it in any case — it is a plant."

Cassidy was sorely tempted to ask about human religion, how they could be different but alongside one another, and if it really came down to one species with one religion and all the dino species grouped together with the other. It was one thing for humans to be united, but such a union of belief between many species? How? She'd pressed the boundaries of her luck and their faith already, asking about the Deep and challenging their views. She hadn't thrilled like this in years, but her head worked at any heartbeat except zero.

"I do not ask you to go beyond your beliefs," she said. "But it seems clear to me — regardless of the specifics — that there's more to these dactyls and the flowers than the knowledge you can share with me. That much, at least, we can agree on."

"In a basic way, yes," Abnir conceded. The dino representatives each nodded as she continued. "But while our beliefs do not hinder us from going with you as humans, we must show solidarity to our dino brethren. And we cannot bear the brunt of another assault like the last one without dino support." Again, the other leaders nodded their agreement with the human.

"I wouldn't ask you to," Cassidy said. "And I'm sure it would be great to live my days out with both your kinds."

"But you would not be home," the ankylosaurus said. Whatever differences the armoured ones might have with her, it seemed they weren't completely without empathy or understanding.

It was Cassidy's turn to nod.

"What then?" asked the tyrannosaurus.

"Lend me a way of covering some real distance," she said, "and perhaps a small amount of supplies or instructions from the humans so I can get by. Send me forward with as small a group as possible — say, one dino who could get me there quickly."

"Where did you have in mind?" the oviraptor folded his claws over one another, curving out his feathered arms.

"Wherever we can find another patch of the flower," Cassidy answered.

"Too dangerous," the armoured ones objected immediately.

"Only to me, really," Cassidy said, then corrected herself, "...and the dino who brings me there. The scouts who find it are only to locate the grove and return, so they shouldn't even be noticed."

"You ask much," the tyrannosaurus remarked.

"But not too much," Cassidy agreed. "It's not just for myself, you see: I could bring back knowledge."

"Some might think you are trying to change our way of life," Abnir remarked. Hers was not a tone of approval.

"How you live is up to you," Cassidy replied carefully. "But it sounds like this quest of yours to stamp out the flower has been going on for an awfully long time. You have so many risks," and she was about to mention what the Deep could do them if it happened too much, too quickly, at the wrong time. Looking at three-quarters of the representatives of the council, though, she saw dinos. Only dinos were affected so immediately and violently. Such a remark would have cost her dearly. "...And so much to be gained. Just let me get close enough to the grove that I could walk to it in reasonable time. Say, half an hour off. Then the dino who brought be that far — and the scouts who might be watching — can back away as far and safely as they wish. I suggest completely."

"Why?" the oviraptor asked. "Do you not think our peoples brave?"

"On the contrary!" she replied. "You've all proven your bravery. But if the dactyls are there and they notice I'm not alone, they might rally their attack — or defence. If it's just me…"

"…they might stop enough to be curious," the tyrannosaurus finished for her.

She nodded. The ankylosaurus said, "We admire your courage in venturing to go alone, and your care for not putting our people at needless risk."

"I believe we can adjourn here," Abnir said. The dinos nodded as she continued, "The Heartwood Council will speak among ourselves now, u-halbu, and we invite you to rest or spend time with our peoples as you choose. You will be informed what we decide."

Cassidy was a little taken aback, as she'd hoped to arrive at the decision together. "Thank you," was all that she could manage as she did her best to walk away with dignity. The yelling started practically the moment her feet landed on soil outside of their circle. She caught something like "another tribe would be better" and something about the importance of belief. Variants of "leader" and "leadership" were bandied about, but she did her best to be out of hearing. It would be all too easy for some scout she couldn't see to report later that she'd been eavesdropping.

This much she knew: there were divisive politics at

play, and she had supporters. It would have to do. Eshkar was waiting for her once she was closer to the common community. "You made it," he joked.

She lifted a dimple. "So did you."

"Come with me," he said, and he did not wait for her but turned and strode along. He kept talking with the expectation that she'd be there to hear him. "The Twin and Belessunu were hoping to work with you."

She was pleasantly surprised. "Oh? On what?"

"I'd like to join you. We were thinking we could talk toolery for a while."

It took two hours for the council to bring her their verdict. In that time, she had some fun with her three unusual new friends. She showed them a magnifying glass she had among her personal effects. They talked about other tools and techniques as well, but that one stood out to them because they thought all glass was black. Most of their stuff, if it were not rope or wood, used lacquering techniques with various resins and gums to create wondrous properties in the rope, wood, or glass — and to just have the amber as its own thing.

Some additional scouts showed up when the decision was reached. "We're to find a grove," they told Eshkar.

"Until the march," he said in farewell, and immediately set about his duties. Cassidy was having trouble with the abruptness of these people, but it made a kind of sense: if you had to keep moving to survive, you'd have a no-nonsense attitude.

The scouts turned to her. "You're to rest and prepare. Some of us will be detailed for your supply, instruction, and guidance."

"What instruction?" she asked.

"You improvised well, and it does you credit," another of them responded. "But there's a proper technique for moving with dinos. We will show you the ropes. We expect that everything will be in step for the morning."

And so it was.

Their operation was prompt, communication was clear and efficient, and she was bouncing along on the back of Mashda the corythosaurus in no time. Her breakfast had been something a lot like honey: they doled it out in little bulbs, and you ate the thing whole. "It'll give you your day's energy and strength for muscle and bone," the Twin had explained to her, "but you can't live off the stuff by itself for long."

"Thank you," she'd said a thousand times, and bid her farewells.

CHAPTER EIGHT

Now roots larger than some buildings she'd seen in her day were zipping by her on either side. The ground seemed to vary in contour, thickness of soil, and so on — but Mashda had no trouble keeping her comfortable and on-track. There were vibrato clicking sounds from high up in the trees every once in a while. By now she'd learned to look for them: they weren't lizards or birds, but scouts using special wooden whistles for signalling while still sounding like wildlife.

Eventually, there was just one sound, and it was high-pitched and drawn-out. The casual observer might have thought it was a lizard declaring its presence to rivals or potential mates. But the corythosaurus stopped, allowed Cassidy to get down, and turned. "May your path be generous," she said.

"And yours," Cassidy said. Her mount looked at her funny, and she was reminded of awkward moments like telling the waiter to also enjoy their meal. Mashda left. Cassidy, now accustomed to the ways of the scouts, occasionally caught small glimpses of them leaping or swinging amidst the branches.

Resisting the temptation to wave — which might give them away to unwanted viewers — Cassidy turned forward. She couldn't quite make out the grove from here, but trusted that the directions she'd been given were accurate. Huffing once, she set out.

It took closer to forty-five minutes, not half an hour, for her to reach the grove. She doubted they'd misjudged the distance. Two dactyls were among the flowers. They hadn't noticed her yet. She took the risk to look up, and had to crane her neck and look hard. But there were more up there. A shadow here, a reptilian caw there. She brought her gaze to bear on the two in the grove, clasped her hands in front of her in plain view, and waited.

They noticed her.

Their shock was unmistakable. They weren't making as many sounds as she'd expected. They looked at each other, then took stock of the plants. She made it a point to show them that she was keeping her distance from the utuki. Broken branches, leaves, fruits, and other bits of detritus fell in a gentle alarm. She didn't bother to look up — winning a fight wasn't an option anyway.

One of the dactyls made its way over. The other watched intently. Cassidy didn't know what to make of that. She allowed the one before her to give her a thorough examination. Its method of walking was peculiar. They had two legs and two wings, whose patagium connected at the leg and not the backs or sides. The wings were so much larger than, well, all of it, that the dactyl used the long edges as a sort of large makeshift foot. Now that she was watching closely, the archaeologist realized that the flowers were growing in an arrangement. Possibly not a true pattern, but it was awfully coincidental that there was always an opportunity for the dactyl to put down a wing in order to walk about.

Which worked well enough — she doubted wings of that size could beat without causing harm to the plants. But why would it care? While she pondered this and examined the dactyl's body, it sniffed at her, stared head to toe, and made throat and mouth movements she couldn't decipher. Eventually, the dactyl made so far as to poke and bump at her.

"Whoa!" she said as she fell.

The dactyl glanced at the flowers at its side, just to be sure. Once she'd stood up and collected herself, with the dactyl watching her warily, she realized it hadn't meant to knock her down — and didn't intend to take another risk yet.

"Cassidy," she said, pointing at herself. "Cass-ih-dee."

The moment she made sound, its eyes narrowed and it tilted its head toward her. It moved its mouth, similar to before, and she could see micro-muscle vibrations running along its upper chest and throat in parallel lines. She pantomimed listening, and faced different directions, trying to show that she wasn't getting it.

The dactyl made two more attempts before Cassidy heard a sound coming from its throat that was somewhere between an avian reptile cry and a large plumping dollop of water. Cassidy's eyes widened and she pointed at the creature. Both dactyls responded with an excited exchange between them that just looked to Cassidy like vibrating at each other.

So they used sound beyond human ears. Or at least, beyond hers. Could the tribespeople hear them, she wondered?

"Cassidy," she said again.

The human and the dactyl made several more attempts. "Hm," she mused. "It doesn't look like this is going to work." She looked around and picked up a stick, then she gestured with it. "Come along," and she headed for a flatter and more accessible stretch of soil.

The dactyl made a sound that was at first a confused kind of surprise, but it did follow when it realized she wasn't coming back to it — or the grove. Its colleague? Partner? She didn't even know how to tell their sexes apart. The other one approached the nearer end of the grove, but did not go beyond. It reminded Cassidy of a sentinel.

She had roughly twenty-four hours before the scouts or a dino would come back to the same spot to see if they could retrieve her. The fact that the dactyls hadn't already eaten her was a good sign that her hunch was at least partly accurate. She began drawing in the dirt. She started with a little stick figure for herself, pointed at herself, and said, "Cassidy."

The dactyl watched. There was a gleam in its eyes. Oddly, she was reminded of Gamgee. She didn't know how that made her feel. Shrugging that off, she focused on how to proceed. She had to avoid confusion. Drawing a group of stick figures, she pointed away and said, "Humans."

The dactyl kept its chin lifted and lowered its head forward before lifting again, as though drawing the bottom half of a circle in the air. It was nothing like a nod. Did it have the same meaning as one, or was the dactyl as out of its depth as she felt?

She tried a few more: a tree, and she pointed at one; she avoided the flowers, but drew and pointed at a near-by shrub-like plant; a rock; the dactyls. She had to keep moving along the ground, and in some cases skipped over little pits or patches of plants, in order to continue using fresh ground. She was worried the act of erasing an image would convey an unintended message. If she erased a dactyl image, would they take that as a threat?

For the time being, it watched. Occasionally the dactyl would perform one of its wing-steps between the different groupings of drawings, bending and turning its head sidelong so it could get a good look at the ground. Her strides were much shorter than the dactyl's, so she had to put in much more work to cover the same space. It seemed to be looking at each drawing separately, then taking them in as a whole. While Cassidy pondered how to proceed, the dactyl abruptly approached a patch of soil and used a wing's broadside to brush an area clean. It was careful to restore the soil to the original position so that it would still have something to write upon. It assiduously avoided disturbing plants, and stopped whenever rabbits or similar critters went to and fro.

It then re-drew some of the images Cassidy had made.

It made one of itself, pointing to itself with the little outcropping of fingers at the topside tip of one wing. It used the pointed end of its wing as a large finger for the soil-drawing. It made another, slightly smaller dactyl, and pointed at its friend — which was indeed smaller than itself. Then it drew three dactyls, hastily and with less detail, and pointed to both itself and its cohort. While the human took this in, it proceeded to imitate the images Cassidy had made of herself and the humans, pointing to the group of three stick men and the three dactyls.

Cassidy couldn't believe what she was seeing. The dactyl was clearly working with her to develop what amounted to a primitive writing system! It was intelligent! But it didn't seem to have any way to easily interface with her outside of this method. Small wonder there was no talk between them and the tribes!

But the way the archaeologist understood things, these groups had been in conflict for a span at least as long as multiple generations. Possibly even into their equivalent of antiquity. If it could pick up on writing this easily, why hadn't dactyls as a whole found a way to get through to the tribes?

Excited and curious, the two began a lengthy process of developing simple methods of expressing things to each other.

She decided to try again. "Cassidy," she said, pointing at herself.

The dactyl regarded her without response.

She reflected and drew a more elaborate person in the soil, emphasizing some of her articles of clothing — like pilot goggles and her leather jacket — instead of the furs and woven plants worn by the humans of the tribe. Then she drew a few extra stick people, circled her image, and pointed again at herself. "Cassidy."

CHAPTER NINE

The dactyl's throat and chest produced vibrations along lines that she could see now that she was closer. It didn't make any sounds that she could detect, though. Then it brushed out the space again and drew two dactyls, one larger than the other. It stopped, looked around this way and that, and sat with a pensive, far-off look in its eyes. Then it drew on the larger dactyl image an imitation of the jagged scar it had on its leg. It made two or three flowers under the feet of the smaller one — which had yet to leave the circle of the utuki.

Cassidy clapped her hands in delight. They understood individual identity and were responding to her attempts! Clearly they saw that she was trying to identify herself to them. She reflected upon the situation. "I'm going to call you Albatross," she said to the one with which she'd been conversing. "Either I win your favour and sail home, or I bring you harm and you doom me. Seems fitting," she remarked with a nervous chuckle.

Albatross, after previously only watching her, this time leaned its head toward her. It had turned to face its ear at her.

"Can you not hear me?"

Turned this way, it couldn't really look at her. She took this as a sign of trust. But it didn't respond when she spoke.

"Oh," she said with a mixture of disappointment and accomplishment. That would go a long way to explaining why human, dino, and dactyl weren't talking — they seemed to use a different sound range!

She decided to call the one in the flowers Roc, to stay on the theme of birds in myth. She didn't bother telling them — that was too advanced for stick men, and they couldn't hear her anyway. She did, however, point at Roc and draw out a hasty set of the two dactyls and herself, with some scratched out utuki to the side. She even drew an arrow starting from the plants and going to the picture of Roc.

Albatross thumped down its wing tip on the picture of Roc and circled the flowers.

Cassidy scrunched up her face, standing back to let Albatross clear the turf and explain itself. It drew Roc in detailed caricature, enlarging the head enough that it could draw a brain inside Roc's picture. It then drew a detailed image of the utuki. Cassidy was surprised by the specifics. The dactyls were so large that she wouldn't have expected them to be able to get down enough to get a good look at the plants. These plants were large to her — not counting the stem, the plant would take up a five-gallon jug — but next to the dactyls?

She held up an index finger, hoping the sign for "hold on a sec" would make the leap over their cultural divide, and carefully made her way over to the grove. Albatross immediately made a single warning bark-like sound. It was too reptilian to be like a household pet, but the sound came with the same biting motion of a snout and it was short and punctuating. Cassidy got down on all fours, well before the plants, and gently made her way closer, exaggerating her investigation in the hopes that they would realize that she was just looking.

Roc was not impressed and made its way over to the human with delicate but precise haste. Its jaw snapped within inches of Cassidy and she backed off. Collecting herself, Cassidy returned to the drawing patch, satisfied that she'd seen enough to recognize that in fact Albatross' pictures were accurate. To her surprise, it hadn't continued drawing, and was watching her now with a combination of worry and consternation.

"Yeah, you warned me," she had to acknowledge. She pointed to the image and watched as Albatross resumed. It tapped near the picture of Roc's brain, careful not to disturb the scratches in the soil, and tapped spots in the soil over the flower, gesturing back and forth between what looked like pollen and Roc's brain.

Are the flowers good for their brains? But they're not eating the utuki. "Are you saying that they're enhancing your mind somehow?" she asked aloud, and remembered that wouldn't go far. Was utuki a kind of pterodactyl peyote? Was Albatross being metaphorical?

She drew a stick man, a picture of the fruits on a nearby bush (pointing as she went), and drew an arrow from the fruit through the mouth of the stick man and pointing at the stomach. She then used her stick to point to the picture of the utuki and the one of Roc, imitating eating as she did.

Albatross hopped side to side, making several distressed half-flaps of its wings and snapping its jaws in consternation. It circled the stomach area of Roc and then X'd it out. It then looked at its compatriot in the grove and they exchanged a bunch of vibrations which were silent to the human, but clearly intense.

With anger, it wiped the whole thing and started again, drawing with such aggression now that dirt flew. A stick man, large and a little silly, with a detailed tube and fire at the end. Utuki with a fire over it. Several different varieties of dino, all with arrows pointing to a picture of an X'd out brain. An elaborate human head with more teeth than necessary, angry-pointed eyes, an X'd out brain in the head, and a line going from the burning flower to two pictures of brains in the human's chest.

Then it redrew the stick man with goggles — Cassidy — and put a brain in the head, making oval circles where it expected lungs to be.

She moved back and forth between the pictures, having to walk for a span in several cases because this was taking significant space (and time, for that matter — daylight wouldn't last much longer), and worked out what Albatross was trying to say. As far as she could tell, it was vehemently opposed to smoking (or perhaps just smoking that particular plant) and it seemed to think that the tribespeople (both human and dino) were brainless beasts or monsters. She, it seemed, was an exception to the dactyl.

Fascinating!

She pantomimed wiping up the images, and the dactyl

obliged. She tapped her chin, thinking about what to do next, and felt she had to make a concession. While she'd been getting used to the dimness of the forest, it was getting late. She pointed at her eyes, and spread out her arms, then pointed up and cupped her hands at the wrists to make the shape of a half-sun.

Albatross glanced at the grove, hop-skipped a little farther away to be safe, and burst into the air. She craned her neck, but lost sight of it amid the branches before it even reached the canopy. She regarded Roc, who was content to furrow amid the flowers and who glanced up at the human only to make an odd shuffling gesture and return to its...work? Play? Something else?

Suddenly illumination spilled about them. Albatross had returned with a bundle of what looked like bioluminescent slugs. They were as large as black bears, and inched along without a care in the world once they were set aright on the ground. Albatross pointed at the drawing patch and sat back, intent.

Well, then.

She set about elaborately drawing counter-points to some of what the dactyl had expressed, eventually getting across that the dinos and other humans do in fact have brains. This seemed to disturb, offend, or irritate Albatross in some way, but it made no move to stop her. She reflected for a second, and decided to take the risk of her hunch.

She drew an utuki, a brain, and X'd out the brain, using an arrow to make sure her message was clear.

The dactyl didn't stomp with its (relatively) tiny feet, but with the sides of its wings. It snapped at Cassidy so hard that she couldn't believe it didn't break its own teeth, and she was knocked back onto her rear by the sheer force of the snap. She also got more breath than she could ever have wanted to smell in her life, and concluded that mint was not among the plants here — or that dactyls must not have liked it.

Albatross cleared the patch and angrily drew a robust image of the utuki. To the side, it drew a large and de-tailed brain-like shape, but made it in segments like a jig-saw puzzle. It then drew a whole brain inside the pistil, rendering arrows from that through the stamens and into the air. At the end of each arrow, it drew individual jigsaw pieces of the brain.

Cassidy stared in disbelief. "You're saying the plants are people? They can think?"

Albatross bumped its own jaw with the nearby point of its wing, as though punching itself in the mouth, and pointed fervently at the drawing patch.

"Right," she muttered to herself.

They spent the remainder of the evening in the light of the slug-things, repeating and counter-pointing their drawings until each was certain the other understood.

Dactyls had a relationship with the plants not unlike human and dino. Utuki could think and communicate, at least in some fashion, and — as far as Cassidy could make out — the dactyls were defending them in what they saw as a genocidal war! That seemed a little out of her pay grade.

In the morning, Cassidy awoke to find that several ad-ditional dactyls (all adults) had joined them. Roc was as-sociating with the others and two different dactyls were now attending, or communing with, the grove. Roc broke off from the others to deliver to Cassidy some objects that had been conveyed by a dactyl who dropped them off and left again. It was a bundle of edible things such as mushrooms, fruits, a nut-like thing, and — to her surprise — a cooked rabbit. She glanced around and could find no sign of any fire. Had they cooked it for her elsewhere? Did they cook their own food? If not, she didn't know if she could trust the meat. She cut into it with one of her knives and found that it had been cooked through.

"All in," she said to herself, and surprised herself with her own gusto.

Being a diplomat for dinosaurs and dactyls was hungry work.

Well, diplomat was excessive, but she didn't know what else to think of it.

Once she was done, she joined them at the drawing patch and noticed that there were bones piled up in the nook of a tree where Albatross had been feeding. She decided not to look at those bones too closely. It seems they'd all been waiting on her, and Albatross approached. It turned sidelong and dropped so that the upper side of its half-stretched wing was exposed to her. The others watched.

"Um, thanks?" she asked, knowing she wouldn't get a response, and decided to imitate its motions. She didn't have an equivalent of wings, but the way she positioned herself effectively exposed her back to it. Satisfied, Albatross stood and resumed its place opposite the sizeable span of flat soil the pair had been using to communicate. The others afforded their comrade and the odd human some room. When Cassidy stood and gazed at them all, she got the vague impression that they approved.

Wasting no more time, Cassidy set about expressing the concept of the — from their perspective — earth in the sky. She had to know if they could get her home.

As part of the back-and-forth, she indicated the canopy and the portal she used. She then drew differing heights of dactyl flight. There was some confusion until she tried a different approach: stepping back, she jumped on the spot — which felt ridiculous, surrounded as she was by giant predatory reptilian flyers. She then drew a stick man with her trademark goggles, and used that next to the picture of a tree to indicate her jump height. She flapped her arms and pointed at all of them and then back to the pictures.

Several exchanges later, she was confident she understood: they could make it to the portal, but it was very high, and took so much effort that they generally only used it for...fighting? Punishment? Maybe something like the game Tag? Albatross' friends, or family, or — for all she knew — co-workers all seemed to be tickled pink by this whole exercise. Sometimes they played, sometimes they did other things that she felt she shouldn't watch.

She was wrestling with how to proceed when Albatross took up the lead. It started with the portal and used lightning bolts and arrows with rocks to indicate explosion or bursting through. It added an image of her Cessna. "So you know that was me, huh?" she asked aloud. If it noticed her talk, it gave no sign. It went on with X'd out pictures of dactyls.

She wasn't having any of that.

"You attacked me!" she said as she went to work establishing the fault.

The process stopped. Albatross snapped its head up and regarded Cassidy for a long instant. She stood up straight and matched its gaze. If it attacked, she had no chance. She didn't care. They'd have to respect her and take her seriously if she was going to get anywhere here. "I wasn't out to hurt anyone. Your deaths are on you," she said.

A predatory lean — heard and felt more than seen — loomed over her from her audience.

Eventually, her dactyl counterpart took up the conversation once more.

Erasing the images so far, it drew itself carrying stick-Cassidy on its back to the portal. Then it drew a simplified image of one of the platforms the tribes suspended from the backs of the deinocheirus, which had become their symbol for a tribe. It made a stick-picture of an utuki with wings -- the symbol for the dactyl version of a tribe. And it made a harsh, jagged line separating the two.

If she was reading this right, Albatross was offering her a deal: I'll get you home if you'll make them leave the flowers alone.

It took a significant amount of drawing before Cassidy was confident that the message was clear: she was going to show the tribe the system she'd worked out with the dactyls and start a dialogue. She hoped her new dactyl friend — at least, not-an-enemy — understood that she wasn't making any promises. She considered indicating that she might return in the future, but thought better of it. Whether she did or not, that should be at a time and for a reason of her choosing.

A new, smaller dactyl arrived and there was a flurry of activity and, uh, chest-vibrating. Albatross was the only one who seemed terribly concerned about how Cassidy fit into this. It drew for her a dactyl-tribe, a curved line at its edge like a border, and a platform-tribe just outside that line.

She drew herself on the line.

Albatross met her eyes again. This time there was no obvious hostility, and she thought she saw something like affection or approval. Albatross turned, did some of that throbbing they do, and the smallest dactyl flew down in front of Cassidy. She couldn't help but remember the scout who'd bent for her to do a piggyback ride, because the body language was remarkably similar. She swallowed nervously.

Time for a test flight!

CHAPTER TEN

Once they arrived at the meeting place, Cassidy was overjoyed to get off the beast. It was like being in a bouncy castle if the balloons were somehow as hard as wood. She hurt everywhere, and would probably show a legion of bruises by tomorrow. In the dactyl's defence, they weren't used to carrying people, and clearly thought it would be easier than it was.

She was much too jostled to notice any scouts in the trees. Before her was Mashda. "It's not as bad as it looks!" she called out as she got off the dactyl in an undignified scramble. She turned to her former carrier. "Thank you," she said, knowing it wouldn't understand her words, but hoping it grasped her expression.

It examined her with some dismay, but made no effort to draw on the ground. First it crouched into an odd huddle, which she got the impression was directed at her, then it backed away two steps before turning and taking to the air again. She tried to remember that there could be cultural mistranslation happening here, but her gut feeling was that it felt guilty for giving her such a rough ride. She'd noticed along the way that it did what it could to glide, which made things smoother, but that brought the dactyl lower to the ground than was comfortable.

The corythosaurus watched it fly away with unsuppressed relief and a tinge of disgust. When it turned its attention to the human, she was already in the process of climbing up the rope on the side that was cleverly aligned along the body and beside the leg, making trips and snags less likely. She was perfectly happy not letting the dino get a good look at her. "Did they mistreat you?" she asked Cassidy as she headed them both back to the tribe.

"No," Cassidy said, "they were suspicious at first and half-tempted to just eat me. I have news for the tribe. We should all talk together."

She spent the day explaining what had happened and trying to get them to agree to learn the primitive writing system she'd worked out with the dactyls as a starting point. She was shocked by how much argument that took: they couldn't get past the idea that the dactyls weren't monsters. When she talked about the utuki possibly having some kind of intelligence or relationship with intelligent beings, they sent her off to the Twin and wouldn't hear anything more until he cleared her as physically and mentally sound. Four of the humans' experts on the ways of the mind — somewhat like shamans, as far as she could make it — examined her at length after that.

The following day, Cassidy was again before the Heartwood Council. Eshkar and Belessunu were also in attendance, along with the Twin and Mashda. Several hours of debate and explanation ensued. After a break for physical and mental refreshment, they resumed.

"We never were clear on why flight is so important for

your return home," Abnir said. She rubbed her bandaged leg as she sat. It was improving, but she'd need at least another week before she was in top-shape.

Cassidy had already made her needs clear to the dactyls. If she kept that from the tribespeople now, things could go poorly. "There's a mountain," she started, "though I can't even point to it now because I'd have to be above the canopy. I'm hopelessly turned about. It looks like the mountain used to be some kind of fortress, and the whole top of it is worked. Above it..."

"The Temple of Hearkening," said the tyrannosaurus, representative of the larger dinos. "Above it, the Ear."

Cassidy swallowed. This was going to be awkward. "I...um...do you remember how I explained that my wings, made of stuff called metal that you don't have, brought me to these lands?" They all nodded. "I flew it here from that cave in the sky. I'm from the Ear."

She expected uproar, hostility, a hubbub of commentary.

Instead, everyone present stared at her in stupefied silence.

"I don't have any way to repair my plane," she said. "Only the dactyls can fly. They're my only way home."

"It is sung that the dactyls come from the Ear," the ankylosaurus responded. "The Temple of Hearkening was re-fashioned by ancient humans while they strove to beat back the dactyl menace. You say there are humans, and no dactyls, where you are from?"

"Well, there are fossils," she corrected. "Ancient bones, of dactyl and dino alike, which we know to be hundreds of millions of years old because of our sciences. Our studies and toolery, as you put it."

"That...that doesn't make sense," the oviraptor said. Several others nodded.

"Our new human friend may be odd, but she has never steered us falsely and often helped us," Belessunu said.

Thank you, Cassidy mouthed as the deinocheirus nodded her support.

"I don't know what we expected," Eshkar said, "when we took a toss of the bones and chanced on the help of u-halbu. The forest has always been the forest. The forest is the world and the world is the forest. The trees are the mountains are the trees. So it is sung."

"So it is sung," echoed many of those in attendance.

"You rode to them," the armoured one mused, "and rode back. Alive. That alone is a worthy feat." He looked at the corythosaurus. "What can you tell us?"

"Not much," Mashda replied somewhat bashfully. "I carried Cassidy, and there were dactyls watching and wary. But they did not attack, I think, because she was right — so few, so cautious, and so far from the utuki, we clearly weren't there for violence. When I came back for her, she was shaken up, but she says this was from the dactyl's lack of carrying skill."

"Is this true?" Abnir asked of Cassidy.

"It is," she confirmed, "and I do not blame them. Your whole way of life includes having dinos help humans cover large distances. Dactyls only have the flowers, and I think they tend to and protect them."

"That much, at least, we seem to agree upon," said the tyrannosaurus. "Have you anything else to add?" he asked the corythosaurus.

"Only this: there was one dactyl, and no more. It seemed to consider Cassidy's well-being important, and made sure she was of sound health before leaving. I did not like to see our u-halbu so shaken, but I cannot deny my eyes — the dactyls did not attack, and I believe her words," she replied.

"I have made my desires clear," Cassidy said, "and my concerns. I assume you take me at my word that they can get me home, and that I need to return. But will you do as I asked?"

"A dialogue with them, and treating the utuki as anything other than a menace, is asking much," the ankylosaurus said. "Far too dangerous."

"But we do not have to come at it all at once," answered the oviraptor. The other dinos looked at him in surprise.

"I, for one, am curious about this writing you spoke of," Abnir said, "though I do not share your hope for what a conversation might accomplish. If all of this is as you say, and they are people, we may still have to fight. What they are harms us, and we have done them much hurt."

"Of course," Cassidy replied. "I don't expect you all to become instant friends. But it's worth a try. And if my guess is right, the flowers are causing the Deep."

"Yet you expect us not to be all the more motivated to wipe them out," said the tyrannosaurus.

"What if they're just defending themselves? Or even trying to communicate?" Cassidy said.

"Again, that is a lot," the oviraptor remarked. "But I have to agree on this: if you must fly above the Temple of Hearkening, only the dactyls can do that. We could offer you no help or protection, even if we wanted to."

"I would like to take some of your toolery — something simple, not too important — for my people to study at home," Cassidy said.

"We see no harm in this," Abnir said. "But it has to be something you can carry; we will not send our people amidst such dangers to carry gifts for you."

"That's fair," Cassidy said. "And I will try to return, perhaps with aid of some kind."

"Would it not be best to have you here for any talk of peace with the dactyls?" the ankylosaurus asked.

"I have started the conversation," she replied, "and I think that's quite enough. Yes, I'm neutral, but there is far too much history between both groups for me to have a valid opinion on what either of you should do. I believe you will have to work the matter out for yourselves, and I have high hopes for both sides."

"Teach us your system, then," Abnir said. "We will have to work and to think, and choices will be made about who should step forward to write with them first. All of this will take time. But you can tell them this: we will send someone. There are no promises here. But we will try."

"That's all I wanted," Cassidy said.

And so it went: she taught several humans and dinos, including Eshkar, Abnir, Belessunu, and the oviraptor of the council, how to communicate what she'd worked out with the dactyls so far. They gave her some bits of amber and resin-worked wood with some of their unusual technological touches to put in her backpack. Suggestions started for ways they might make the drawing process more efficient.

Cassidy spent the remainder of her time with them in minor games, discussions, and meals — bidding them farewell. Mashda returned her the following morning to the meeting spot, and found that the dactyls were watching for her well outside of the grove. Roc took her from there, and gave the corythosaurus a conspicuous amount of space until Cassidy was on her back. But it let the dino go, and proceeded to attempt to fly the little human itself. This time, there were dactyls at various angles and it made many stops, sharing vibrations with its colleagues.

"Good job!" Cassidy congratulated them. She was still on Roc's back, so there wasn't much more she could do, but she realized they were working on developing better techniques for carrying her. Oh, the chats she'd have with Gamgee when she got home!

Albatross was at the same flat drawing patch when Cassidy alighted, still sore and thoroughly thumped but better than before. "Hi, everyone!" she said with a wave.

None of them responded, of course.

Albatross began by drawing her backpack. She was shocked. "What, why?" She drew an arrow from the pack to a picture of herself. Albatross immediately jabbed the tip of its wing at the picture of the pack.

"Okay, okay," she said somewhat grumpily. She was truly excited about what studies might yield of the materials she'd collected. One item at a time, hoping to demonstrate that her stuff warranted respect, she laid out each item with care. She spaced them far apart, so that the dactyls would have no trouble getting close to them and would not disturb one thing while looking at another.

Her first aid kit, rations, and other gear that clearly

didn't come from here were examined with curiosity and at great length. But eventually they were returned to her. She saw with some annoyance that they were collecting the amber tech, resin-covered materials, and — while shooting her a dirty look — the smokes and an utuki plant she'd smuggled out of the tribe's belongings.

She knew that much, at least, would never get past either the tribespeople or the dactyls. What did surprise her was that they took everything that came from this world from her possessions. Even a fruit she'd been given purely as a snack, a bit of bark from one of the trees, and oviraptor feathers. Frustrated, she avidly pointed with the nearest stick at the picture of herself and the arrow, drawing more to emphasize: "That's mine!"

Albatross didn't waste effort on detail, drawing a simple down-open parabola for the Temple of Hearkening and a circle, somewhat above it, to indicate the portal she'd used. It then drew an utuki next to the circle, a double-headed arrow pointing at both the portal and the flower, and an X in the middle of the arrow's shaft.

They spent several hours going back and forth, refining their communication system even as they strove to work out the terms of an agreement. Cassidy inwardly accepted some time ago that they weren't going to let her take anything from this world on her return. What she was really struggling with — despite passing herself off as still arguing — was why they cared, why they were refusing *everything*. What did they care if she took tools and tech belonging to the dinos and humans that neither utuki nor dactyl could use or understand?

Ultimately, she concluded that this was partly the

price they were demanding of her. They weren't taking her to that cave in the sky without a cost to be paid. Which was fair. But everything from here? Yet she was allowed to keep the materials that she'd brought with her? Sighing, she conceded defeat. She couldn't risk dragging this out too long, as she was hoping they'd bring her back while she still had daylight.

They used a tight formation of not less than a dozen dactyls to get her above the canopy. Most of them were below or to the sides of Roc, who was carrying her again. Albatross had taken her effects, including the utuki, and left the circle of discussion with some ceremony. Cassidy couldn't hope to follow all of it. But it looked like they were taking care to have plenty of backup to catch her in case something went wrong.

Once free of the rainforest, she struggled to pull out her cell phone and get in some snapshots. It was like trying to take pics while on a canoe in the midst of rapids. Once they approached the portal, the flight slowed. From here, all she could see was the small span of a rocky cavern. Gamgee's team had made sure that she'd have to turn to go through the portal, because they didn't want anything or anyone who came looking to find them too easily.

Half of the group of dactyls flew around the portal every which way, clearly fearing and mistrusting it. Roc hesitated before getting close. Cassidy was profoundly disappointed that she hadn't gotten a chance to bring back anything from her exploration, but consoled herself that she'd learned a great deal. She'd be back.

Roc was trying different approaches.

"What's wrong?" Cassidy called out.

No response. Obviously.

Eventually, the dactyls around Roc and Cassidy gathered, facing the portal. They gave their friend some space. The human, being the person she was, looked down. Every time she did, it sent jolts of vertigo and joy through her gut and her spine. Roc's flight climbed a little, so that they were on par with the top borders of the portal. Its breaths came in the same way a human's does when bracing themselves.

As the dactyl brought her in for a landing, Cassidy shouted at the top of her lungs, "INCOMIIIING!"

"Don't shoot!" she added when she landed. "This is just my Über driver!"

THE SECRET OF THE OHKS

AJ RYAN & JD RYOT

CHAPTER ONE

Shouts erupted close behind as Cassidy beat a path through the tall grass. She huffed and puffed, pushing her legs to the limit, shoving through the huge blades of green. The local strong arms were hot on her heels. She could hear several pairs of feet crashing through the grasses as well.

She finally broke out of the line of green, making for the blue cobblestone road. The road led downward, between the halves of a rocky hill. It had been cut open to build the road through it instead of going around. She glanced over her shoulder, seeing the guards with their red capes flapping behind them as they gained on her. She just had a little further to go. She pushed what little reserve she had left to bolster her on down the road.

At last, the bridge came into sight. She thumped along the boards, feeling the structure stretch a little, but the tight ropes held strong. She glanced back again and saw her pursuers were gathering at the edge of the bridge, but not following. She frowned, scrunching up her bright eyes as she brought her attention back ahead of her. That's when she stumbled to a halt.

Waiting on the other side was a similar group, except they were clad in blue. Two opposing peoples. Neither likely to let her through in peace. She looked behind her at the Red capes. They were pointing at her, shouting in their long syllables.

"Sorry?" she held up her hands.

Shouts began on the other side. She whirled around. These guys were quicker at making decisions. They were already marching onto the bridge. The shouts gained a new pitch behind her. She could already guess why, but she looked anyway.

Just as she expected, they were also beginning a march onto the bridge. They increased their strides.

The Blues did too.

The Reds compensated, breaking into sprints.

"Only one way out," she thought aloud, waiting until her blood hammered through her veins at the same fast tempo. She ducked under a rope, drew in a quick breath and sprung off the bridge, swan diving towards the waters below.

"Professor Cane?"

"Hm?"

"The water table tablets, right?"

"Huh?" Cassidy looked out into the lecture theatre where only half the seats were filled. The department head had noted a fall in the numbers for her classes. She had received an email from him before class. She was going to be audited. She blinked hard, bringing herself back into the present.

"Oh. Yes. Correct. That was the artifact we were hunting for. And, uh, who was the pivotal researcher that led us to the most likely area?"

A half-dozen hands raised. She pointed to the closest student. However, the voice faded out, her eyes no longer interested in what was beyond the tip of her own nose. The boredom was like a massive blanket, muffling everyday life.

Then she was in her office, but she didn't remember going there; not one part of the journey.

Autopilot.

Mundane life just ran on its own for Cassidy Cane nowadays. She had passed on the last expedition that had come her way. She had something way more exciting on the horizon. Or she thought she had. Gamgee had hinted at another portal about to clear for her, but that had been over a month ago.

She sat back in her chair, making it squeak as she leaned into the cushions, thinking. All she got was irritation and maddening expectation. Did you bring a skydiver up into the air and forbid them to jump? She actually didn't know the real answer to that, but her point still stood. Her eyes caught sight of the papers on the end of her desk. Essays that she had yet to read. Cassidy found her attention ran away whenever she tried to comb through them.

She clasped her hands together, her fingers feeling along the line of a scar on her palm as she attempted to concentrate, even a little. On the shelves of her tight office were trinkets from her earthly adventures, A chunk of amber from the British Isles, a fossil from Mexico, and a polished disk from a dig site in Africa. However, there was one that did not belong to the same category. It had no earthly origin. It looked to be a piece of glass with dyes caught in it. Though the outside was solid, the inside appeared viscous. Blue and red swirled like ink in dense water, only briefly mixing and then pushing apart again.

She groaned upon glancing over her collection. "This is impossible." She pushed herself onto her feet, hauled on her worn leather jacket and made for the door.

It opened before she could reach it. Cassidy took a quick step back as Margo stepped in. Seeing her big sister standing before her, Margo quickly shut the door behind her. "Going out?" she asked.

"Margo, what are you doing here?" Cassidy asked instead of answering. Her mind ran through a bunch of possible scenarios in the meantime.

Her sister sighed, crossing her arms. "I told Mom you were checked out."

"Huh?"

"Yep," she agreed with herself, walking over to the nearest shelf. Cassidy began to feel the judgement rolling off her middle sister. It really didn't rub well with her.

"You totally forgot I was coming for a visit." She outlined, "You probably have other plans, too." She picked up an artifact and turned it over in her hand. It was a little stone statue Cassidy had brought back from South America.

"As a matter of fact," Cassidy reclaimed the artifact from her grasp and put it back where it belonged.

"Running off on another big trip?" Margo continued to lead on, her hint of sarcasm hitting Cassidy square in the face.

"Well it *is* part of my job," she shot back, forceful enough to say that Margo should have put those facts together by now.

"Doing your job is one thing, Cass, but this pace is something else altogether."

"Geez, Margo, you've really been working on the theatrics." Cassidy almost groaned with flat wit.

Margo shot her a glare only a sister could appreciate.

"What are you trying to say?" Cassidy rested her hands on her hips.

"You've always been fast. Remember how you used to drag me when I was a toddler? You could never just walk anywhere." She shook her head, "but lately you've been ratcheting up even more than usual."

"Okay. So, I live fast." Cassidy shrugged, then crossed her arms over her chest, still waiting for a logical problem to be presented to her.

"More than that, Cassidy. Ever since Dad got sick, you've gone off to places that are more remote, and much more dangerous. Now after Dad's relapse, it's like you are constantly taking these trips to unknown places without hardly a break."

"I think I can thank you for your concern, at least it seems like concern, but there's nothing wrong with any of my work." Cassidy took hold of her shoulder to direct her out of the way of her door.

Margo steadied herself in place instead of being ushered out. "What are you running from?"

"What?" Cassidy edged to a stop, hesitating, wondering whether she should look at her sister directly or not.

"Or maybe you think you're running to something?" Margo thought again. Then she shook her head, meeting Cassidy's gaze.

"Rica says you've always been racing ahead of yourself, but that's not true. You might have been determined, but lately you're pulling away. It's like you're becoming someone else. You're obsessed with whatever it is you say you're chasing, or running away from," Margo explained simply. Somehow, her words dug into Cassidy.

"I have to keep on top of things in my job." Cassidy's statement came out in a defensive tone, giving Margo license to drive forth in her own righteousness.

"You need to slow it down, Cass. No one can race indefinitely."

"Look, I'm sorry I got our schedules mixed up, but I have somewhere I have to be." Cassidy reached around her, taking her time so that Margo could sidestep out of her way at last. "I can email you a list of the good restaurants in town."

"Wow, Cass." Margo leaned her weight to one side, arms crossing again.

Cassidy waved her toward the door and straight into a young man.

"Oh, sorry." He stepped back, fiddling with the papers he held in his hands.

"It's okay." Margo eased up, speaking gentler toward him than she had to her eldest sister.

"Professor Cane," he stepped up to Cassidy as she was closing the door to her office.

"Yeah?" She looked him over. He didn't look familiar to her.

"I was wondering if we could talk."

"Sorry. I have another engagement. Next time you can email me to schedule office time," she said, then zipped up her coat.

"But - but we did schedule a time," he stammered.

She paused. Then she hesitated on going back to her office. The mundane blanket over her shoulders felt too suffocating. She had a mission to get. Something to blow this stuffy slow pace of life right off her.

"Sorry. We'll have to re-schedule." She worked to keep Margo from catching her gaze as she quickened her pace down the hall.

"Sorry if I took up your time." Cassidy could hear her sister speaking to him as she pulled open the door to the stairs. It didn't matter.

CHAPTER TWO

She got herself to the lab of Dr. Herbert Gamgee straight away. She'd sat with the uncomfortable and prosaic pace long enough.

"Gamgee," Cassidy called as she entered his warehouse lab. She looked down from the walkway above, but found that he was not in the fishbowl space below. Brushing a loose piece of her red hair out of her face, she looked around again. "Gamgee," she called, using more force this time. "Gamgee, are you here?"

"Professor Cane." His voice paused between the first and second syllable of doctor, giving the T-sound centre stage. She looked around to find him on the southern walkway.

"Good day," he prompted, brows rising over his thick glasses while he dipped his chin.

"Hey."

He led the way down to the lab floor where he began to make coffee. Gamgee held up the cup and raised his brows again in question. "Sure," Cassidy agreed.

"What brings you to my little operation, Professor

Cane?" he asked, pouring her a cup and handing it over.

"Well, I was in the neighbourhood…" she trailed off, waiting to see his reaction.

Gamgee smirked as he rose to his feet and walked past her to his workstation, resting a hand on the back of the chair. "I'm not the kind of guy who gets a lot of idle visitors," he told her, raising his cup to his mouth, breathing in the aroma of the brew, "and I think I know you well enough to say that you're not the kind of woman to make such idle visits."

"Oh, well," Cassidy shuffled her feet, scuffing one of her boots on the floor.

"I don't have a disaster to fix right now, Professor Cane."

"Come on, Doc!" she burst out. "It's been ages."

He took a sip of his coffee, putting it aside, "Junkie."

"That's why you picked me for this whole business in the first place, right?" she challenged him, gingerly taking up her own cup. Just because she was itching for adventure didn't mean her mind had dulled any, and her wit remained just as sharp.

Gamgee chuckled, "Maybe."

"We both know it is, Doc." Her gaze hardened. "Come on. I saw your map. There are so many places to go. There has to be something you've been working on with them."

"That's classified." He sniffed, walking away from the console.

"Doc, what if you couldn't tinker? What if someone locked you out of all the labs?"

He paused. "Come now, Professor Cane, it isn't all that bad," he said, rubbing some dust off his white coat.

"Just think about it." She pushed further. "Gives you a little itch, doesn't it?"

He raised his eyes to look at her, searching for sensibility. She held his gaze, determined not to back down.

"Well that's because I'm a junkie."

"Come on, Doc!" she reiterated, taking the reins and marching up to the console. She reached for some of the buttons to search for an interesting case on her own.

The doctor's hand snatched one of her wrists away. He was faster than she thought, and stronger than he looked. His actions caught her off guard. She looked to him with surprise. His expression was already falling into a smile though. "Please don't touch the merchandise, Professor Cane." He stepped around her to begin typing for her. "If you're so gung-ho on another operation through the slipstream portals..."

She waited with bated breath, but only got passing minutes of keystrokes until she couldn't hold her breath anymore. "I am." She leaned in, laying her cup near his own discarded drink.

"There was this one portal I've been looking into, but—"

"I'll take it," she declared, already feeling her blood bubbling with anticipation.

"Now hang on," he begged. "This world isn't safe. Despite my belief that this artifact could have a number of uses for us, I've been hesitant to even mention it," he warned.

"Are you starting to doubt me, Doc?" she teased, but also defended herself, hands on hips.

"That's not it. No. I just want you to listen to me. You

must be very careful in this world. It's an extremely dangerous place, and if you don't keep your guard up, then I'll have more troubles than a missing artifact to deal with. Okay?"

"Just give me what you know, and I promise to take any precautions I can."

He hesitated at the console, looking her over with concern once more. His hand drifted left on his three-dimensional model of the earth. She widened her stance and squared her shoulders, exuding as much assurance as she could until he sighed. His hand switched direction and clicked on a portal icon. He typed in his password and released his digital file to Cassidy's email. Her phone beeped in gratitude.

She pulled it out to read what the objective was. "The Lord Stone, huh?" She couldn't help but smirk, "I'm on it."

CHAPTER THREE

Cassidy read her phone as her plane flew over Nebraska. The new portal was almost directly across the country from Plainsfield, Massachusetts. She was heading for the state of Washington, all the way to the Olympic National Park. Once upon a time she had almost hiked the Pacific trail, but had chosen an assistant position on an anthropological study instead. If this portal didn't do enough to get her blood pumping, then she decided that she might just take some time to hike part of the trail.

The commercial plane touched down at the Seattle-Tacoma International Airport. Cassidy went through the motions of disembarking. None of it put her off. Travel was her life, and plane rides were the most mundane part of her travels. She quickly collected her gear and headed for a rental company. While a ferry ride might be more fun, she figured she might as well enjoy driving a car and the climate controls it offered while she could. The file warned her that she would be technologically advanced to the native citizens of this portal world. That meant leaving her phone behind.

As she drove toward the mountain range, she went over the file in her mind. Gamgee called the world Ohkshhon. The inhabitants, the Ohks, were likened to East Asian warriors. They were in a similar situation to the feudal era or middle ages period. So, she decided she would choose her hiking boots in preparation for having to ride horseback.

 She arrived at the Olympic National park – making good time - and got everything settled away for the car before she had a small brunch. Then it was time to set out on the trail.

Cassidy walked the path where it was crowded, but took her time to let the majority of her fellow hikers break away from her. She lagged as much as she could, knowing she would soon have to stray from the marked trail. She found a stream that had been noted in the file and followed it downhill. When she came to where it turned back east, she saw a tree with white painted bark. That was her signal to turn west. Hiking over the next hill and back down again left her with sweat soaking the sides of her head. It wasn't uncomfortable to her though. Rather, the sweat of a hard trek served to give her a nostalgic feeling. It also gave her the expectation of an adventure on the horizon.

Speaking of adventures, she reminded herself, she had to keep her eyes open for the next part. The portal was positioned where the trees were older and much larger. They soon became so large that they were open on the bottom, roots supporting them even though the ground had fallen away over years of erosion. Or one could look at it as the trees raising up, able to stand on their own merits, confident in their own strength.

Cassidy closed her compass when she arrived at the tree grown so far from the earth that it looked like an archway to the kingdom of the forest. Just to be sure, she checked her GPS. She was in the right spot. However, to be absolutely one hundred percent sure, Cassidy took off her hiking pack and lay down on the soft earth. She shifted until she had the right angle on the light. She leaned to one side to see the light beaming around the trunk of the tree, and then the other, seeing much the same. Then she focused on the archway. Just as Gamgee had said, the light was wrong. What little light got through bent wrong. It was coloured differently, too. A purple hue in spite of the bright day around her.

"You're definitely the portal," Cassidy concluded, hopping up onto her feet, brushing damp dirt off her jacket. She grabbed her pack and took a new breath, walking up to the archway, sizing up the opening. She had a foot of clearance over her head, so no worries there. Taking a step back, she readied herself, rehearsing her plan over in her head again.

Three...Two...One...

***

Cassidy tensed as she passed through the portal, concentrating on the task of breathing out. She had decided that it would be best to be ready when she landed in a new world. 'Always be ready to run,' was the motto that played through her mind more with each portal excursion. If she started at a run, she could have the advantage of surprise over the native denizens.

She felt fresh ground under her boots and started into a sprint before her new surroundings became entirely clear. Luckily, her other senses were quicker than her head. She came to an abrupt stop as quickly as she had set off. Her muscles tensed over and over, wanting to move forward, but before she could question why she wasn't moving, the rest of those senses caught up. She found her nose was just shy of a short stone obelisk. She had almost run headlong into a sculpted rock! So it looked to her that she would have to rethink her entrance strategy again.

There were locals in the area too. They jumped into action once they swallowed their surprise, just seconds short of her senses coming back to life. So much for getting away. They were in close quarters, and it was dark.

"Careful!" One put out his arm, wrapping it around her front.

"Vaso!" another hissed in criticism. But was that a criticism of her, or the man leading her a step back from her near collision?

"It's fine," the man replied. "Go and tell them the promise has been delivered."

The sound of quickened footsteps upon stone soon dissipated.

"Vaso, be careful," the other warned again, sounding as if he felt she was some viper that could lash out at them without warning.

"We're fine, Qui," Vaso insisted confidently.

It took her a few extra seconds to follow the conversation. It wasn't English, but it wasn't indecipherable, either. Judging by their tones, she was able to guess at the roots of their phonology. The language was very close to modern Mandarin. When she looked at the one called Vaso, Cassidy saw he had every reason to be calm and confident. He was decked out in armour and belted with more than one weapon.

If she were to guess a comparison, she'd say the world of Ohkshhon was definitely in a time similar to the Middle Ages, except a little more fantastical. While he appeared to have all the layers of garb, his armour was far from a full suit. The only plates she could see were on his shoulders and forearms.

That's when Cassidy realized how fantastical this world she had arrived in truly was. Vaso was holding fire. In his other hand was no torch, no lantern, but just fire.

"What is it, Promised One?" his mouth twitched with amusement in response to her uncomfortable expression.

"The name's Cassidy. Cassidy Cane. And I'm alright on my own, thanks. No chance of crashing into any of the statuary," she said, testing out her interpretation of their tongue. His brow scrunched a little, but he definitely understood her. She directed his arm away from her, but her gaze continued to linger on the open flame in his hand. Although he held it safely away from her, it was still unsettling.

She pulled her focus back to take in more of their surroundings. Since she appeared to have found herself among peaceful inhabitants, or at least those who were peaceful towards her, Cassidy couldn't help but look around her to take in clues about the culture she had landed in. It felt like they were underground. The room was damp, and old by the look of the stonework. She even saw some cobwebs catching the flicker of light from

Vaso's hand.

A man, dressed similar to Vaso and Qui, came down the path, holding a lamp aloft to illuminate the way. He was leading a woman to them. She was tall, and strong looking with the width of her shoulders. Her raven hair was loose and damp, clinging to her breastplate. She wore a dark sash draped from shoulder to hip. Cassidy guessed that this represented a station of importance that the woman held. That and the fact that Vaso stepped aside to allow her a full view of Cassidy. He shifted to hold the flame in his hand upward in order to help illuminate Cassidy better. Both women inspected one another.

The woman's dark eyes narrowed upon Cassidy. "Where is your weapon?"

"I don't need one. Usually," Cassidy declared.

The woman's expression made it clear that she didn't entirely believe that.

"What sort of protection is this?" she tapped the back of her hand against Cassidy's jacket.

"I like to think I'm fast enough without all that metal," Cassidy hit back with quick words.

The woman snorted, "You speak so strange."

Cassidy could only respond with a shrug to that one. At least they *could* speak to one another.

"Honoured Guardian," Vaso urged, but he earned himself a harsher glance from her.

She took in a stiff breath through her nose, staying focused on Cassidy, "I am called Saka. The prince's safety is my sole purpose."

Cassidy hesitated over this fresh bundle of information. They seemed to expect that she knew more about them than she actually did.

Vaso gasped, waving his hand. The flames fell to the floor in cinders where they fizzled and extinguished. "Demon's tongue." He growled into the darkness.

The unnamed man came forward to illuminate their circle with his lantern. Saka took the light from him. "What are you called?" she asked.

Cassidy's eyes drifted to Vaso who was carefully trying to remove his charred glove. "Is he alright?"

"Your name. **Now**," Saka demanded. The flame within the lamp flickered wildly as if in response to her impatience.

"Sorry. My name's Cassidy. Cassidy Cane."

"Cane." Saka breathed, exchanging a look with her peers. "Take her bag. Let's get back to the fresh air." She waved and then took the lead once Cassidy had surrendered her pack.

CHAPTER FOUR

They came out into a land of grassy hills with the odd stone jutting out like they had long ago been dropped by giants. The path worn into the grass led further on toward a wood. Just aside from the entrance of the wood sat a group in similar Middle Ages armour. Saka trotted up to a rather large and well-kept man. Cassidy thought that must be the prince.

"Ohto." She bowed her head, "The one of Cane is here."

"Finally," a different man replied. Maybe not a man, though. He looked no older than a teenager. As he rose to his feet, everyone around him immediately bowed their heads in reverence. He paused to re-assess his guard's expression. "What is it, Saka?"

"She is far from expected," she muttered.

He leaned out around her shoulder to look at Cassidy with bright but sunken eyes. "Ah. But she is what was promised," he declared.

Cassidy couldn't help but worry about the boy. He looked like his armour was weighing him down, and it wasn't even as extensive an outfit as those who were with him.

"Promised by who exactly?" she pondered out loud.

Saka turned upon her, eyes aflame with insult, "Do not speak out of turn."

"It's fine, Saka." Ohto sounded exhausted by the few words. "Your coming was foreseen."

"Huh." Cassidy's mind raced around the ideas of what that could mean. Was there an actual seer imbibing hallucinogens? Or a really vague legend from ages past? Or maybe it was a shaman who was rather adept at reading people, like modern fortune tellers?

Then again, with the slipstream portal, there was also the chance that others had been here before. Possibly even Dr. Gamgee. No doubt any visitor would not be as cognizant of their difference in technology before arrival. So, legends of all manner could quickly form around this area.

"Honoured Guardian." The larger guard that she had mistaken as the prince interrupted. His face was showing markings that Cassidy was sure hadn't been there before. The marks were glowing from under his skin.

"Guard, form up!" Saka barked, pushing in closer to the prince.

"Any sense of what to expect, Biren?" Vaso asked, sword in hand.

"Not yet."

Suddenly, the ground erupted in white flame. It travelled in a line like it was following gunpowder that had been laid down and aimed right for Cassidy. Vaso jammed his sword into the earth before the fire could reach them.

When it met his blade, they heard a crash. The energy visibly dissipated. Cassidy felt it push through her hair as it passed over them like warm winds of the west coast. Qui thrust his hands upward, spreading a dust which took form over their heads. He had done so just in time. A projectile met the form and exploded like fireworks, leaving a shower of static that fizzled along Qui's barrier. The sparks that hit the ground outside of their safety field burned the grass and blackened the soil.

"It's Ghost People," the big glowing guy, Biren, announced.

"I think we can *see* that." Vaso grunted, pulling his sword free from the ground to then parry the blade of an enemy who had attacked at a running pace. The whitest creature Cassidy had ever seen had rushed through their protective barrier to attack with force. Her brilliant blade was aimed for the prince. The woman's hair and skin were as white as milk, while her eyes were impossibly dark. It brought to mind the representation of demonic possession in some horror movie she'd seen once.

"Eyes on the other two," Saka commanded.

"Right, there's always three," Biren thought out loud, scanning around their group.

Cassidy looked around them. It wasn't like she could be of much help otherwise. Truthfully, she could hardly keep up with everything going on around her. It was enough just to push her beliefs to agree with what her eyes took in. Suspending disbelief in a theoretical study was one thing, but when the impossible was happening all around her, it seemed to make her head spin.

"Shimmer. There!" Qui pointed. With his other hand,

he appeared to be rolling something across the ground. Smoke shot out of the soil like a geyser. Within the steam were two pale women. The first one had her hair and garments loose. She waved one palm over the other and grew a ghostly flame between them. She made a witch-like silhouette with her cape fluttering, black as night around her. Meanwhile, the second, who had tightly braided lengths of white hair and more fitted clothing, charged toward them, drawing a set of peculiar blades. The same ghostly flame the witch summoned began to flicker down the curved lengths of her twin swords.

Oh no, Cassidy thought, seeing that she was in the line of fire.

Vaso had pushed the larger ghost woman away from their group while Qui was busy sending volleys at their two new foes, forcing the second woman off her course and then to retreat a few steps.

Cassidy drifted back to Saka and the prince. "You have a plan?"

Saka was about to answer but Ohto touched her wrist and she closed her mouth. "They are pressing us toward the wood."

"A trap?" she asked.

"Most likely."

"Do you have a counter?"

"Only faith," he replied, a glint in his sunken eyes. "Let's go."

She looked worried, then conceded to his will. "I will cover you as far as I can. Let us try to avoid triggering this trap."

He nodded. "Ready, Cane?"

Cassidy smirked, feeling a rush coming over her. Their group began to edge back, losing ground to their attackers with the wood looming larger and larger. Their big guy was knocked to the ground by the woman with twin blades. She took her chance and leaped toward Ohto and Cassidy. Saka intercepted, catching her by the neck. "Go back to the shade," she shouted, driving her pale foe into the dirt. With a swift kick for good measure, she turned to make a run for it. Ohto did too, grabbing hold of Cassidy's hand, towing her along.

They crossed into the forest, finding it tightly grown and dim. Cassidy could hear her blood beginning to thrum through her veins. The odds of walking into a trap were highly likely. They made it down the path and took a turn before phantom flames cut them off. Saka threw herself in front of them and waved the end of her sash over the surrounding fire, killing most of it. The fabric glowed in her hold, showing there was more to it than expected. "I'll block them here as long as I can."

"Don't overdo it," Ohto begged.

"As you command, my prince." She dug her hand into a pouch. "Go now."

Spreading glowing stones before her in a fluid motion, Saka created a chain reaction of elements. Cassidy didn't get the chance to appreciate the power of this display, though.

Ohto pulled her along as they ran further down the path. They took a fork to a lower and less worn part of the woods. They ran until they were crashing through the brush, speeding downhill, and then they lost traction. They tumbled down in a heap.

"Are you okay?" Cassidy gasped. "Oh." She rubbed her shin, realizing they had run into a line of little standing stones. Ohto looked at his bloody knee, then found a deep gash on his hand. He began to shake.

"Hey. Hey. It's okay. I have clean bandages." Cassidy reached into her pocket. "Can I check the wound?" If they hadn't taken her pack, she could have cleaned it too, but that would have to wait. He gave her his hand without argument.

"Why do you trust me?" she asked, looking to distract him as she dabbed the bloody wound, squinting in the waning light of dusk.

"You are the one who was promised. The answer in Cane," he replied, fully believing that his words made sense.

"Was it a prophecy?"

"Not entirely. I just know," he muttered through the stinging. "I can tell you have a good heart," he said, though he winced again and paled.

Maybe. But not the best of intentions, Cassidy thought to herself.

"Why are they attacking you?" she wondered.

"They want to stop me from being anointed in the capital," he murmured, drawing his gaze downward. "I am heir to the throne, which my father has ascended from."

"They want to destabilize the region?" Cassidy interpreted. He didn't sound too keen when he mentioned this anointment, though.

Noises of battle echoed from up the hill. "We must hurry," Ohto urged, fear coming to his voice.

"All done." Cassidy tied the bandage and sat back

on her heels, looking at their surroundings. "We should probably get away from the path altogether."

"That is a sound plan," he agreed, though his voice grew weaker with each crashing sound that reached their ears.

Cassidy looked at the standing stones they had tripped over, brushing her hand over the carved symbols on the one closest to her. She looked at all the other stones. They were placed in a kind of pattern around her and the prince. The symbols reminded her of native etchings, telling others of safe spaces, good hunting grounds, and of home. Following a similar symbology, she read the stone telling her to look to her right, then the next right, and a left. She followed them until she walked into a piece of a statue. A large head, gawking at them from overgrown shrubbery.

She pulled back the leaves and recoiled from the horrible expression forever contorting the face of stone.

"Whatever's the matter?" Ohto followed her at a distance, then shuddered to find the face as well. "What an awful omen."

Sounds of thunder reached them, followed by lightning strikes flashing in the distance.

"Actually," Cassidy began to ponder to herself, "if I'm right..." She began to press her hands around the stone crevasses of the head, trying the mouth, the eyes, ears, but nothing budged. She felt like she was about to be disappointed.

But far from it, in fact! The challenge posed by this puzzle gave her a nagging sense that she could not let go of. It was a special sort of excitement that seeded within her. With the added pressure of the danger drawing ever closer to them, she was simply, pleasantly, abuzz. Cassidy took her time, walking around the structure. Once she was at the back of the skull, she pressed in and felt the surface give under her force. She tried again and noticed the surface bounce. "I think this could be our way out," she announced, gaining his full attention, though the prince looked aghast at the option she offered.

Another clap of thunder boomed through the forest, and lightning screeched through the air, making Ohto duck in fright. The battles were getting closer.

"How will this help us get away?" He made up his mind, eager to get away safely.

Cassidy smirked, "It's a false back." She dragged her hands down along the superbly crafted seam. Anyone could have mistaken it for a crack placed there by age. Near the ground, she found space for her grip. Taking hold, she lifted the false back to show it was a cleverly disguised hatch that now welcomed them into a hidden path.

"Wow." Ohto breathed. Quickly, he ducked again from the increasing noise of combat. "Can we go?"

"I thought you'd never ask." Cassidy took the lead, ducking under the hatch and descending into the unknown.

***

Once they were inside, the hatch closed behind them and plunged them into darkness.

"Do you have a torch?" Cassidy asked, remembering that her things were still in the care of his guards.

"I have better than that crude solution," he informed

her. She listened to his breathing as it changed in the darkness. First, he gave a directed exhale, then another, but more open this time. Light began to form between them.

"Woah," she exclaimed.

The prince was holding up a faceted crystal. "You have your talents, Cane, and I have mine," he offered with some cheek. Dust fell from overhead, bringing his expression down as well. "Let us move onward."

As they walked along the cobbled underground path, the sounds of battle faded away. Cassidy observed the construction of the path they were on. It was well-made, but had no remarkable images added and no ornaments. The path was only for utility. At least, on this end. So it couldn't hold her interest for very long. Instead, her focus shifted to the crystal. She had a mission here.

"How does it work?" she asked, pointing at the shard that lit their way.

"Be careful! Don't get too close." He shifted to the other side of the path. "Don't you have Vital Stones where you come from?"

"No. Not ones that can do that at least." She paused, "Is it the stone doing that? Or you?"

"I am only the spark. A conduit. Men cannot create what isn't already in the essence of the stone," Ohto recited as though he were recalling text like one of her students in the lecture hall.

"So, it's naturally occurring?"

"That is the basis of it," he murmured.

Cassidy took a moment to ponder the depth of this new information. If the stone held such energy that it could be coaxed to create light, or fire, or lightning, along with any number of feats she had witnessed since coming through the portal, then it was definitely a hazardous material. "Then it must be dangerous to obtain."

"Warrior societies are the only ones who really use it. We hone our knowledge and skill to wield Vital Stones in the service of the people and the Master Kings."

Cassidy's eyes widened.

Ohto laughed bitterly, "You're surprised to learn that even I shall have to answer to another." He huffed again with self-mockery. "Though the warrior societies are few, they are kept in check by those who speak for the majority. Or such was the theory."

Cassidy had so many questions, but she forced herself to stick with what would help her to uncover the artifact she came here for. "There are bigger stones, right? Stronger ones?"

Ohto sighed, "I supposed there is no one who wouldn't know." He glanced at her. "I wonder how much simpler all this could be if such things could remain legend."

"What do you mean?"

"Out of the five kingdoms, ours is said to be the strongest. This is not due to our numbers, but simply because we posses the Lord Stone."

"And that's a big deal?" she chose her words carefully.

"Well the king ascended and now the only one with knowledge and access to the Lord Stone is me. The stone with powers to recharge any Vital Stone, among many other mysteries." He sighed again.

"Wow. It's a very big deal then." She breathed, doing her best not to let on what a relief it was to finally have clues and know that she was on the right path to her objective.

"It makes for a big target." He grumbled. "The kingdom hasn't known a moment's peace since the Lord Stone was uncovered." Ohto sliced the air with his free hand. The light in his other hand dimmed for a moment and then renewed its strength with a surge that was not unlike Edison's bulb.

Cassidy let herself fall behind by a step as a precaution. "I'm sorry," she murmured.

"It's of little consequence now. You are here. And my fortunes are in the wind."

"Come again?" she stopped walking altogether.

"Hm?" Ohto paused. "Oh. Pay me no mind. Just simple musings," he assured her with a gentle smile.

Cassidy felt that whatever his musings might be, they were definitely not simple. He continued on without her but stopped a few feet away. "Ah. I think we are here."

Cassidy jogged to catch up and found that they had come to the end of the path. Before them stood a door with an ornate steel design.

"What do you think?" he asked. "Are we about to interrupt someone's dinner?"

Cassidy looked the door over, noting the caked dust and the undisturbed webbing. "If we are, I'd bet we'd be disturbing the kitchen maid," she joked, lifting the latch and pushing the door open.

CHAPTER FIVE

The sound of the hinges would certainly alert anyone to their intrusion. However, Cassidy soon concluded that they were likely alone. What little provisions that were left in the room were long past rotten. The place had been picked over by smaller creatures and possibly wanderers. She wished she could have seen the architecture better, but Ohto led the way with his light, having no interest in the tight lower quarters of the building.

Together they passed through an archway and found her conclusions to be entirely true. The floor of the main room was rotted and collapsing. The ornate window that overlooked the entire space was broken. Once upon a time it had probably lit the area with brilliance through its coloured glass. One staircase had fallen in at the bottom, leaving the other staircase as the only means to get to the second level. That is, if they wanted to. Cassidy was all for exploring, especially with uncertainty at hand, but Ohto seemed to be a far more cautious person.

As if in spite of her assumptions, he continued to walk ahead of her, leading the way up the stairs. He seemed to be looking for something. She followed him to keep from being swallowed up by the darkness of the space. On the first landing, he paused, holding up his glowing gem to a nearby statue. It had its face smashed off and was missing the end of its outstretched arm below the elbow. She glanced to Ohto who surveyed the statue like a scholar in a museum. She looked back to the statue, noting it was definitely the likeness of a man. His other hand was rested on his chest, like he was pledging to something.

"Nobu," Ohto named him. "The ancestor who almost united the kingdoms."

"What happened?" Cassidy leaned in to try and get a better view of the statue without falling off the landing. There were no obvious crests, only simple leaf motifs embellishing his armour.

"Greed." Ohto murmured, "an inability to close the gaps in our differences." He shifted, casting the light around the landing until he found another statue. This one was of a woman with half her face smashed. Her ears were small and pointed and she even had the same markings down her arm as the Ghost People.

"Tela-Na. Nobu's chosen partner. It caused great scandal." He huffed in amusement, "It scandalizes to this day, though they are but history."

"So, people don't like to mix with those who are different?" This land wasn't so detached from her own, Cassidy thought.

"They don't like what they don't know, and if they have power, those people make laws about what everyone else can ever know."

Cassidy admired the boy. He was incredibly intelligent and perceptive for his age. Heck! Even for his rank. Most that were fortunate enough to be crowned in their youth had a tendency to rest on their laurels; a sad Commodus to the Marcus Aurelius.

The light dimmed, causing Cassidy to look up. It was then that she saw Ohto wiping at his cheek with his free hand.

"Hey, what's wrong?"

He shook his head, making sure to stand straighter. That just made her heart go out to him even more. Like watching JFK Jr. saluting a casket. She took a deep breath, "I'm nobody. I'm not from here, just passing through. So... you can talk to me, whatever you say will be safe."

He looked back at her, trembling as he continued to wipe away tears, sniffling. "Nobu gave up his crown to be with Tela-Na. He did everything to lead the way through his example...and the people followed him, for the most part." He took in a calmer breath before continuing, "My father, the Ascended King, Juto. He was a great man too. He brought the clans of the region together, bartering with feuding clans to establish one of the greatest hubs for our warriors." He took a shaking breath, getting to his point. "I am no leader."

"Why would you say that? Saka and the others seem pretty dedicated to you," she countered.

"I make them fools." He sneered, "They will die for naught."

"Don't say that." She felt her mouth turn down.

"I have no plan, Cassidy. I never do. With all I have, all I could manage back there was buckling to my own wants to run."

He was only a boy. To face such burdens, Cassidy wanted to shake her head. She'd studied different types of monarchs throughout history and while they all coped differently, with varying outcomes, there was never any doubt of the strain such a position placed on them. The hardest for anyone to watch, even through the pages of history, were the young.

"It's normal to be scared." She said, "That was a serious life and death situation back there. There's nothing wrong with being scared in that."

"No."

"You're not a coward," she declared, feeling certain of that. She saw the look in his eye, a mirror of what she knew she held in the face of dangers that promised adventure.

"You misunderstand." He broke her bubble. "It wasn't just the battle that made me want to run. It's all of it. The duty, the relations, the power, everything to do with the Lord Stone."

"Oh."

"It weighs on me like a curse." He breathed, "I didn't want this destiny. And I knew that when they came to me," He reflected.

"You accepted anyway?"

"It wasn't simple. But also, I must admit, I wanted the power. Some of it at least. Just not the bulk of it." He sighed, "But you can't break it apart." He mused.

Cassidy stayed quiet for a couple minutes, going over the situation in full. What he said did nothing to change how she felt about him, but she felt it would be rude if she couldn't control her elation. He had just shown her an opening, the chance to make this mission easier. Plus, while she didn't mind a challenge, war zones were a whole other story. Gamgee had been right in his assessment of this world. It was mortally dangerous.

"Well, what if you could get rid of it?"

"What?" he demanded.

She was surprised to find her pulse quickening, but continued speaking, or perhaps her increasing adrenaline was why she did. "What if I took it away? No Lord Stone, no feuds," she offered. "Maybe then you might be able to step back from all the pressures, at least until you're ready for all of the duties," she declared sagely.

His eyes shifted away as he pondered her offer.

She turned her head to look out into the darkened sky. A falling star appeared. The drifting spark caught Ohto's gaze as well. Cassidy cocked her head to the side, focusing harder. The star looked odd. She watched for a couple more seconds before she figured it out.

It was falling toward them.

"Get down!" Ohto cried, shoving her to the side as he dove away. She hit the floor hard, but that didn't matter. They were overtaken by the sound of something crashing through the rest of the glass. The 'star' exploded in the centre of the landing. Cassidy was thrown back further, catching herself on the pillar by the old stairs.

Scrambling upright, her eyes darted about in search of the prince. She strained to see through the darkness and the dust. Then her gaze focused on movement at the epicentre of the explosion. Steam continued to roll out from the spot where a man now stood. Markings on his arm glowed painfully bright. That was when she realized that it wasn't dust or steam, it was fog. The Ghost People had found them.

CHAPTER SIX

Ohto straightened himself up, taking his time. His foe watched, unmoving.

It was hard to hear the prince. The air crackled while the entire structure was still settling from the disruptive intrusion.

"I don't want this," Ohto murmured, hesitating over his next move.

The Ghost Man lifted his arm. The mist came to life, forming a stream that raced toward the prince. Ohto took the blow, stumbling to the side. With a turn of his wrist, the Ghost Man brought the stream back around, knocking Ohto in the other direction.

Using both hands, he directed the stream to split and come at Ohto from both sides. It raced so fast that Cassidy winced at the thought of the strike.

But the prince caught it this time. When the streams met his hands, they ignited into clouds of fire. Cassidy shielded her face while the area illuminated among the blaze. The heat hissed through the air around them.

The Ghost Man was unmoved though. His eyes widened, but that was all.

Cassidy thought he might yield.

There was no such luck.

"What have you done with it?"

Ohto jumped forward, taking a chance to attack. He unsheathed his blade, diving straight into the man's chest. However, Ohto only tumbled to the floor behind him, rolling onto his knees. Resting his sword down on the floor, the prince frowned. "What is this?"

"A message, boy."

The Ghost Man wasn't really here. He stood before them like a hologram.

Then he captured Cassidy in his dark gaze, eyes piercing the darkness and the fog. "You've brought a Streamer into this?"

Cassidy managed to tear her eyes away from his to look at Ohto. No one had mentioned that they understood Slipstreamers before.

"This world has no need for their kind." The Ghost Man growled, throwing his hand down in her direction. Cassidy flinched out of instinct, even though she knew he wasn't physically here, and the fighting seemed to have come to a halt.

"You're wrong." Ohto got back to his feet, returning his sword to its sheath.

"What do you plan on doing, boy?"

Ohto refused to answer.

He shook his head, chuckling. "Then take your message and see what your Streamer can do."

Ohto glared, crossing his arms in waiting.

"Bring the stone and your men might survive."

"What?"

"Follow the beacon. Then maybe we can put this to rest." He held up the black sash Saka had worn.

Ohto's frustration boiled over quickly. He yelled, thrusting his hand into the ethereal image of his foe, burning off all the fog in a single blast.

The image of his foe evaporated. A wave of heat ran through the air, making the space humid like she was back on the Pacific trail in Washington.

The prince fell to his knees with a groan.

"Ohto," she dashed to his side.

He was shaking all over by the time she placed her hands on his back. She thought he was crying, until the shaking became worse. He dropped to the centre of the blast scar in the clutches of a seizure.

"Oh crap." She knelt, pushing her legs and hands under his head. "Did that creep do this?" she asked no one, counting the seconds as she squinted over him in the darkness.

She hadn't counted very far before he settled down, although it felt like it could have been ten times longer.

"Take it easy." She rested one hand upon his arm.

He groaned.

"How do you feel?"

"Tired," he murmured.

Unfortunately, Ohto's last blast had been powerful enough to destabilize the building.

The landing careened under them.

"We have to go," she cried, pulling him up awkwardly. Somehow, they stumbled down the stairs and out of the crumbling building. As they escaped, she looked back to see that the entire front of the structure had let go and collapsed. The trees out front were blackened as well. They looked like they had been caught in a flash fire, burned to a crisp and left with nothing to feed flame. Some of the trees even crumbled as they ran by.

They came to a stop a short distance away, catching their breath. The cold began to set in now that they were away from the range of the magical fire.

"You said this was about your crown." Cassidy led into the heart of her discovery. That encounter, while threatening, had given her more truth than these Ohks had.

"It is. The stone is part of my responsibility. We are not supposed to talk about it."

"Why?"

"Because it corrupts." He stamped his foot into the hardened soil. "My father's ascension was not by his choosing."

Cassidy began to wonder what exactly they meant by that phrase. At first, she thought it was her slip of translation, a mistake due to a difference in dialect, but they seemed rather intentional with the words and order they chose. "When you say ascended," she began to ask.

"He died, mortally." He began to pace, "A living god ascends to his full power when he completes his mortal journey."

She blinked, curiosity igniting her mind with this new information. This culture was becoming increasingly fascinating.

"But the Lord Juto didn't choose to complete his journey so soon. They murdered him."

"The Ghost People?"

"No. The men he trusted. His government of the people. They killed him for want of the stone. They think they'll have it too, holding the kingdom for me, thinking we don't know any better."

"Won't they kill you too, when you arrive? Why weren't they arrested?"

"Plans for my banners are in place. Saka will bring order, and we will establish new governance."

What a mess she had run herself into, Cassidy thought.

"I need her." He kicked the ground, unsettling a tuft of dry grass.

Cassidy raised her chin, looking over the next tree line.

"You're insulted by my failures?"

"Huh. No. I don't see that at all," she argued. "But I do see how you're going to get your guards back." She pointed to the twin of the star that had fallen. "He said follow the beacon, right?"

He returned to her side to check for himself. "That's exactly it." He nodded, then took her hands. "I know I was not entirely forthcoming with the state of our nations. But I do agree with your previous solution. Help me to save them, and the stone will be yours to take from this world."

She wasn't sure how she could help these people, but how could she refuse the offer?

"Deal."

***

They started their hike as thunder began to roll in the atmosphere. The environment had begun working to balance itself again. Cassidy felt a chill the closer they got to the location of the beacon. The journey took a few hours, but the forest was so thick, daylight never reached them. Cassidy paused to take a drink, fixing her red locks back behind her ears. She shrugged her shoulders against the cold and dampness that clung to her. "So, this is probably a trap, right?"

"Hm?" Ohto raised his head from his waterskin. "I expect no less."

"But you only have one plan?"

"For you." He nodded. "With you as a distraction, Saka can choose the best course of action," he said, taking a short sip of water.

"Fine." She glanced back to the beacon, noting this was their last rest before they reached the location under the false star.

Ohto set a faster pace this time, marching hard toward their foes.

Cassidy pushed through wet branches, careful not to slip on the moss beneath her feet. "Hang on."

"We're almost there." Ohto pushed, hesitating in his step.

"Yeah but look." She waved her hand through the air, her skin picking up water droplets from the air around them. "Isn't this their modus operandi?"

"Excuse me?" he frowned at her.

"Oh, uhm. Their usual methods?" she held her hands up on either side of her.

"Yes," he agreed.

Cassidy thought back to the encounter with the phantom image and how the fog had hit the prince. "What if we're ambushed? Maybe we could look for a way around this?"

Ohto opened his mouth to answer, looking tired, but someone else spoke for him.

"No, dear thing, you're already in it."

Ohto looked at her, the colour draining from his face as the fog collected around them, growing dense.

"Where is the stone?" The witchy woman appeared from the murky fogs.

"It's nice of you to ask," Cassidy thought out loud, "but does that ever really work?"

She frowned at Cassidy before taking a bolt to the side. Cassidy smiled, seeing that her distraction had worked, letting Ohto land an attack.

He almost grinned but didn't get the chance.

"It wasn't a question." She crooned, holding her side as the other two stepped from the fog. "It was a command."

She summoned a white fire, throwing it down at Ohto's feet. "You will tell me," she commanded, waving her hand.

Ohto readied a defence but eased up when no attack came.

Instead, her sisters dragged their captives out of the fog. They tossed their prisoners onto the ground before Ohto and Cassidy.

Vaso, Qui, Biren, and Saka. None of them looked ready to take up the fight.

"Saka." Ohto ran toward her. White fire torpedoed between them, cutting off his path to his trusted guards.

"Tell us where you hid the stone," the witch demanded again.

Ohto hesitated. "Saka. Please say something."

Cassidy looked from her allies to their enemies. Maybe she should have pushed for more of a plan. He had seemed so sure in the abilities of his guards. He never thought that they could be too roughed up to mount a counter attack.

"Saka," Ohto begged.

"Ohto, remember who you are." Saka coughed from the dirt.

"What?" Cassidy wondered.

"You don't need to say anything to them," she insisted to the prince.

"Shut up," the witch barked.

But Saka continued, "You never have to say anything to anyone."

"Saka, I can't," he argued.

Cassidy's brows scrunched together, wondering what on earth they were talking about.

"But you can!" she insisted.

"Stop talking." The witch stepped forward, taking Saka by the arm, lifting her off the ground and pressing a palm full of fire to her forearm.

Saka screamed, though Cassidy could tell she was trying to resist the primal urge to show pain. She gritted her teeth, cringing at the sight.

"Do it!" Saka cried with what little breath she had left.

"Enough." The witch took hold of the back of Saka's head. "Kill them all."

Her sisters brandished weapons above their captives.

The men did their best to face down death with courage. Cassidy knew she wanted to look away but, at the same time, couldn't deny their show of honour. Then there was a new sister who took Cassidy's arms behind her back. She got the feeling she wouldn't be included in the execution order. Somehow that made her feel worse.

Something hit the ground, making her look back at the prince, fearing he might be hurt, or worse, having another seizure. All she got was an eyeful of head-splitting bright light.

"What?" the witch screamed.

Cassidy could feel so many things that her mind was quickly overcome. She watched as the witch's arms lit up; all the markings that she had used to craft her spells with were now causing her pain. At least, Cassidy interpreted the contortion of her expression as such. She couldn't hear anything anymore.

She continued to watch as the markings on the witch's arms began to spread, the light bleeding out and pooling together. It looked as though she might be consumed by the power entirely.

Then, Cassidy began to hear again. She heard the strangled breathing of the witch as her knees hit the ground. She heard something else hit the ground behind her again. This time the prince was down. He was on his hands and knees.

And that was all Cassidy could grasp as she was overcome with the pain in her head.

CHAPTER SEVEN

"You did well."

Cassidy gasped for air as she came to. She sat up on instinct, but the swirling in her head protested the act. She rested the side of her head in her hand, blinking to gain better sight of her surroundings.

Saka was sitting nearby. She nodded toward Cassidy upon noting she had awakened.

Ohto turned to face her, "You're awake."

"Seems like it," she mumbled, rubbing her head lightly. She was still seeing stars behind her eyes.

"I'm sorry you were caught in that." He leaned in closer to her. She still felt woozy, like they were moving, or swaying a little.

"It's fine. Nothing broken, I think." She checked her arms and hands, then looking down at her legs. Her pants were dirty and scuffed in the knees, but everything was intact.

"I cannot apologize enough." Ohto bowed his head.

Saka glared at him, leaning her head in close as well. "You finally showed them a taste of what they get by attacking our people."

Ohto visibly deflated.

"If only you allowed your conviction to shine through. Then you would truly have shown them the might that we hold," Saka insisted.

Cassidy glanced to the prince. He clearly didn't like those words. He looked physically weighed down all over again.

"What's going on?" Cassidy finally realized they really were moving. All of them. She looked past the others and noted canvas walls and a roof over them. It flapped, dulling the sounds of nature beyond. They were in a covered wagon. She could hear the wheels grinding along the terrain, and they bumped around painfully.

"I failed," Ohto murmured, dipping his chin.

"You did very well. Next time you will succeed," Saka assured him. She hadn't given up in her push to sculpt him into a warrior more like herself.

"We have been captured!" Ohto argued, throwing his hands down in frustration.

"Yeah. It seems the end is coming closer," Vaso insisted. He was seated in the corner close to the driver box beyond the wall. His hands were bound, though his leg appeared to be burned on top of the bruises and contusions he had suffered in battle.

There were too many holes in her knowledge. It didn't feel like Cassidy had been hit in the head. She just felt groggy. Questions raced into her mind, but she took a moment to sort them. Qui was not among them but she felt that she knew the worst had come to him in their last encounter. Why would they not have brought him, otherwise? The most appropriate question seemed to be: "How? How were we captured?"

"I overpowered their magic," Ohto admitted gravely. "Only, we all got caught up in it."

"I see." That didn't answer her question in the way she had wanted.

"They prevailed through the attack this time." Saka sat back with confidence, "Next time they won't be so lucky."

"Saka." He fretted.

"They're taking us to our deaths!" Vaso argued with her.

"You should trust me," she snapped back at him. "Or rather, you should trust in our prince."

Ohto shifted uncomfortably.

"They demanded the stone. He is leading them to the border." She smiled.

"That's where you called your banners to meet you, right?" Cassidy thought out loud. "Before you were marching on the city."

"Precisely. Even this foolish Streamer sees the plan." Saka cocked her thumb in Cassidy's direction.

Cassidy looked to Ohto instead of letting the guard see her insecurity with the presented prospect.

"Cane," he leaned over to take one of her hands in his. "Your coming was not coincidence. You are meant to help us."

"Uh..." She looked down to avoid everyone's eyes. His hands felt so bony.

"I think you were right. You can help with this burden. You can free this land of its curse." He gripped her hand firmly. His bones kind of hurt. But his intention was made clear. He still wanted her to take the stone.

The plan did make sense. With all his men gathered at the border, their captors would be outnumbered, and quickly overpowered. Then he could give her the stone and be on his way to the capital to win his throne. So, there wouldn't be much to worry about. She could sit back and let it play out. Yet Cassidy no longer felt very good about that fact. Of course, she thought to herself in an attempt to shrug it off, this would be an utterly boring conclusion to her trip.

***

They bumped along for a while. On Saka's orders everyone rested in relative silence. When the wagon finally jerked to a stop, they all perked up, stretching a little while they waited to be let out. But no one opened the gate on the back of the wagon. No one came for them.

"What are you doing here?" the witch's voice demanded from the driver's box.

"You thought you could leave me behind, Sister Noh?"

"My sisters have done the bulk of the work in securing the stone. I'd rather be drained by the shadow before I let you take the credit, Pun-ni."

Cassidy perked up. The voice was from the man that had given them the ultimatum. Only now did Cassidy realize that he had been absent from their rendezvous at the beacon. It sounded to her like that hadn't been his choice, though.

"It is not about credit, Sister Noh. We have a duty."

"A mission to get the stone, we are all very much aware of that," she growled out her annoyance. "Now get out of the way."

"You are mistaken, Sister."

"Shut up and get out of the way." Another sister rocked the wagon with her movement. Probably the larger one.

Silence passed over them all.

"So be it. Run him over," Noh ordered.

They clattered forward once more.

"That's right. Stay off the road, Pun-ni, if you know what's good for you."

The group in the back exchanged looks with one another, but no one saw fit to comment. Cassidy looked to each of them, until her eyes were caught by the prince. His eyes shifted from side to side, lines creasing around his mouth and into his forehead with the force of his thoughts.

She wondered what he might have perceived from the encounter. She wondered if the schism among the Ghost People might prove to be a benefit to them in the coming surprise they were approaching. There would be no telling until they arrived.

***

The wagon drove for hours more. There had been a couple stops for their captors to check on them and give them water. Cassidy stayed awake throughout the entire journey, while the others dozed. She couldn't get comfortable in this situation. Although she was sure a way out would present itself sooner or later.

"How much longer?" Vaso mumbled to Saka.

"Not long. They'll probably drive right into our legions." She smiled over the thought.

Biren, their larger guard, shifted on his seat, grunting his discomfort.

Eventually, Saka leaned over and nudged Ohto awake, "It's almost time."

He nodded, drawing himself up to sit as if he wanted to make himself smaller.

***

They arrived at last. All of them were led off the wagon and into the strong winds coming through the valley. Cassidy looked at the cliffs looming overhead, and the mountain at the end of the road.

"There is an old structure up this mountain." Ohto gestured his hands toward it, not missing a beat in finding the road completely abandoned.

"We know." The witch muttered, pushing him ahead of her.

The way up was steep. The red silt where there wasn't slate was very loose. Even the Ghost People stumbled from time to time. Soon they came to steps hastily driven into the mountainside. Ohto continued, though sweat had stuck his hair flat to his head.

He looked ready to collapse by the time they saw the top. The slate rock had grown up around them, the steps twisting, having been cut into the stone itself. The way was pitted, but at least it was stable. Their captors ushered them to the final landing.

One storey below them Cassidy could see an unexpected temple laid out.

"Huh." Cassidy looked around at the carved pillars

that held nothing up, and the markings on the walls that remained. It was more like an open amphitheatre, perhaps. This wasn't unlike the Parthenon of Athens, albeit it was adorned with the remnants of Ohks symbology and colours. The pillars had been washed dark, and red sand was running along the floor, laid down in designs. She wondered what it would look like from a higher vantage point.

Saka huffed, garnering a shove from the larger sister.

They descended in single file. Though the walls protected them, the sound of the wind was still fierce. It made this place feel even more desolate and detached from the world. It was probably how so many warriors were able to elude their notice though. At least, until it was too late. The warriors collected to fight for Ohto marched out and surrounded them once their group hopped off the last steps.

The sisters looked from the soldiers to their captives while Cassidy basked in elation. There was nothing quite like the figurative cavalry to move your heart to thanks. Not quite the right buzz, but she'd let it slide this time.

Saka shoved the witch, Noh, out of the way to keep her from grabbing at the prince in desperation.

The other sisters brandished their swords.

"You can't be serious." Vaso gaped at them, "You're outnumbered."

"It's actually not that simple," Biren stated, stepping forward from the back of the group to join the sisters. The shorter one cut the ties off his hands. At the same time, many of the soldiers attacked their own men.

"What?" Saka cried out, looking around them in disbelief.

Ohto took a step closer to Cassidy.

"We knew what would be waiting here all along," Noh told them, ignoring the battle that broke out before them.

"It's too bad our main informant perished in the last encounter, but Biren will just have to manage with double the payment." She smiled to him, and his face broke into a grin as he accepted a blade from the larger sister.

"How dare you." Saka sneered as she ducked under his first hearty slash.

Noh zeroed in on Ohto and Cassidy.

"If I were to guess, I'd say they took your magic Vital Stones away?" Cassidy shuffled back one pace, only to hop aside as a pair of soldiers tumbled through.

"Something like that," Ohto stuttered.

"I'll ask one more time, boy. Where have you placed the stone?" Noh stalked toward them. Her movement reminded Cassidy of a cat on the prowl. Ohto grabbed Cassidy's arm and pulled her back. To her surprise, Cassidy saw the witch pull away too. She jumped quite like that proverbial cat, caught off guard by a wall of fire erupting between them. More to the point, it was white fire.

"This is going too far, Sister Noh." Pun-ni rushed in, placing himself in front of the prince.

"You are depraved." She laughed. "I told you to stay away. And yet you insist on blocking our victories with your twisted beliefs? You need recognition that badly?" She waited, but he did not stand down. "Then you'll suffer the consequences."

"Sister Noh, yield now. We can take care of this together without bloodshed," he said, attempting to appeal to logic.

"You think you can stand up to all this?" she waved her hands wide, encompassing the growing battle. She definitely had more on her side now. The surprise betrayal had reduced the number of Ohto's men before they could even act. With the balance of numbers shifted from the outset it seemed likely that they would soon be entirely defeated.

Pun-ni turned his head to the side, then back to Noh. "I will have to try." His arms ignited, fog billowing from him, gathering and forming into the shape of men, interrupting the final slaughter and pushing back their foes.

"Take this and run." Pun-ni held out a knife. Cassidy took it, using it to free Ohto's hands and then letting him free her.

The prince took her hand and dragged her around the battles until they found a room that was cut into the mountain wall.

Cassidy saw the statues that stood over rows of sarcophagi. Each with its own stone to light their faces and the space itself. Her stomach dropped. They were in a crypt. The prince didn't seem to care as he led her to the end of the row, hiding behind the largest statue.

"Ohto, what are you doing?"

"I can't. Last time I burned up their magic, I...no. I won't do it."

"Okay, then let's protect the stone," Cassidy offered.

He shook his head, "It might be best to destroy it. You see how it twisted that woman? How greed has seeped into my own trusted guards, ones I would have called friends. My own sworn swords are tearing each other apart for its power."

"Where is it, Ohto?" she demanded in desperation. If she could grab it and get away before he smashed it, then things might work out. Or so she told herself weakly.

"Very close."

"You mean it's in here?" she turned to try and see him in the dim light of the room.

"Yes."

A thud shook the space, dust rushing over them.

"I have to show you," Ohto insisted.

"What? We have to be quick. This is a dead end," Cassidy countered, looking from him to the billowing dust coming in from the only way out. Or more likely, it was the fog of the Ghost People.

Ohto grabbed her hand. Cassidy tried to pull away out of instinct. "What are we doing?" she looked at him, but his grip only tightened, bones digging in, adding to the tension.

"Quickly," he hissed. "You need to understand. You must take it!" he pressed her hand into his chest, along the lower ribs. He exhaled completely, and her eyes widened.

What is that?

Something was under the skin. Something that shouldn't be there. A foreign object. Her eyes widened again, and she gasped, not wanting to believe it was true.

"Yes," he said lowly and nodding. "Take it quickly, before they get here. Break it on first strike if you must. Save us all from this curse."

She strained her eyes to glance back at the entrance. Crashes echoed down the path and throughout the crypt.

Enemies and traitors alike were working to get to them, to capture prince Ohto. How long would it take for them to figure out that he'd had the stone with him the entire time? It was a wonder they hadn't known with traitors among them. The secret must have been held by very few. She shook her head to get her racing mind to one side.

"I can't." Her words tumbled out of her mouth. She had never made someone bleed if it wasn't in self-defence or through sheer mistake. Cassidy's hands began to shake.

He held up the knife, like offering a totem to be used in sacrifice. "You can. You said you would take it from here. You're the one who will free this world of its troubles."

"Ohto." Her mouth had dried up incredibly fast. She swallowed with some difficulty. "I can't hurt you."

"You will free me," he begged.

Shouts could be heard, echoing down the passage and into the space of the dead.

Done with asking, he turned the knife around and pressed it to his shirt.

"No." She grabbed at his arms.

"I'll do it for you. Then you can take it for yourself," he assured her.

"No, Ohto. I don't want it," she argued further, straining against his arms, trying to pull them away from the stone in his torso. This was too much.

"Do not lie, Cane. You have always wanted it. From the moment you came here. I saw desire in your face. Determined need. It's all that mattered."

"Not like this," she begged.

Had she caused this? Had she been so driven that she

looked past a boy's need and pushed him to self-sacrifice? There had to be another way.

She struggled against him, locked to a standstill. "Ohto, the people need you," she begged again.

"It doesn't matter what happens to me. This is the best action I can do for them."

"You said you didn't want to give in to your desire to run from power," she snapped back at him.

"Cane," his expression softened, his sunken eyes becoming glassy. They both relaxed in their tug-of-war. "This act will be me wielding all of my power. I will take on the burden to protect this world from the evils that tear into it."

"By dying for them?"

A crash sounded, shaking the room. They lost grip of the blade and it clattered to the floor. Ohto bent to retrieve it. Cassidy caught him by the shoulder, pressing her finger to her lips.

Footsteps echoed louder than the distant sounds of battle. They listened to each patient and purposeful step. Each heel strike fed into Cassidy's sinking sense of unease.

"Nowhere to run, Boy. Bring out the stone and your little Streamer friend," Noh ordered. She sounded more tempered than before. Victory, or confidence in one's victory, could do that.

Cassidy looked into the prince's face, holding his gaze. "I believe," she murmured, pausing to listen for their enemy. They froze in the moment, anticipating words, and fearing attack. The prince waited for the answer, and Cassidy was stuck feeling more than thinking.

It was as though she stood on a precipice. Her heart was thrumming, no longer hammering, but her blood picked up speed none-the-less. "You are worth more alive," she declared before she snatched up the blade and strutted out from behind the statue.

"No. Wait!" he whispered after her. But he was too late.

"Don't worry about him. I've got the stone," she announced loudly.

"No!" Ohto cried. "No, she doesn't," he insisted, racing out from the opposite side.

"Quiet," Cassidy hissed.

Noh laughed despite her battered looking state. Punni had obviously given her a difficult fight. "You speak strangely, Streamer, but your kind has always been...useful," she mused. "Now show me the stone." She held out her hand.

Cassidy took her time, reaching into her jacket with purpose. She stretched out the seconds for as long as she could.

"It's here." Ohto had removed his mail shirt to show the shape protruding from his chest, and the scars that told of how it came to be there.

"Well isn't that novel." She crowed, lighting her hands with magic one final time. She held fog in one and wiry flames in the other.

Cassidy turned her attention to the prince, utterly despondent. If she was responsible for this, having ignored his needs, ignored him through her selfish insistence to race forth and snag even a moment of that rush, then she had to quit her focus to win and show him better now. She had to do whatever she could to reverse the damage she had caused. He needed more time.

Thus, she found herself racing forward, sprinting between them. The magic roared in her ears. She met it in an instant. The force hit her like a freight train. Just as loud, and just as disturbing. The power rocked her clear off her feet.

Hitting the ground didn't stop the thunder inside her chest though. Noh came into her view as the world grew frightfully still. Shock had coloured the witch's pale face. There was something else in her expression as well. Horror?

"Cane," Ohto spoke in a tone that reflected the witch's expression. "What have you done?"

"..." Noh's mouth fell open, but no sound was made. Everything had grown painfully silent.

"Sister Noh," another voice spoke, strong in conviction, but wavering in mortal strength.

Cassidy let her head drop to the side, seeing Pun-ni, one arm limp at his side, legs threatening to fail. His long white hair was now dishevelled and stained with smoke, ash, and blood.

"You have committed the unforgivable sin. You have acted against the laws of our very world." He shook for a moment.

She seemed to know as much. For the first time since Cassidy had met the woman, her angry front had broken. She continued to look down, whether at Cassidy or the floor, she couldn't be sure.

"It is not for us to curb the fate of Streamers." He exhaled, though the breath was unsteady. His remaining mobile arm flickered with magic. The fog was slow to summon forth, and this time it was blacker than night.

"No," Ohto interrupted.

She watched the witch's eyes flicker away from her as a blinding light began to cover them once more. Noh sank to her knees, hands held before her like a prisoner bound. Ohto's magic began to overtake them. However, it failed to impact Cassidy this time. Her body was already preoccupied with its own damage.

"Oh." She realized that fact at last.

CHAPTER EIGHT

"What have you done?"

She woke up warm, with the lingering smell of a fresh-ly lit fire tickling her nose. Cassidy looked at her hands. They were perfectly fine.

"Back again," she heard a voice.

Saka sat down next to her. She was no longer wearing her armour. Her arms were bare, though there were some bandages covering where she had been burned. Her tat-tered black sash was tied around her waist. Her long hair, half pulled back, tumbled over her shoulders when she leaned forward. "You were incredibly foolish, Cane," she began, her face dour.

Cassidy felt down her torso, finding no pain.

"You could have died. Then we'd be in even more mess." Saka shook her head, more of her hair coming for-ward.

"What happened?" Cassidy sat up, finding she wasn't even bandaged. Surely she couldn't have dreamed the overwhelming pain.

"He saved you." She crossed her arms and sat back,

like she was satisfied with whatever she saw. "An even enough exchange," she added.

"What?" Cassidy touched the side of her head, not quite keeping up with all she was saying.

"He told me. Everything."

"Oh." She tensed, ready for the hammer to fall.

"How dare you come into our world, into our lives, and seek to destroy our future?" Saka growled.

"Your future? What about his? All this responsibility was killing him," Cassidy argued back, not standing down, even though Saka loomed over her.

"I'm not finished." The formidable guard held up her hand. "You fed into his insecurities. You pulled the loose thread. I can't say why you would do that...I might have called you an enemy, if you hadn't sacrificed yourself like that." She bowed her head. "To your other concern, you should have asked."

"Why?" Cassidy frowned.

"Because I could have told you. I know, without question, that he can do this. He is the only one who can be king," Saka declared.

"What makes you so sure that he can?" Cassidy challenged, ignoring the accusation against her person. She was thinking about the young man this time. Ohto, the brilliant, caring, and sick boy who had been burdened with the weight of the world of the Ohks.

"Because he is my brother."

Saka's statement shocked her into silence. The guard took a moment to bask in the quiet before continuing with her explanation. "Half-brother," she amended. "Same father." She paused again, glancing over Cassidy. "However, I was raised as the household slave. Our father was quite ferocious, you see. But Ohto, he was always kind to me. And he challenged me to learn and grow. He never mistreated me, only ever believed in me. When he was chosen to inherit the seat of Lord Juto the Ascended, he set me free." Saka paused to let all of that sink in. "I sense he might have agreed to be adopted with such eagerness in order to prevail upon the power it gave him. That way he could order my freedom." She smiled.

Cassidy wanted to comment, but it was a lot of heavy information to absorb. She merely blinked, mouth open just a little.

"He encouraged me to work hard, to train, and found me somewhere to go. Two years later, I asked to be his guard. I had gained the skill so no one could challenge me." She concluded, "So, you see, I have no question that he is the best person for the crown. Because he knew how to help me. Most of all, because he wanted to when no one ever taught him how."

"You think a lot of him."

"He is everything." Saka admitted, her eyes focusing into the distance, "Not often is a world graced with such a pure soul. Even less that they are given the chance to make a difference."

She was right. "Okay. I'm sorry."

"He showed you, right?" she looked at Cassidy directly, flicking her long hair back over her shoulder. "He shared the secret of the stone with you?"

Cassidy nodded, keeping as quiet about it as she could.

"We call Lord Juto a god, but Ohto will be more of a

living god than he could ever have hoped to be." She explained, "Ohto and that stone, they're not separate, they are something else together now." She concluded, wrapping her arms around herself as if needing comfort.

Cassidy stared at her, although she continued to be preoccupied with the information.

"You were correct in that belief." They both looked to the open tent flap. Ohto and Pun-ni had arrived.

"We're back." Ohto smirked. He looked taller.

"And?" Saka asked, her gaze on Pun-ni who had a sling around his arm, but any other damage was covered by robes.

"Everything checks out. It's more than any scripture could tell. Certainly, more than I could hope. His solution to the stone has stabilized it in a fashion my people never would have dreamed."

"So, you are satisfied?" she inclined her head.

"About that," Ohto piped up, "I have asked Pun-ni to stay with us. Should I ever become a danger to the people, he can stabilize the stone...by whatever means necessary." He spoke with finality.

"Although I don't see why he can't remain alive. Your words prove true, at least as far as I can see. He is one with the stone on some level. It's an untold marvel," Pun-ni told her excitedly.

"While I appreciate that, it doesn't mean I trust you," Saka warned him.

"Told you." Ohto smirked.

Pun-ni shrugged his shoulders, ending in a brief wince.

"He'll also act as an ambassador." Ohto moved his

chin to the side in response to her indignation. It was clear that he was set on this decree and unwilling to negotiate with his sister.

"We'll see," Saka concluded, folding her hands.

"It's time we shared secrets. If we had understood each other properly, this bloodshed might have been mitigated."

Silence passed between the siblings, as they leaned wills against one another.

"We only wanted to stabilize the stone. It's our duty to tame such powers and prevent unthinkable destruction. As I said before, the loss of the Red Kingdom, and the people who had built this temple, the subsequent creation of the dead lands, was all due to the previous Lord Stone that graced our lands." Pun-ni outlined his stance.

Saka dropped her hands and sighed, walking out of the tent.

"She agrees. Just give her time to say it." Ohto smiled then nodded to Pun-ni.

"I'll try not to provoke her." The Ghost Man gave a short bow before taking his leave.

"Cassidy Cane, the promised one." The prince finally addressed her. He still looked pale, and thin. His eyes remained sunken in his head, but she hadn't really noticed that until now because she was wrapped up in the feeling that he had changed.

"How are you holding up?" he seemed older than she remembered too.

"This journey has been incredibly self-informing," she admitted, running her hand through her fiery hair sheepishly.

"I couldn't agree more." He set himself down beside her. "I think it's time I came clean with everything. At least, I'm finding that to be an approach with far greater benefit to me now."

"Alright. By all means," she ushered.

"You see, you came at a time of great change for me. I had just recovered from taking on the stone, which was a short time ago. Only Saka was supposed to know the full truth."

"That it was with you. Literally," Cassidy filled in.

He chuckled, though with a hint of discomfort.

"You remember what I said about the Lord Stone, what it was known to do?"

"It recharged your other magic stones," she said.

"Right."

"But you also said that was among other mysteries," she added.

He smirked. "Ever the clever mind." He mused, "Thank the father for that." His hand drifted to his chest for a brief moment. "The foretelling of your arrival...that was from me."

She cocked her head to the side.

"You witnessed the future come to me." He explained, "When Pun-ni first appeared to us." He touched her jacket that rested beside her bed, feeling the leather for a moment. "They are visions, mostly. Their meanings are incredibly layered and elusive."

"Ah." She nodded, "That's par for the course as I understand it." Out of all the strange and unimaginable things she had encountered in this adventure, soothsaying was one thing she could give a quick reference to.

Most academics studied Cassandra, or they heard of the Oracle of Delphi somewhere along the way.

"I still wish they could be more useful." He rubbed at his neck and shoulder.

"Everything has turned out okay so far," she argued. "And, if you don't mind me saying, I think you'll do very well in the future to come."

"Thank you." He touched her hand before he got up. "Rest. We will be making plans for our next steps soon," he concluded, then left her alone in the tent.

***

News of the battle at the temple seemed to have taken off like wildfire. The prince received word from the capital, which led to a hasty meeting in their large tent.

"It's about time we pulled up stakes and made for the capital," one of Ohto's trusted bannermen began.

"With haste," another chimed in.

Saka sighed before placing a scroll on the table. "Things have changed." She announced, "There's been rebellion in the capital."

"What?" several of the bannermen cried, others gasped.

"General Shoka has written to us with his witness account. He tells of the people rioting, chasing the enemies from the city. Young Toza."

"That plucky captain," someone commented.

"He led his men in and retook the city in the name of our prince," she insisted, smiling.

"And they sent you an invitation?" one man crossed his arms.

"More or less." She nodded.

"How can we trust that this isn't another ambush?" a much younger bannerman worried.

Saka hesitated.

"We don't," Ohto spoke up. "Not entirely. We will advance with caution, send runners and scouts ahead every step of the way. I will ask that we meet again after midday to establish plans should we be betrayed upon returning home."

With that, he had signalled an end to the session. Everyone filed out, leaving him with Saka and Cassidy.

"What can I do?" Cassidy asked, wanting to help them. She should at least try to make up for the mess she'd made for them.

"It's time you returned through your portal," Saka announced.

"What?"

"They don't know it," Ohto glanced to the tent flaps, lowering his voice to protect their secrets, "but the battle is done. We will find no attackers of substance in the capital." He declared, "Of this, I am certain."

"You had a vision?"

"Yes."

"I see." Cassidy felt deflated but she knew the time was right to leave. "I guess I'll start my way back."

Saka snorted, "We're not kicking you out. We're sending you with an escort."

On cue, Vaso entered and bowed to them. "We'll be ready to leave soon."

"We have already decided to establish a permanent settlement at the portal," Ohto said.

CHAPTER NINE

The return trip to the portal went smoothly, making for a dull journey. Cassidy didn't mind though. She got to know more about Vaso, and that he was entrusted with putting down roots near the portal. He was so pleased at the prospect, and that all his relations would meet him there, that his company had been delightful. After travelling on edge the entire time, it was refreshing to hang out with relaxed people who were ready to just live their lives and enjoy a new start.

Vaso took her back to the portal alone and waved her off with a smile.

"I'll be guarding, should you ever return."

"I promise not to come barrelling through next time," she joked, gaining a chuckle from him.

Then he stepped back and watched her march back through the portal and to the woods.

***

After a long hot shower followed by a relaxing bath at the motel, she hopped into her rental car and drove back to the airport. Everything fell into place, and before long she was on a plane back across the country toward home.

After they reached cruising altitude Cassidy set to work, checking her emails. She sent one to Gamgee with the information about her flight. Then she clicked on an email entitled "Research paper assistance." Thinking back, she recalled the young man who had visited her office before she left to see Dr. Gamgee. Trying to recall his features, she could only see those of Prince Ohto. She would do better now. Especially since this student had done as she instructed and emailed her again, looking for a new time to go over his research paper.

She emailed him back, offering a time later today after she settled in, or tomorrow. Then Cassidy switched to her contacts. She scrolled over her family category and looked at Margo's name and photo in the bubble. It was a picture taken from her last work on a production of Grease. Cassidy had snapped the pic of her in a 50's outfit before the stage makeup. Her thumb hovered over the image for a minute or two, before she tapped through and then chose the envelope to take her to the messenger app.

Hey. Maybe you were right. Back in town soon. Dinner?

With all attempts to make amends complete, she put her phone away. She sat back in her seat and waited for time to pass. Feeling particularly restless, however, she soon indulged in a mid-flight movie. Once that was over and she still had a couple hours to go, Cassidy fished a box out of her coat. The craftsmanship was lovely. Its joins were built without nails or screws.

She opened it to study the crest they had given to her. Saka had gifted it to her before they parted. The seal of Ohto's house included a double crown. Between its two layers was the shape of a gem, lines suggesting its magical glow. To Cassidy, the idea was similar to the triple crown of the Papal seal. Below Ohto's heavenly crown were his royal symbols. A sword crossing over a cane in an x-fashion. She touched the x, tracing along the walking stick.

"The one who was promised of Cane," she mused to herself, admiring the mysteries of all worlds.

***

Dr. Herbert Gamgee was at the airport when Cassidy's plane landed. "This is a surprise." She smirked, wondering if he had read her feelings in the tone of her email. Maybe he was here to tell her off. Maybe he would fire her from the project.

"How were the Ohks?" he asked.

"Pretty dangerous." She brushed strands of her hair out of her face.

"I told you." He sipped coffee out of a reusable cup. "Did you get the artifact?"

She stopped as she opened the trunk of her car. How could she explain everything that happened? All her feelings were still running in opposite directions. "It got lost," she admitted.

Silence passed between them.

Still, she waited for the hammer to fall.

But then Gamgee broke out of his statue state and lifted her bag into the trunk for her. "I'm glad you got through alright."

She dared a glance into his face, and found he wasn't angry. At least, not on the surface. If he was angry at all, he was very good at hiding it. "Yeah. Thanks." She stuffed her hands into the pockets of her jacket.

"There's always the next world," he assured her, turning on his heel and walking back to his own car.

"...Yeah." She wasn't sure why she hadn't been completely up front with him about the Lord Stone, but something held her back. All she knew was that it wasn't her ego pulling the strings this time.

She hopped in her car and drove back home. Once she had her things unpacked, she found an email from David, the student from her class. He wanted to meet up in thirty minutes. She was more than willing to help him. He deserved that much. However, by the time she was heading out the door Margo called her back.

"I'm ready for dinner when you are," she insisted, sounding much more amiable.

"Oh," Cassidy bit her lip, hesitating on how to break it to her little sister that she'd have to wait again.

"What is it?" She sounded ready for a let-down.

"You'll have to wait a little. I have a meeting with a student first," she said, scuffing her foot on the doormat gingerly.

"Oh! I don't mind waiting for David." Margo's beaming came through the receiver.

"David?" Cassidy frowned.

"The guy with the research paper," Margo cemented her knowledge. "Take your time, if you have that setting," she joked. "I'll check out your campus library."

"Thanks."

"Anytime, since you're buying."

Cassidy opened her mouth to protest, but the line was already dead. She could only breathe out a chuckle. The point wasn't whether Cassidy had a slower setting or not, it was about the placement of the heart and the head.

EPILOGUE

Tallis awoke with a start, his black hair matted and damp with sweat so much that it clung to the shape of his head.

His black shirt was off and draped over a chair near him. He was in a bed made of long bows of wood with a thin mattress of foam over the top, and the dichotomy of those two things shook him for a moment. He was in a large, gray tent that looked like the type the military sometimes erected.

He looked down at himself.

His chest and stomach were wrapped in gauze and bandages, covering his entire midriff and forming a sash from his left shoulder down around to his right side. He moved to rise, but winced, and made a pained sound.

"I wouldn't move too quick, if I were you," came a haggard voice from outside the door flap.

He stiffened, then loosened as he was joined by an old woman with soft eyes. Her hair was pulled back in a bun so tight that it pulled the skin of her forehead back with it, a permanent facelift. There was a pinch made from tree bark keeping it in place.

Her nostrils were askew, one on each cheek. The slope of her nose continued down into the cleft of her lip, a bump there from when the nostrils had been properly placed somewhere far back on the evolutionary tree.

"You were banged up when we found you. There was an explosion in the forest, and when we went to investigate there were parts all around, and you: not far away. You seemed like you got away from the crash – ejected, maybe – but not far from it." She pointed to his chest. "You punctured your lung."

His hand went gingerly to his solar plexus.

"It's fixed now."

He nodded, remembering the crash. He had been flying a mining pod, escaping the Xik'en asteroid station, when he'd found his way to a portal. He went through to the other side, but had found himself too close to land and unable to veer up in time to miss it, especially with the engines transitioning too quickly from no atmosphere to low. He honestly didn't remember hitting the eject or crawling away, but must have.

His hand went to the side of his face, and felt the gold wiring that lined his jaw where the Branch of Languages still sat. He smiled, then checked his pockets. He seemed panicked for a moment, finding them empty.

"We put it over there," the woman said, motioning to a bedside table.

Tallis turned, seeing his small, thin stress ball on the table. He breathed a sigh of relief and picked it up.

"I'm Clarn," she said, in a tone that indicated he had waited too long to ask.

"Hello, Clarn. I'm Tallis. Thank you for your care."

She smiled and nodded respectfully. She then motioned to the left side of her face, in roughly the same place where the Branch of Languages occupied his. "We tried to remove that but it resisted, and we thought it not best to try again."

"Thank you," he said again, rising from the bed to stand. "I'm on Cortex, then?"

"You shouldn't get up. Your wounds aren't ready," Clarn said, reaching out tentatively.

Tallis checked his wristwatch. The screen was cracked, but it seemed to still be functioning. He pressed the buttons on its side and it bleeped happily. He smiled, sighing in relief. He turned back to Clarn and motioned to her nostrils. "This is Cortex, right?"

She nodded, though she wasn't sure what he meant by the gesture. He was the one that was odd; she wasn't sure how he could tell where she was from by the features everyone had.

"That means the one to the east that leads to Earth is closed..." he mumbled to himself, checking his watch and turning in a slow circle. When he was facing due west it bleeped again. He smiled and pressed another small button along the side. The screen glowed red to indicate it had accepted the command. He grabbed his shirt off of the chair. "I wish I had something to thank you with..."

"It's fine. But you can't go. There's nothing even out there, that way."

He placed a reassuring hand on her shoulder and smiled. "There's at least one thing. Home."

JD Ryot is the reclusive creator of the *Slipstreamers* series from Engen Books. JD is an avid fan of young adult literature and adventure serials. When asked if they had come to this world through a portal themselves, JD Ryot refused to answer. No record of their birth has ever been found... on this world.

Lisa M Daly is A native Newfoundlander, **Lisa M Daly** is an archaeologist, historian, professional ballroom dance instructor, crafter, and avid baker. Previous non-fiction writing credits include essays *Sacrifice in Second World War Gander* and *An Empty Graveyard: The Victims of the 1946 AOA DC-4 Crash, Their Final Resting Place, and Dark Tourism.*

Matthew Daniels is an author currently living in St. John's, Newfoundland. He has over a dozen writing credits both locally and internationally, and his work had been featured in bestselling anthologies on five separate occasions. Stories include 'Grey Anatomy' in *Paragon*, 'Where With All' in *All Borders are Temporary*, and too many stories to count in the *From the Rock* series.

AJ Ryan is a freelance fiction editor, writer, and artist based in Mount Pearl, Newfoundland. She holds a BA in English from Memorial University of Newfoundland and Labrador and also received a diploma of Independent Illustration from Seneca College. Ryan is passionate about conveying stories with clarity and creativity. She also works to expand diverse representation in the industry by supporting 2SLGBTQIA+ writers and stories. Along with her freelance editing work, she has been a regular editor with Engen Books since 2018.